Paul was born in his grandmother's house on the High Street in West Ayton in 1958. Much has changed since then and with artistic license added to the mix, the fictional characters in the novel live in a village which resembles but does not accurately reflect the real place. The author has lived and worked in the UK, East Africa and now Western Australia, sharing life with his partner and soulmate Kerryn, who invariably is 'right' in all matters. His four offspring range from mid-thirties to mid-teens and he is proud of all of them.

Paul Coates

AN UNFORESEEN MURDER

First Edition.

© 2022 Paul Coates.

This is a work of fiction. Names, characters, places, and incidents either are the products of the author's imagination or are used fictitiously. Any resemblance to actual persons, living or dead, businesses, companies, events, or locales is entirely coincidental.

Specials thanks to Jo for reviewing and editing.

Cover design, illustrations, editing and typesetting by
Karren 'Wren' Payne

ISBN 978 0 64556 370 2

"MURDER IS ALWAYS A MISTAKE. ONE SHOULD NEVER DO ANYTHING THAT ONE CANNOT TALK ABOUT AFTER DINNER."

-Oscar Wilde

In 1390 Sir Ralph Eure built a tower, known locally as Ayton Castle, in the small Yorkshire village of West Ayton.

Three hundred years later it had been gradually dismantled, as villagers used the stone to rebuild a bridge over the nearby river. Most of the current inhabitants maintain that not much of any note had happened since.

This was about to change.

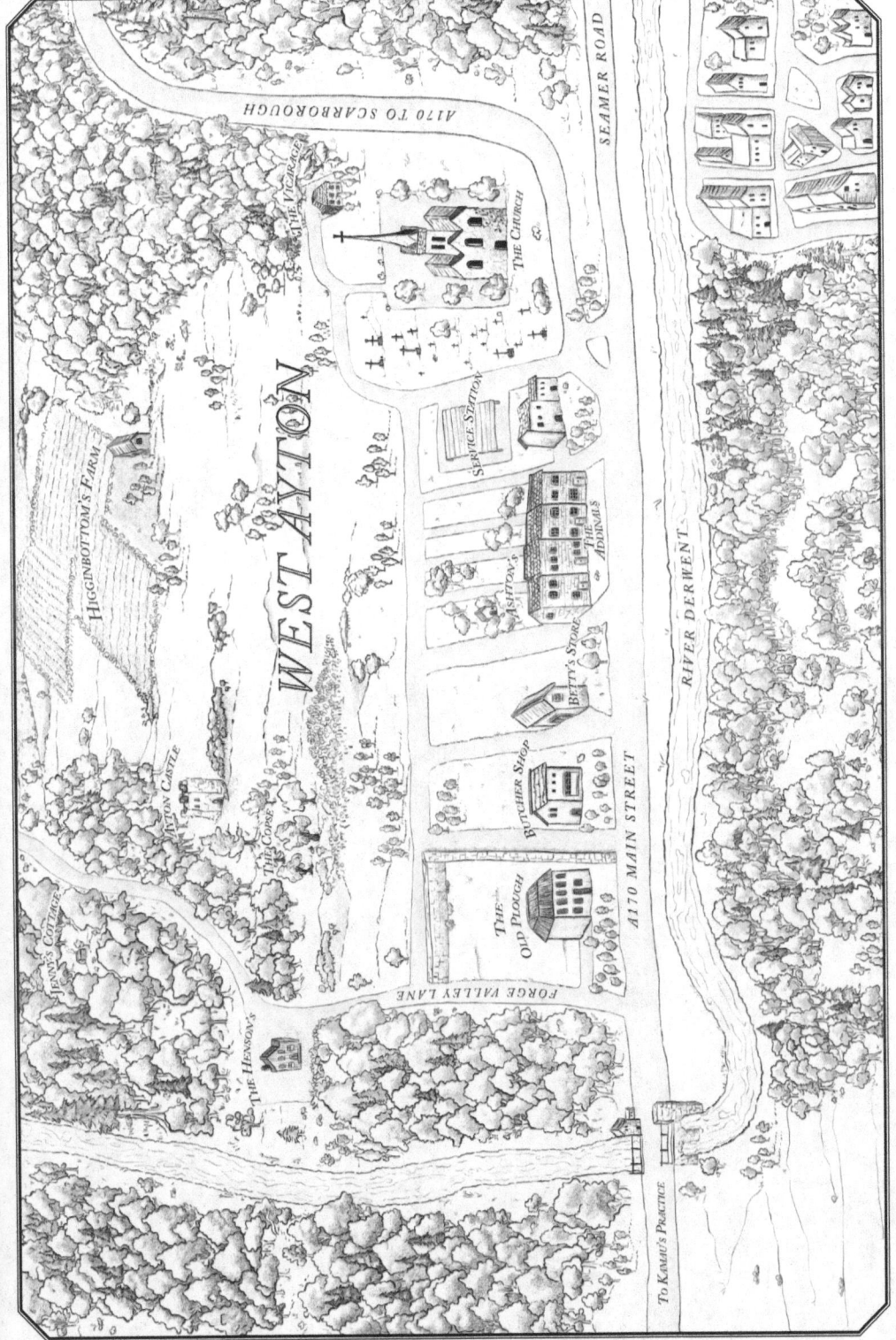

1

WEST AYTON IS a picturesque village, comfortably typical of many others scattered along the main road which runs, undeviating, inland from the North Sea towards the Yorkshire Dales. High Street buildings occupy one side of the road and the Derwent River runs parallel on the other side, until it breaks ranks at the village end and turns northwards under the bridge. Unerringly, the road continues westwards over the bridge. In moments of silence the babble of the river and cows mooing can be heard, but these sounds are increasingly drowned out by the drone of traffic as locals journey to work, school or wherever their routine takes them. All of them too busy to take in the beauty of the village's surroundings.

A passing cloud slowly crosses the sun, casting a shadow that glides across the village like a benign spectre. It travels cautiously westward from the coast, enveloping the village landmarks one by one. Progressively the sunlight disappears from the church, the graveyard, a small service station, four terraced High Street houses, the grocery store, the butcher's shop, and lastly, the village pub. The whole village is temporarily in shadow once the sunlight bathing the pub submits to the darkness. In the northern corner of its car park a wooden fence meets a dry-stone wall and, as the spectre continues its journey, Hairy Bob sits on his rucksack, glancing skyward whilst chewing absent-mindedly. Betty, who owns Betty's Provisions provides a free lunch to Bob every day that she is open for business - and for that matter, most days that she isn't. Bob had hopped over the wall into the car park for a change of scenery before settling into today's sandwich.

Further down the High Street, a lorry reverses ponderously through a narrow pathway at the side of the church guided by the site manager supervising works on the western wall. The other side of the church has been cordoned off with yellow and black striped tape as men in white coveralls busy themselves at the main entrance. One carefully examines a pool of blood near the steps. Oblivious to this activity, the truck driver clumsily lowers the empty skip which crashes noisily onto the concrete reverberating through the village. The loud jarring noise startles Bob who winces as his mood darkens. Bob is exhausted, his recurring nightmare had snatched him from sleep to wakefulness in the early hours of the morning, sitting bolt upright screaming 'Wadarega'. He quietly mutters that word, reliving the dream, and feels an encroaching dread as the warmth of the sun on his face disappears behind the cloud. Crumbs escape from his mouth as he repeats that word whilst chewing the last bite of his sandwich.

On the other side of the car park wall is a field which marks the southernmost tip of Higginbottom Farm and the owner, Gerard Higginbottom, allows Bob to set up camp on occasion in the corner where he won't disturb the cattle. Bob is homeless. Bob has PTSD. But Bob is popular and a well-liked resident of the village.

Church bells herald midday, prompting Bob to rise from his rucksack and make his way to the rear door of the pub, the Old Plough. The welcoming sound of a sliding bolt precedes the opening of the door which reveals the smiling face of Dolly Wilkes. Bob's mood immediately lightens at the sight of the woman he has grown so fond of. It is mutual.

"Ow do, Bob! In yer come," she cheerfully ushers him forward until, sniffing him, she blocks his entrance with her arm. "Now then, hold on luv, smell like you're well due yer shower and y'know the rules. Can't 'av you gassing the place owt."

Bob nods in agreement running his hand through long unkempt hair, "Okay, fair enough, sorry, Dolly, the shower in the park is out of order, local kids vandalising it I reckon."

"Well, you can't come in smelling like one of Higginbottom's herd, wait here." She goes back inside the pub, leaving Bob waiting patiently in the doorway scratching his chin through his thick beard. With a cheery waddle Dolly reappears with shower gel and a towel that has seen better days.

"Here you go, use the shower in the outhouse and dig into yer rucksack and change yer clothes. It was only last week I gave you some of Ken's."

"Cheers, luv," and off Bob trots like an obedient child bowing his head, muttering indistinguishable words to himself.

Dolly tracks his journey all the way to the outhouse, shaking her head fondly and when he disappears, she bustles back into the pub to go about the daily routine of preparing for her customers. Tying her apron behind her rounded waist she tuts then busies herself switching on lights, stocking the fridge, straightening chairs, putting menus on the tables, and finally opening the front door.

Built in the late nineteenth century, the Old Plough comprises one main L-shaped bar decorated in an eclectic mix of horse brasses, banners of local sports teams and a variety of seaside paraphernalia hanging from the walls and on randomly interspersed wooden shelves. The front of the wooden bar presents a collection of almost fifty saucy seaside postcards behind a framed sheet of clear Perspex. Being only five miles from Scarborough, the local seaside town, the pub carries a fusion of seaside meets country life, with the main showpiece being an eighteenth-century wooden hand plough resting in the corner of the room, hemmed in by five wooden tables and chairs. Pouring a pint of Guinness, Dolly walks over to the small table nearest the plough and places the drink carefully on a beer mat. She returns behind the bar and starts polishing glasses. The silence, punctuated by the ticking of an antique clock resting on the wall behind the bar, is broken as Bob shuffles into the bar, greets Dolly and sits down taking a sip from his Guinness.

Suddenly, the hum of traffic, punctuated by the sound of a car horn, enters through the front door of the pub followed by a wiry, black-haired man who oozes a natural athleticism as he seems to glide through the across the floor to the bar. As the door closes behind him, peace is restored as the external world is once more cut off.

A beaming smile lights up Dolly's face. "Ow do, Chris luv . . . not seen you for a few days, an' ow come you are in so early today, of all days?"

"Taking a day off, Dolly, creative juices have stopped flowing and fancied a cold beer on a hot day. I'll have the usual." Chris Ashton takes a seat at the bar, staring expectantly as Dolly tilts the glass under the flow of amber liquid. Smiling as the glass fills, Dolly breaks the silence.

". . . 'ere you go, Chris. Are you sure you're okay? You look a bit peaky . . . off colour? Not much in the way of company in here at the moment, just Hairy Bob and Kenneth."

Surveying the room behind him, Chris's eyes rest first on Bob sat next to the plough in the corner, and then to a four-foot toy Koala placed on a rocking chair in the other corner who had been christened Kenneth by the locals in deference to the imposing bear-like landlord. Bob returns Chris' nod of acknowledgement, but Kenneth just stares at him glassy eyed.

"You do look a bit peaky," insists Dolly.

"Well, it's been a bit of a shock. Haven't you heard? Have you not seen what's going at the other end of the High Street?"

"No luv, I haven't been out all morning."

"Check it out, I'll watch the bar and make sure Bob doesn't drink all the Guinness." Chris almost apologetically smiles at his weak joke as he looks over to Bob who just stares back at him with his lips on his glass.

Dolly rushes to the front door and goes onto the street. Through the glass in the door Chris sees her shielding her eyes from the sun and bending forward as she tries to focus on the ruckus near the church. After a moment she rushes back in.

"Good lord, Chris, there's police cars, a girl with a microphone in front of a bloke with a big TV camera and a load of other blokes in white suits who look like they're going to the moon! They've blocked off that bit of the High Street. What's gone on?"

"Not sure but it looks like someone has been hurt."

"Shall I put the telly on?" Dolly asks and Chris nods as she picks up the remote and flicks through the channels until she finds a local news programme. Speaking animatedly, the young woman that Dolly had seen with the microphone was directly addressing the camera. Dolly turns up the volume to hear the young reporter talking to the host in the studio.

"Yes, Warren, the Church, surrounding grounds and this part of the main road has been cordoned off by the police. The public are being kept at a distance and at this stage the police are unwilling to comment. There is a large blanket on the ground near the church door and it looks as if there is a body underneath it. One local lady who passed by told me that she had heard that the local vicar, Peter Dibley, had been hurt. There is certainly no movement under the blanket so, if there is a body under there, then it doesn't look good."

The news report continued with the host and the local reporter recirculating the same scant information until a producer had clearly decided it was running its course. The host touched his earpiece in response to the producer's instructions and moved on.

"Thanks, Sue, I understand you're staying on location and may be able to give us an update later... And now on to Roger in Scarborough who is at the seafront talking to local celebrity, Jack O'Nelly, who is attempting in the next half hour to break the world record for oyster eating. Tell us more Roger ..."

The TV screen turns black and Dolly places the remote back on the counter. She looks over to Bob who has begun to silently rock back and forth, and then to Chris who is staring straight at her.

"Oh, my Lord, Chris, you don't think that was the vicar under that blanket, do you?"

"Don't know, but it looked as though there was somebody under it and no movement underneath. Couldn't see a face so who knows? Looks like a fatality to me."

Placing her hand over her mouth in shock, Dolly looks over to Bob who glances back at her and, almost guiltily, stops rocking. Dolly turns back to Chris and Bob resumes his metronomic movement.

"De'yer know, it was weird, I was making breakfast for Ken—"

"What, the koala?" Chris smirks.

"No, yer daft apeth, the hubby!" Dolly laughs, "And I am sure I heard gunfire . . . thought it was those idiot Messruther lads shooting rabbits in Higginbottom's field at the back." Her face screws up in thought, "But come to think of it, it sounded more from the direction down the road as opposed to behind the pub."

Sitting in silence in the corner Bob has tuned out of the conversation between Dolly and Chris as his mind reels him back to Afghanistan. He is on patrol, stood in a field with a local farmer screaming at him and pointing to a rugged plateau in the distance. Imploring Bob to assist, the farmer falls on his knees to the ground, he grabs at Bob's belt, crying, shouting, urging him to intervene. Looking at the plateau, his eyes scale a sheer rock face that runs to a summit some forty metres from the ground. At its highest point three figures shadowed by the sun behind them mark the horizon. Two soldiers are looming over an Afghan teenager and forcing him to kneel at the cliff edge with his hands behind his head. Three buzzards circle above them, a portent. Bob recognises their uniforms, they are SAS, but not from his regiment, they are Australians.

The farmer stands up shakily and tries to push Bob in the direction of the plateau. Tears are running down his cheeks. Bob struggles to understand his screams but knows enough Persian Dari to work out that the kneeling teenager is the farmer's son. Gesturing with a flat open hand to indicate that he understands the farmer and is going to try to help, he starts to jog across the field, rifle held across his body. Within thirty yards from the cliff-face he can hear voices of the soldiers screaming at the teenager who shouts back nodding wildly. Bob pauses, cups his hands around his mouth and shouts up to the soldiers. No response. The wind is carrying his voice away from them. He renews his effort, yet still they neither respond nor even look down in his direction. Bob can see that one soldier is a Captain and the other a young Trooper. Turning to the Trooper, the Captain starts to shout directly in his ear, barking an order repeatedly. Gusts of wind sweep the words away from Bob, but it becomes clear that the Captain himself is growing increasingly frustrated with the Trooper who is looking anxiously sideways between the Captain and the kneeling boy.

Bob shouts once more but his words are strangled into silence as he stares in horror. Dragging the Trooper aside, the Captain places his boot on the boys back and violently propels him over the cliff. Somewhere behind Bob the farmer shouts. "Wadarega! Wadarega!" to no avail as his eyes follow the plummeting body. In shock, Bob's world momentarily stands still and is then reanimated to the sound of a sickening thud. Lifeless on the stony ground at the field's edge, the boy's body slowly oozes blood and life. His face a bloody mess. Tears blurring his vision, Bob sinks to his knees, sobbing as the father's screams pierce his ears, etching the enduring nightmare into his psyche.

ARTICLE IN THE MELBOURNE HERALD SUN.

"Investigations are ongoing and today we have spoken to two SAS patrol members, witnesses to a newly uncovered killing. What they have told us is astonishing and horrifying. They allege that a disabled Afghan man was shot in the back of the head as he was trying, in their words, to 'limp' away.

'We came in loud in the helicopters. All the village was in a panic. I get it, we were intimidating, scary. This guy ran off which was fair enough. I get it,' said one patrol member.

'I could see the bloke was intellectually disabled. [Soldier X] shot him through the back of the head. It was just so unnecessary, I was appalled.' Another patrol member says he saw [Soldier X] raise his gun to get what he thought was to get a closer look at the unarmed Afghan man through the sight of his weapon. 'I thought that it was not right, why was he doing this? But then he raised his weapon, and then shot him,' said the patrol member. 'There was no need for what happened. No need whatsoever. In my book that was war crimes — murder.'

Our investigation has tracked down the victim's family and identified him as Ziauddin, a farmer in his early 20s from the Paryan Nawa region of Kandahar Province.

'Ziauddin had a mental illness . . . because two years ago the Taliban beat him,' said his relative Kalimulla, who spoke to an Afghan journalist engaged by the ABC.

'Because of those beatings, he developed a mental problem.'

This latest reported incident follows a number of investigations prompted by a report by a British SAS operative in 2018 of an incident involving a local farmer and his son who was found dead after falling off a cliff. The resultant investigation concluded that the soldiers involved were guilty of unlawful killing."

Dolly and Chris are at the bar chatting and Chris points to the TV.

"Hey, Dolly, I reckon the local news will be on again. Flick on the telly and let's see if there's more information about what's happening down the road."

"Okay, Chris, luv." Dolly points the remote at the TV and its noise fills the room snapping Bob out of his dream. He is back in the Old Plough and stares at the screen. Advertisements eventually give way to the morning show. After a brief rundown by the host telling viewers what to expect in the next hour, he cuts across to the feed in Ayton. Sue, the reporter, once again smiles earnestly at the camera.

"Thank you, Warren, there have been a few developments here in Ayton. We now have confirmation that the local vicar, Peter Dibley, has been shot with what the police believe is a rifle. I am sad to report that the wound was fatal. It is currently unclear as to whether the Police have located the weapon at this point. I am told that they believe it is some sort of high velocity weapon and given the location of the wound this was an intentional killing. I can tell you, Warren, the atmosphere is tense as news travels

around the local community in this small, peaceful village, but the overriding reaction is one of shock."

Lowering her voice for dramatic effect the reporter concludes her report. "A serene Yorkshire village in an idyllic part of the countryside is now the scene of an inexplicable murder. It will take some time to unravel exactly what has occurred and why the vicar would be the target of what appears to be a professional killing."

Pausing to let the summary settle in the mind of the audience, the host then thanks the reporter with reverence for the subject matter. After a further pause he then lightens his tone as he segues onto the next news item.

"Now let's get back over to Roger in Scarborough with the disappointing news that Jack O'Nelly has failed in his record-breaking attempt. . ."

Turning down the volume Dolly, ashen faced, turns to Chris. Her concern mirrors the worried expression on his face as he looks across the bar. Climbing off his stool he walks over to Bob whispering in the corner of the pub.

"Awright. mate?" Chris approaches the corner table and waves his hand in front of Bob's eyes.

Blinking at the movement, Bob eventually responds "Yeah . . . ye-yeah sure, Chris, sorry mate . . . was miles away." Placing a reassuring hand on Bob's shoulder Chris smiles and returns to his bar seat.

"Jeez, Dolly, those trance-like states that Bob gets himself into are bloody disconcerting. D'yer know what's going on inside his head?"

"Aven't a clue, luv. World of his own I reckon."

Chris shakes his head, "When I went over there I could see there were tears in his eyes. Whatever it is, it isn't good. Wonder if it was about the vicar? Didn't think he had much to do with him."

Getting on her tiptoes, Dolly strains to look over Chris's shoulder to check on Bob. "You okay Bob, luv? Yer not looking yourself today."

Ignoring Dolly, Bob mutters ". . . Wadarega . . ." to himself and takes another sip of his beer. Seconds later, without warning, he sits up rigid exclaiming "Shit! Shit—Shit—Shit!"

Concerned, Dolly calls over, "Bob? Bob are you—?" but her voice is drowned out in a cacophony of scraping noises as Bob shoves his table aside to clear his exit, but remains seated. Like a cornered rat he scans his surroundings, desperate to find an escape route. His eyes become fixated on the rear door of the bar and without warning he leaps to his feet. Knocking the table as he runs, it screeches in complaint against the stone floor. In his wake a nearby chair topples over and leaves Dolly gaping in surprise. Chris calls after him but it falls on deaf ears, Bob is in full flight disappearing at speed through the door. Dolly's head spins to the door, then the table, looking at the spilt beer. Her eyes settle on Chris as she tries to process what had happened.

"Bloody hell, that's strange, even for Bob." Chris mutters to himself. Pale faced, Dolly nods in silent agreement.

If they had seen him, any villager would have struggled to believe the speed and agility with which Bob crossed the car park and vaulted over the back wall. Like a man possessed, he runs across the field into an adjoining copse and comes to an abrupt halt in the middle of the group of trees. Agitated, Bob feels the trees close around him like a sylvian sporting huddle. His eyes settle on one with a small, barely discernible cross carved near the base. With purpose, he walks over to it, turns around placing his back against the mark and takes a deep breath to calm himself. He walks ten paces in a straight line, drops to the ground and begins to dig like a demented mole. But within seconds the blur of his desperate hands morphs into a slow and careful scraping. He first finds the side of a large brown holdall, then the handle which he carefully eases from the soil. Its weight comforts him and he draws back the zip, revealing a clear plastic bag inside. Bob smiles with relief at its contents as he pulls out the L129A1 designation rifle. The gun had been his close companion when on duty in Afghanistan. He breathes a sigh of relief, which trails into gentle sobs.

"Thank God," he whispers, ". . . it's still here." Bob lies on the ground, covering his face with his hands, his chest hitching as he cries. Next to him rests the rifle. The cloud floating over the copse passes by. Sunlight breaks through the gaps in the trees, bathing Bob whose breathing begins to slow. Caressed by the return of warmth on his face, he brushes his hands aside and exhales; in the branches above him a sparrow chirrups comfortingly.

2

TEN HOURS AFTER THE SHOOTING

LOCALLY, JEFFREY MANDELSON and Ronald Neaves were not well liked, and at first glance they seemed an unlikely pair to be close friends.

They had grown up together in Scarborough and had known each other throughout their childhood attending the same schools. Short, skinny, pale, nervous, and studious, Mandelson was the inevitable target of bullying; years of taunting had carved a certain bitterness and meanness into his personality that endured through to adulthood. His father was a Yorkshireman of a certain generation and this physically underwhelming boy whose whining voice grated with him did not fit the picture of the son he'd envisioned while standing in the hospital watching the ruddy ball of new life come screaming out of his mother's womb.

Pneumoconiosis prematurely took the life of Mandelson's father, with the source of the disease uncertain. 'Indeterminate' was the conclusion of the judge after the lawyers got their teeth into the legal wrangle. Somehow the sand blasting business escaped any form of liability but paid a meagre ex-gratia payment to his mother more as a public relations exercise than out of any concern for the family. At the funeral Mandelson displayed little emotion for the loss of his father, nor any ill feeling towards the sandblasting company as the bitterness that gnawed away deep inside him was a product of his childhood and not the events leading to the demise of his father. With age he learnt to hide it, developing a thin veneer of charm which made him appear both sincere and caring to those who were less astute. For those who saw through to the real man, his presence sent a mild shiver down the spine and an uneasy feeling in the gut. Chris Ashton, being one of those sharper villagers, described it like biting into a juicy steak sandwich but discovering you had bitten through a still wriggling worm hidden under the meat.

Unfortunately, not everyone in the village had his perspicacity and Mandelson fooled enough people to secure his election on the local council. He used his office of power very effectively and at every opportunity to further his personal interests.

Neaves was the only real friend that Mandelson had. Physically and mentally they were polar opposites. Head and shoulders above Mandelson and as wide as the proverbial barn door, Neaves had spent his childhood coming to the rescue of his unpopular friend when things got a little physical in the schoolyard which was reciprocated when Mandelson willingly completed his saviour's homework assignments. Ginger haired Neaves cut the figure of a country stereotype with a ruddy complexion and bulbous ears that had spent many an hour in the scrum at the local rugby club. He played weekends for the Danesmen club's third team, The Third's. An amalgamation of Scarborough and village-based players, described on the club's website as a side set up for those with a passion for the sport, but not looking to play at a competitive level. For Neaves it offered a physical outlet for the frustration generated by needy clients and difficult sub-contractors in his construction company. Complaints about the standard of workmanship were his main headache, causing a weekly build-up of stress requiring some form of release. He chose the pathway of physical rather than spiritual relief; opposition players in the Saturday afternoon games often left the field with a few bruises to prove it.

The pair sit in the living room of Mandelson's cottage located in Forge Valley Lane. About two hundred metres off the High Street, the drive cuts through the forest and on to a series of back roads winding a route towards Scarborough. Mandelson lives alone with few visitors besides those paid for their personal services, but Neaves had come to the house to tell him about the disturbing events on the High Street.

"Well, that should solve a few problems" Mandelson sneers angrily as he sips his whisky.

"Can't do any harm at least," agrees Neaves, mirroring his friends' movements he takes a sip of his own drink and winces slightly when his heartburn flares as the amber spirit trickles into his stomach.

"Well, the court case isn't going to happen any time soon now, is it? So, the fear of jail time subsides a little . . . still, perhaps a good lesson for your brickies, not to mention the rest of your crew. Even I have to say, and I am no builder I grant you that, but the restoration work on the church is absolutely appalling. The spire looks like the bloody leaning tower of Ayton."

Neaves shifts indignantly in his chair. "Alright mate, don't go on. Wasn't exactly a straightforward job and restoration of historic buildings isn't exactly our specialty. It'll be fine. That building has stood for over two hundred years."

"Well, it will be lucky to stand for another two hundred days after you lot had a go at it. Those supports you had to put into the side wall to stop it collapsing already look as though they are going to give way at any minute," sneers Mandelson. "And if it's so fine, how come you got the letter from the church's solicitor?" Neaves didn't respond which only served to give more fuel to his friend's lecture.

"And another thing," Mandelson waves his hands in frustration, "I am in the middle of, shall we say . . . *financially* encouraging two councillors to get through the plans to build the hotel on the site next to the church. If anyone makes the connection on that little deal of ours then I am going to be drawn into the shit storm you have created." Emphasising his points, he jabs his finger at Neaves. "Almost looks as if you are destroying the church on purpose. Doesn't look good, the vicar was vocally opposing the hotel plans and your sub-standard work on the north wall looks set to bring the whole church down. Oh yeah, a total collapse would be convenient for removing the planning impediments to the hotel development wouldn't it just. If anyone finds out that you have a finger in both pies, we are in trouble. You need to sort it, and sort it soon. There is no way I am going down with your sinking ship."

"Well, things are working out, aren't they? Neaves shakes his head defensively. "The future of the church looks dodgy according to the Scarborough Evening News. Apparently, the congregation is practically non-existent and there was talk of closing it down anyway. The Bible Bashers can bugger off to the church in Malton."

Mandelson's face reddened. "Working out well! Working out well, are you kidding me? On top of everything else the vicar of bloody Dibley has been shot! The vicar has been shot! Shot! For God's sake. Gone. Kaput. Killed. And let's face it some of your associates are hardly choirboys, are they? It's not as though the bloody vicar has a long list of enemies, certainly not ones that are slowly demolishing his church and being taken to court. It doesn't take Sherlock Holmes to work out that you are worth having a

4

JULIA HENSON WINCES as her husband slams the phone down onto its cradle. Sitting in the drawing room of her house overlooking a picture perfect pristine front garden, she sets down her magazine and looks over to see his face turning crimson.

"Sebastian, please be careful. You insisted on retaining a landline and that phone is a genuine antique, it didn't come cheap."

"Sorry, darling, that man is a bloody nightmare." Sebastian Henson sinks into the expensive cream embossed Edwardian sofa which blends perfectly in with the tasteful décor of the room. Its centrepiece is a large early 20th century Chinese rug with exquisite green flowers and silver-grey butterflies almost invisible within white weave.

The five-bedroom house was a monument to refined taste and the envy of many of their golf club friends. Whilst Henson's wardrobe matched the décor with his Versace loafers, light blue chinos and cream polo shirt, his physical appearance did not keep pace. No amount of elegant fashionable attire could hide his middle-aged paunch and drooping jowls held up within a frame that barely reached five-foot five in heeled shoes. Neither did his personality compensate and his golf buddies had nicknamed him Danny DeVito: outwardly, he took this with good humour; inwardly, he raged. Especially when one added, thinking he was out of earshot, "Without the humour."

Julia's image, on the other hand, would sit comfortably on the cover of Vogue resting underneath the copy of the Tatler on her side table. Slender, with shoulder length blond hair and a clear, slightly tanned complexion, she wears her Dior sweater and slacks in the sort of casual effortless way that would make any designer cry with joy. Rotating her hand as she addresses her husband, his head circles mirroring her movements as he becomes mesmerised by her perfectly manicured nails polished in Hermes Rose Indien.

"I take it that the nightmare you are referring to is Ronald Neaves. What is that ignorant pig of a man up to now? I really think you should just drop him as a client. It's not as though you need the business."

"Oh, nothing darling. Won't bore you with it, save to say he never learns . . . as usual. Making bad decisions and false economies. You must remember the issue with the insurance when his factory offices burnt to the ground having ignored my advice to increase the insurance? Well, he's at it again."

"What a bore." His wife picks up the Tatler and resumes reading her article.

Conflicted emotions wrestle in Sebastian's mind as he stares at his wife. True love for her ran deep but he has never been convinced that it's reciprocated to the same degree. This hurts far more than the bitchy comments of supposed friends and associates. Clichés in overheard conversations at the golf club about punching above his weight and marrying him for his money. Snide sideways glances at the tennis club during his ponderous attempts to return the ball whilst his wife and doubles partner move gracefully around the court. He buries the hurt. These circles are all about keeping up appearances.

Self-awareness was a strength that Sebastian possessed. He knew he was no oil painting, and he knew that he may not have the most charismatic witty personality, but he had intelligence and a razor-sharp business sense. These qualities had funded a very comfortable lifestyle for his beautiful wife and himself. There was plenty of money in the bank, much of it safely resting overseas away from the prying eyes of The Tax Man. Not all his wealth was acquired legally, and he was not averse to having clients with conflicted interests, including McCarthy, the orchestrator of the downfall of Ronald Neaves. Gentile white collar crimes like fraud and embezzlement were one thing but having McCarthy as a client drew him into a far shadier world. Not that this association was without benefit. On occasion he had strayed out of his depth with disgruntled clients whose business interests would not bear scrutiny, and this is when his symbiotic relationship with McCarthy served him well.

On McCarthy's part his financial empire blossomed under Henson's financial guidance and acumen. Henson had established a company structure that not only minimised tax liability but provided a money laundering outlet for McCarthy's less respectable concerns. McCarthy valued the skills of his accountant highly and recognised him as an important cog in the machinery of his empire. Though never a big one for defending the vulnerable, McCarthy had taken a shine to his short accountant and was intuitive enough to observe the insecurities that came with a wife as stunning as Julia Henson.

However, no cog is irreplaceable, and this was a lesson Henson had learnt particularly when he needed the more unsavoury physical services available to him from within the McCarthy empire. The disappearance of one individual who had threatened Henson with police involvement shocked the accountant, who expected that McCarthy's promise to "Deal with it" meant the putting on the hard word and nothing more. Discretion being the better part of valour, Henson chose not to ask questions. On reflection he realised that any threat to expose his accountant would have put McCarthy under scrutiny through association. This was probably the prime determinant of how the problem was resolved so expeditiously. It did, however, cause him to rue the wisdom of baring his soul to McCarthy during one whisky sodden evening 'business' meeting.

Rumour had it that Julia was having an affair with Peter Dibley. In contrast to most village rumours this did not defy credibility. She seemed to spend a lot of time supporting the blond-haired, blue-eyed vicar, with his effortless charm and easy good looks. Dibley, who physically towered above Henson when they conversed at social events also played full back for the local rugby club, and his looks did not go unnoticed amongst women of all ages in the village, whether or not they were in his congregation. Struggling to recall his exact words on that evening with McCarthy after a few whiskies had been sunk, he was concerned that he may have given the wrong message. Or at least the meaning of his offhand comment that he wished Dibley was out of the picture may not have been interpreted as he intended. McCarthy may have had a different understanding from Henson's wish that the vicar would just move on, get promoted, then bugger off to a bigger parish. Do vicars get promoted? Henson had no idea. Nodding sagely and murmuring sympathetic understanding, McCarthy had drawn his own conclusions which Henson feared had not aligned with his own. As McCarthy ushered him out of his office, he gave Henson a reassuring pat on the back and a few words of comfort. Henson left the club with

McCarthy's words ringing in his ears. "Don't you worry Seb, it'll work itself out—with a little help from your friends."

Afraid to directly address the rumour of infidelity, fearing confirmation of its veracity, Henson had spent many hours mulling over how he could keep the woman he loved happy and content. The Beatles sang "Money Can't Buy Me Love", but Henson was not so sure. Unknown to his wife he had bought her a surprise birthday present, a small apartment with a view of the bay in her favourite French resort of Biarritz. His plan was to suggest that they split their time between the village and the retreat in France. His hope was that absence would not make the heart grow fonder when it came to Dibley He was not even certain that there was any truth in the rumours, but he lived by the adage that prevention is always preferable than having to find a cure. Little did he know that irrespective of the truth of the matter, a cure for this problem had been found that morning.

"Julia, love, I thought you were meeting friends for a coffee this afternoon?"

Shaking her head with her eyes still fixed on her magazine, Julia lets out a bored sigh. "No dear, Maggie sent me a text saying not to bother as the High Street was blocked off."

"Blocked off, why?"

"She didn't know Sebastian, she thought that maybe there had been another car accident. The speed they fly through the village I am surprised there isn't one every day."

"So, you're not going out then?"

"Perhaps later, I said I would catch up with Peter, he asked me yesterday if I would be willing to help organise the Church Fair this year. He wants to raise money to help fund the restoration."

Henson's barely concealed scowl goes unnoticed as she remains transfixed on her magazine article. Struggling to get her attention he raises the pitch of his voice. "It's your birthday tomorrow, would you like to know what I've got you?"

Still no eye contact. She replies, "No darling, don't spoil the surprise. Give it to me over dinner. I've booked that lovely French restaurant in Scarborough, 'Maitre D'. It's been ages since we went there, and I love the duck and, for pudding that yummy Tarte Tatin."

Deflated, Henson tries to give a cheery acknowledgement, but it descends into petulance. "As you wish." Julia picks up on this instantly.

"Oh, don't be like that darling. You know I love surprises and I am sure whatever you get me will be the epitome of good taste." If Henson were a puppy dog, he'd have wagged his tail with joy and, tongue lolling panted for more. Flattery from his wife, no matter how small the scraps, always appeased him.

"I know, it's just I love you so much Julia and I am excited about what I have got you. You bring sunshine into my life."

She had zoned out, so the words escaped, unheard. Flicking over a page of her magazine she sighs with boredom. Patiently and hopefully, he waits. No further scraps are to be thrown. Expectancy rises when she eventually looks up. Sebastian's eyes widen.

"Okay dear. Do you know, I think will pop out for a short while. I need some fresh air. Won't be long. I'll call in at Betty's and grab a couple of things to make us a small salad for lunch. We need to make more of an effort with your diet and healthy eating. Wouldn't do your waistline any harm either, we are both getting to the age where we need to take more care of things like our diet and health."

Smiling at his svelte wife he knew this was all about him, perhaps she cares deeply for him after all. Or perhaps his growing rotundity is becoming an embarrassment to her in the social circle in which they move. Insecurities wrestle inside him as he watches his wife rise from her chair and leave the room with easy elegance. Hands tighten into fists and his knuckles turn white at the sound of the front door closing. Did she slam the door? In his mind it had a finality about it as if a metaphor for their relationship. Insecurity gnaws and gnaws inside him.

Julia starts to reach into her bag for the car key but the singing and twittering of birds in the trees above draws her eyes up to the blue sky and a gathering of perfectly white altocumulus clouds. It was such a beautiful day, she decides to walk to the High Street, setting off down the driveway and then right into Forge Valley Lane. This short walk always raises her spirits as she strolls along the narrow pathway bordered by a variety of trees: Ash, Wych Elm, Holly and Rowan shade her from the sunlight. Nuthatches, Tree Creepers and Blackcaps twitter and warble hiding up high amongst the leaves and branches. They elude her despite her attempt to spot them. As usual the walk ends too early. She turns into the High Street and comes to an abrupt halt, standing stock still, she tries to take in the scene before her.

From her position at the western end of the High Street she sees the church in the distance overwhelmed with vehicles, flashing lights, people in uniforms and high-vis. There are two marked police cars, two saloons and an ambulance. With growing trepidation, she slowly makes her way down the High Street passing the Old Plough. Passing the butcher's shop, she lets out a short squeak of surprise when the owner materialises through the shop doorway.

With a white cap perched on his bald head and his arms folded across his striped apron, Stan Proudfoot appears with a cheery "Hello," but his smile quickly turns to an expression of concern. Realising he had caught Julia by surprise he immediately apologises. "Oh, terribly sorry, Mrs Henson, didn't mean to startle you. Are you okay?"

"Yes, Stan, sorry, I was too busy looking down the road at all the commotion. Do you know what's going on? Looks very serious. Is somebody hurt?"

The heavy-set man leans against the door jamb, looks down the High Street as if he needs reminding, and then speaks. "Not entirely sure Mrs Henson but I hear someone has been hurt, apparently shot. Not sure who but possibly the vicar and . . ." he pauses as he takes in the expression on Julia's face. "You okay, Mrs Henson? You look very pale, d'you want to come in and sit down for a minute?"

Julia was trembling. "Er, no, oh, sorry Stan, just was a bit of a shock. Are . . . are you sure that Peter was shot?"

"Peter? oh what, y'mean the vicar? I forget he has a name; I just call him Reverend. Yeah, he . . . rather no . . . to be honest I'm not certain. Just what I heard from Betty. Now do you want to come in and sit down fer a couple of minutes?"

Immediately she rushes along the pavement calling back, "Don't worry Stan must rush, in a bit of a hurry." Scratching his head in puzzlement, he watches her disappear through the door of the neighbouring grocery store.

"Ow do Mrs Henson," comes a disembodied voice from behind the counter. A short woman with a welcoming smile and tightly curled blond hair appears from the back room directly behind the serving area.

"Hello Betty, I popped in to get some things to make Sebastian a salad but just had a nasty shock. Stan says there has been a shooting down the road?"

"I've got some lovely fresh cucumbers, tomatoes, radishes, and some lovely butter lettuce."

"And the shooting Betty?" urges Julia, her brow furrowing in concern.

"Ooh yes, I went down there but the police will only let you go so far. It's all been blocked off. Could only get as far as Chris Ashton's place and they wouldn't let me go any closer. Even the petrol station is closed off.

T'was a crime scene they said and that I should go back to my shop and let 'em do their job. Very rude if you ask me."

"Stan told me that you said someone has been shot. Is that right? Is it Peter?" Emotion begins to creep into her wavering voice.

"Not entirely sure, Mrs Henson, but they are all over the church grounds and I couldn't see the vicar anywhere, so I was telling Stan that I wondered if it was the vicar? You'd 'ave thought he would be around about given all t'commotion, but couldn't see him."

Speaking from the shop doorway, Chris Ashton nudges into the conversation. "Hi Betty, hi Julia, how are you both? And yes, I saw it on the news when I had a quick half in the Old Plough. They seem to be confirming that there was a shooting, and it looks as though the victim was Peter." Betty gives a strangled squeal in alarm, prompting Ashton to tense up and swing round towards the shop door thinking someone was behind him.

"No Chris, it's Mrs Henson!" Turning back towards Betty he sees her pointing to Julia and darts forward, catching her as she rocks sideways. On the verge of fainting Julia sways as he takes her arm and guides her to a stool that Betty was setting down.

Reassuring her customer, Betty whispers "There, there, luv, just sit down while I get you a glass of water," and promptly disappears into the back room.

"You okay, Julia?" asks Ashton with a concerned calmness.

"Yes, thank you, Chris, I don't want any fuss. It was just a bit of a shock. This sort of thing doesn't happen in Ayton. Guns! Killings! Murder even . . . and Peter is — was — such a lovely man . . ."

"He was Julia . . . but I am not sure that anyone has confirmed it was murder to be honest. Doesn't make sense, why on earth would anyone want to murder Peter anyway? Could have been some sort of accident. Those idiots are always shooting rabbits, birds or whatever across the road but the police can't seem to catch them and prove it. Bloody dangerous."

Returning with a glass of water in hand, Betty passes it to Julia who nods in thanks and drains the glass in three long gulps. Setting the glass on the counter she thanks Betty, pats Ashton on his shoulder and starts to leave.

"Oh! 'ang on Mrs Henson I'll get you your salad veggies. Don't want Mr Henson to go 'ungry do we?"

Betty fills a carrier bag and passes it to Julia telling her to that she will put it on her account. Nodding gratefully Julia takes the bag, gives Ashton a final nod of thanks and quickly leaves the shop.

"Blimey!" exclaims Betty as Julia disappears out of the doorway. "She's in a state and an 'urry. I know it's a bit of a shock with the vicar 'an all but she has taken it very badly 'asn't she?"

"We're all different Betty. It is bloody awful though isn't it . . . anyway, I also need to get off, just popped in to see if you had got my tea in? The Darjeeling."

Without responding Betty bends underneath the counter and passes a package to Chris. "Here you are luv, just arrived yesterday."

"Cheers Betty," Chris quickly pays and jogs out of the shop leaving Betty muttering to herself that the whole village was in a hurry today.

5

ALONG AYTON'S HIGH Street, four cottages sit side by side adjacent to Betty's store. Chris Ashton owns the most westerly cottage next to Betty. Each plot of land occupied by the cottages is narrow but runs deep, almost sixty metres, onto a small back road called Carr Lane.

When he had first considered purchasing the cottage, Ashton had been concerned about the proximity to the main road and the noise as he'd listened to the hum of traffic leaking into the front living room. His concerns were soon allayed as he explored the property. Filtering out the sales pitch of the estate agent he made his way towards the back of the cottage through the kitchen discovering a large back room with French windows framing a sea of green. A verdant long and narrow back garden, dissected by a worn paved pathway, led to a wooden shed at the northern end. He'd almost missed it in his initial viewing, until the estate agent had pointed it out, because it was fully hidden by a blossoming white Dogwood tree. For him it was perfect: despite the proximity to the road, the depth of the back garden and its lush vegetation provided a peaceful retreat and the psychological space to create.

The shed became his workshop. Forsaking his natural skills as a wood carver he redirected his talents to stone sculpture and his initial works had sold quickly. Generating income from his art was neither important nor necessary to him but the appreciation of his pieces gave him the confidence to continue to develop this newfound skill. A pragmatist at heart, the foundation of the art form appealed to Ashton. He embraced its honesty and humble origins, historically rooted in the skills of tradesmen rather than the high-minded society of painters. Michelangelo had changed the game for sculptors. Chris Ashton knew he was no Michelangelo, but recognised he had talent.

A quiet and outwardly modest man, Ashton soon became popular in the village. Women would gravitate towards him, drawn by his good looks, easy manner and charm – not to mention his slim muscular build. In his mid-forties they could see he clearly took care of himself, and his athletic fluidity of movement gave him an understated but very real animal attraction. Some women would gossip, purring to each other that he was a man who ticked all the boxes; artistic, and single to boot. Was he too good to be true a few wondered with more than idle curiosity? Surely he must be gay because there was no woman in the picture, nor did he seem to have any interest in the female sex despite the less than subtle "come-ons" that local women had given him on occasion. Doing nothing to encourage this attention, one or two unwelcome incidents had occurred due to the dangerous mix of alcohol, flirting and insecurity.

At the recent New Year's Eve party hosted at the Old Plough, the girlfriend of a young villager had sidled up to Ashton a little worse for wear, becoming very tactile despite his best efforts to extricate himself. Seething at the bar, the boyfriend decided he had seen enough and marched his considerable bulk across the pub. Most locals gave the short-tempered labourer a wide berth being of a size that was a workable impression of a Mack truck. Shoving his drunken girlfriend aside with enough force to cause her to totter precariously then fall clumsily on her behind, he took a swing at Ashton, fuelled with the misguided confidence that the artist would be easy meat. In the alcoholic fog of the occasion no-one really saw what happened, other than Ken Wilkes whose second nature as a landlord was to always keep an eye out for trouble. For a big man Wilkes moved quickly, and although halfway around the bar in seconds to break up the developing fight, the situation resolved in an instant. Reading the telegraphed blow with ease, Ashton ducked in a measured economic movement just sufficient to evade the blow. As the bully's weight carried him forward, Ashton aimed a short but powerful punch to the man's solar plexus which winded him, followed by a second to his left kidney. The boyfriend fell to the floor in a heap like a very large sack of the proverbial potatoes. Wilkes was taken aback at the speed and power of the blows and the dramatic effect they'd had on the young labourer. By the time Wilkes had picked up the man, dusted him off, admonished him and started to frog march him out of the pub, Ashton had gone and was unlocking the front door of his cottage. He'd worked hard to blend into village life as anonymously as possible, but these situations did not help his cause.

Relatively new to country life, Ashton had spent most of his years based in London and discovered Ayton when he was in the area and a client of the security business that he worked for suggested Sunday lunch in the Old Plough. Subconsciously he was looking for a life change. He had tired of the big smoke. All the things that used to excite him about living in the capital began to rankle and irritate him like a persistent mosquito. In his younger years he embraced the noise, the hustle-bustle and the diversity of the people and cultures that the city had to offer. Over time his mindset altered, he had Capital Fatigue. Observing the peaceful life in Ayton triggered a yearning for change. Life was also becoming a little too difficult in London. Too many people knew him and where he lived and, in his occupation, this was a hazard.

Serving in the Intelligence Corp for fifteen years and highly trained in firearms, self-defence, and counterintelligence, he found upon discharge that he had skills in high demand. An ex-army colleague spent many months persuading him to enter as a partner in his security business and eventually Ashton relented, but only on the basis that he was an employee and could pick and choose what he got involved in. He did not want to be tied into anything long term and quickly began to regret this decision, even if he had written the narrative of his contract. Gradually it became clear that the legitimate façade of some of his friend's business clients hid an dark underworld that he wanted no part of. After all, what sort of person needs the security his friend's company had to offer? Not the normal man in the street, that's for sure. On the verge of resigning anyway, the decision was made for him when he was assigned as a bodyguard for a previous client, Edward Fraser. Working for the uncompromising Scotsman turned out to be his final job, bringing a dramatic turn of events that shaped his future.

To Her Majesty's Revenue & Customs, Fraser's Freight was a reputable company specialising in the transportation and import of heavy machinery. Occasionally the machinery was slightly heavier than indicated in the specification's manual, particularly with deliveries sourced from South America. Edward Fraser had inevitably made a few enemies, and, like himself, many were typically not people to be messed with. One recent deal had put him on edge. A Columbian businessman had berated him during what seemed like a never-ending phone call accusing him of underpaying for the weight of a recent delivery. Barely disguised accusations of theft, coloured with exotic South American insults, riled Fraser, who was made to feel like an errant child rather than an equal. Feeling a perverse sense of injustice and standing firmly on what he considered was the moral high ground, the bruising to Fraser's ego spread. As far as he was concerned, he had paid the agreed rate for the weight of the extra merchandise being delivered to his bonded warehouse in Portsmouth. Concluding that the fat greedy dago was just pushing boundaries, he simmered, and the angst ate away at his insides.

Who the fuck did he think he was? *Threats, really? Who gives a shit?* Once he'd calmed down, he decided that perhaps he should beef up his home security for a while as this business partner was due to have one of his regular trips to London.

It was at this point that Ashton's destiny was determined. Not wanting to waste his own men on babysitting duties — they had more important business to attend to, including escorting the entourage of the South American — Fraser contacted Ashton's friend who had assisted him in the past. The call resulted in what appeared to be a straightforward four-week assignment to keep an eye on Fraser's home and live-in girlfriend, Katja.

Two uneventful weeks passed, causing Ashton to question the wisdom of the assignment and whether it would suit a more junior and less experienced colleague. Was Fraser overreacting? Probably. Most jobs were mind-numbingly uneventful, nothing more than childminding neurotic clients, but there was only so long he could sit in a big house staring at Katja. He was bored and more than a little claustrophobic in the self-imposed prison. Katja never seemed to go out and spent her days watching television, drinking wine and ordering Uber Eats. Despite the size of the house the walls of Fraser's nine-bedroom mansion were closing in on him. Located on Bishops Avenue in north London, the house was in one of the most expensive streets in England outside central London. Neighbours were rarely seen but Katja, with no small degree of relish, gave Ashton the lowdown on an impressive list of neighbours, including a wealthy publisher, an industrialist, a philanthropist and two property tycoons; the biggest house on the street was supposedly owned by the Sultan of Brunei.

Relief for Ashton came from the most unlikely source. As much as he disliked Fraser's business partner, Hoskins, he could have kissed him when, on one of his frequent visits to check on the trophy girlfriend, he told Ashton that he could have the weekend off. Checking in with Fraser by text, Fraser confirmed what Hoskins had told him and he did not need to be asked twice. His weekend off was authorised.

Returning in a far more relaxed and refreshed state two days later, he rang the doorbell but got no response. His internal radar told him something was amiss even before he spotted the girlfriend's silver Mazda MX-5, a recent birthday present, sitting unused and forlornly in the garage having been delivered straight from the showroom.

The woman never leaves the house, her car is still there.

Shielding his eyes from the sunlight reflecting on the window, he peered into the living room but saw no sign of activity, so he decided to let himself in with the spare key. Curiosity ramped up to mild concern as he checked each room systematically all the while calling out to see if anyone was home.

No answer. Not good. Perhaps she had gone out for one of her rare jogs up to Hampstead Heath? Surely not, far too early for her, given her usual routine.

He began to check upstairs continuing to call out, not too loudly as he didn't want to give the woman a heart attack. Still no response. His final call caught in his throat when he entered her bedroom through the wide-open door.

Lifeless on the bed, he looked into her eyes. Glassy eyed death stare. The bed sheets soaked with her urine, her throat dark with a collar of bruising. Examining the room, his eyes rested on the white residue on the bedside table and then her small silver straw on the floor. Whatever had happened it had ended in a fatality and there was no sign of Hoskins nor his BMW. He called Fraser which, unsurprisingly, did not go well. Anger and shouting swiftly transitioned into accusation and blame.

The Scotsman was not a man to see reason when he was told news he did not want to hear and often it was the messenger who got shot. Fraser's normally faintly disguised Glaswegian accent had dredged up its Gorbals roots as he became increasingly agitated.

His father still lived in the housing estate that had shaped the man Fraser had become. Festering like an infected sore, Fraser's abusive childhood had crafted his own uncompromising personality. His father, an old, alcohol-sodden, dementia- ridden bastard could rot in his hovel. Fraser never went back to what could laughingly be called a home after his mother died a broken woman; thirty years of marriage had finally taken its toll.

As he took in Ashton's news, Fraser exploded

"And where the hell were you . . . playing with your fucking dick?"

Ashton calmed himself. *Deep breath, make allowances for the situation, be professional.* "As you will recall Mr Fraser, I had your permission to be away for a couple of days, so I was not here this weekend. She was meant to be under the care of Mr Hoskins."

"And where the fuck is he?"

"I am afraid I have no idea. I only got here a few minutes ago and there is no sign of him or his car. I am about to call the police. It's going to have to be reported."

"Calling the fucking police, are you serious?"

"Yes, Mr Fraser, I am here to protect people not to hide and bury them."

"You need to watch your tongue, sonny. Protect them! It doesn't look like you did much of a job at that either," snarls Fraser.

"As I explained, I was not on duty, Mr Fraser. We texted and agreed that Mr Hoskins would be staying here. I am trying to make allowances for you because of your loss and the shock but you are going to need to calm down."

"Oh! You'll make fucking allowances for me, will you? Thank you very fucking much. Keep talking like that and you will be making allowances to pay for your funeral. Do you know who I am?"

A further expletive-charged ten minutes passed until Fraser calmed down sufficiently to accept that the police was the only option given the circumstances. Not that they were much use.

Clarity on what had happened eluded the police in the days and weeks that followed. Ashton's tracks were covered by several corroborating witnesses, attesting to his presence elsewhere in the window of the time of death confirmed by the coroner. Much to Ashton's surprise the same could be said of Hoskins, though the veracity of the statements of those who backed up his story would probably bear less scrutiny. Not that Fraser saw it this way. Blinded by misguided loyalty to his partner and fuelled by his nagging insinuation that Ashton's relationship might have been less than professional, Fraser began to concoct a fantasy that Ashton was the man not to be trusted. Keen to avoid blame, Hoskins poured fuel on the fire. Eventually fantasy became the reality and rumour of retribution reached Ashton' after a serious conversation with his friend and soon to be ex-employer.

Retirement and a move from the big smoke became an imminent necessity and he knew exactly where he was heading.

Officially, the cause of death was recorded as strangulation due to clear evidence of petechial haemorrhaging, as well as the bruising on the throat. Detectives continued to regard Hoskins and Ashton as prime suspects in the absence of any associated crime. A house full of valuable items including the girlfriend's jewellery in the bedside cabinet ruled out the likelihood of a burglary gone wrong. There was no sign of forced entry. Since both Hoskins and Ashton had stayed in the property and no forensic evidence or DNA of other unknown parties was found in the house the case was left hanging.

Months passed and the death of Fraser's girlfriend remained unsolved and became just another cold case in a city where the list grew daily. Hoskins and Ashton remained persons of interest despite their apparent alibis but, as no one was actively investigating the case, it remained in limbo. For the Police they were just names in an investigation file. No charges laid. Diminishing interest in pursuing an old and seemingly unsolvable case, as fresh more straightforward crimes emerged, shunted it to the bottom of the pile.

6

THE DESK SERGEANT smiles mischievously to his colleague behind the counter who responds with a wink, as Detective Sergeant Len Hardy and Detective Constable Keith Stanley enter the reception area of Scarborough Police Station.

"Morning detectives, your witnesses are in Interview Room Three. I will buzz you through." A jarring sound and a large click indicated the security door, allowing access to the back of the station, was now unlocked. Stanley grabs the handle to open the door for his boss and as Hardy crosses the threshold the desk sergeant whistles the "Dance of the Cuckoos" theme tune to the old black and white films of Laurel and Hardy.

Hardy shouts back as he disappears down the corridor. "Very, very, very amusing. You two need to get a new joke, it's wearing a bit thin. Why don't you just bugger off and find a lost dog or something and leave us proper coppers to do our job in peace."

"Yeah, do that," adds Stanley as he follows his boss through the security door.

"Oooh! Young Laurel there has got his brand-new little detective knickers in a twist," mocks the desk sergeant to the loud guffaw of his colleague. "A few months as a detective and he thinks he's Sherlock *bloody* Holmes."

Although the similarity of the names had helped to give rise to the desk sergeant's nickname for the pair, it was their physicality that sealed it in his mind. The resemblance of DC Stanley to the famous comedian did not take a great leap of imagination. Tall, thin and pale skinned, DC Stanley looked almost malnourished and had an unfortunate resting face that gave him the appearance of a man mildly surprised that he had made it through thirty-two years of life relatively unscathed. Unfortunately for the pair, DS Hardy was shorter, approaching fifty years of age with a middle-aged spread that had settled stubbornly around his body. Hardy's diet and lifestyle was that of a single man who had long given up the chase. If he wanted female company, he hopped between the options of Tinder or professional services. Recently the latter was his preferred option. Less hassle. Less disappointment than that which came with the inevitable stream of awkward encounters from social media connections. He was sick of sitting opposite women who only vaguely resembled their photograph on social media and, on meeting them face to face exuded an air of desperation. Not only that, but the women opposite him invariably thought the same thing and dates tended to end abruptly. And to be fair, they had a point.

Shaking his head in irritation at the antics of the desk sergeant, Hardy briskly enters the interview room to find two ladies a few steps beyond retirement age sitting expectantly behind the table in the stark, grey, windowless room. Around the table rests four chairs composed of metal and vinyl which were clearly designed for functionality above comfort. Easing themselves down onto the two chairs at the opposite side of the table, the detectives adjust themselves to achieve as much comfort as the furniture will allow. The table is lodged against the side wall and on it sits the only other meaningful item in the room, a recording device.

"Hello ladies. I am DS Hardy, and this is my colleague DC Stanley," Hardy gestures towards his colleague and forces himself to give as close to a welcoming smile as he can muster. Stanley nods to the two women in acknowledgement but says nothing.

Reading from a sheet of paper in his hand Hardy addresses the women who look startlingly similar with short black curly hair, rosy cheeks and both wearing cardigans, one beige and the other pink.

"You are Miss Addinall?" Hardy enquires looking directly at the woman in beige nearest the wall. She nods in confirmation.

"And so am I," interjects the other woman in pink, cheerily.

"Sorry, you are both called Addinall?"

They nod in unison. "I am Freda, and this is my twin sister Mary," explains the woman sitting nearest to the wall, she then taps the recording device and asks, "Don't you need to switch this on?"

"Er, no Miss Addinall, we just want to hear what you have to say first, and it is not as though you are under arrest," replies Stanley with a forced chuckle. He was met with a vacant stare from the sisters and then an acerbic comment from his boss.

"Okay, DC Stanley, I'll do the talking. I understand Miss Addinall and, er, Miss Addinall that you both wanted to talk to me about the recent shooting of Peter Dibley. "

"Yes, yes," said Freda.

"Absolutely," confirms Mary.

Freda adds, "And you were on the TV, Mr Hardy, and you encouraged people who may have information on the shooting to come forward. We saw you …. you were very good."

Hardy manages a vague smile of appreciation, "Thank you. So, let me clarify, were you in the church at the time of the shooting?"

"Oh, no we weren't," respond the sisters in unison.

"Okay, so did you see or hear anything?"

Freda's brow wrinkles in thought. "Not really, we didn't see or hear much other than a gunshot that morning."

"Okay, that is very important, tell me more. You heard a gunshot, so I assume you got worried and went to see what had happened . . . perhaps?"

The sisters shake their heads in the negative.

Hardy continues his questioning with a frown. "Okay, so you were not worried, nor did you go outside to check what was happening." He scans the paper he is holding and then prompts the two women to say more. "I understand you live at one of the cottages on the High Street."

"That's right," replies Freda.

"Next to that nice Mr Ashton. He is such a dish," gushes Mary.

"A dish? The vicar?" asks Hardy.

"No, Mr Hardy, not the vicar. Mr Ashton is the dish," explains Freda.

"Mind you, so was the vicar," adds Mary.

Silence hangs in the air like damp washing on a clothesline. The detectives wait fruitlessly for further information or elucidation. Breaking the conversational standoff, Hardy continues, but with exasperation gradually creeping into his voice. "So, you heard a gunshot and this did not strike you as unusual?"

"Oh, yes we heard it," explains Freda earnestly. "But it's not uncommon, is it Mary?" Her sister nods in agreement but adds nothing further.

Hardy's exasperation doubles, they are not getting anywhere, but he manages, through gritted teeth, to push for further clarity. "Not uncommon?"

The sisters nod in agreement.

Hardy's exasperation turns into sarcasm to elicit a reaction and more information. "So, the vicar getting shot is a common occurrence then?"

Stanley's snigger is cut short by the withering look from his boss.

Impervious to the sarcasm, Freda cheerfully offers up an explanation. "Oh no, that's silly. We mean that we hear shots all the time from the fields. Young local men shooting at rabbits and other defenceless creatures— even Mr Wilkes from the Old Plough frequently goes 'hunting' as he calls it. Believe me, we have raised it with the local police on several occasions, but they do nothing, so we have given up even mentioning it now."

Audibly drawing breath to calm himself, Hardy summarises. "So, ladies, what you are saying is that you saw nothing, heard nothing unusual and have nothing that you can say to help our investigation . . .? So, what exactly can we do for you?"

Mary chirps up. "Well, we did a lot of work for the church, including the cleaning and we knew Peter quite well."

Renewed hope washes over Hardy. "Okay, so you knew the vicar well. So, did he have any enemies, Miss Addinall? Do you know who might want to hurt him?"

Watching her sister fall silent Freda responds. "It's only gossip mind, and we don't gossip . . . and we have never actually noticed anything obvious but . . ."

Silence descends once more. Hardy waits but his patience gives out and he finally snaps. "But what?! But what, Miss Addinall? Please tell me, but what?"

"Well, I . . . we . . ."

"Yes . . .?"

"Go on, tell him Freda," urges Mary.

Freda nods to her sister, appreciating her encouragement. "We are not saying it is true but . . ."

Hardy finally breaks down and bangs his fist on the table, causing the sisters to yelp. "Just tell me what you know! Please, just bloody tell me what you know!" Realising his tone, he feels contrite and glances sideways to Stanley whose expression is a mixture of admonishment and surprise. "Look, I am sorry ladies, I am really sorry, but we are busy and there may

41

be a killer at large. And if so, we need to catch him before more harm is done."

"It could be her, not necessarily him," offers Stanley. "The shooter could be a woman." He immediately regrets interrupting his boss when presented with Hardy's withering stare once more.

With a slight quiver in her voice, Freda accepts the apology. "That's okay detective. We are just trying to be helpful, and it was an incredible shock when we heard what had happened."

Mustering up his best conciliatory tone which still comes out as barely concealed frustration, Hardy tries once more.

"Okay take your time, just tell me what you know."

Freda takes a deep breath. "Well . . ."

"Yes . . ." encourages Hardy.

"Well . . . there is a rumour that the vicar — Mr Dibley, was having an affair with a local lady of some standing."

"And?"

"And we just wondered if this had something to do with it," suggests Mary.

"What are you implying Miss Addinall? Is it that you think this woman shot Mr Dibley?"

Stanley nods vigorously and with encouragement, feeling his suggestion that the killer could be female was vindicated. Luckily for him Hardy did not notice.

"Oh no, surely not," gasps Mary, staring at her sister in horror and dashing Stanley's hopes.' "Mrs Henson couldn't kill anybody."

"No Mary," replies Freda. "But *he* could have. I have never liked her husband; a horrible, rude and arrogant little man."

With his boss stunned to exasperated silence, Stanley, despite the previous warnings to stay quiet, speaks up. "Are you saying ladies that you think Mr Henson shot the vicar because he was jealous of an affair his wife was having? —"

"Oh, who knows," interrupts Mary. "But we did see an interesting documentary on the crime channel last night which featured real life crimes of passion, or *crime passionnel* as the French call it. They seem to think it is okay. It is, in their eyes, apparently justifiable to kill someone if you are jealous."

"Whose eyes?" snaps an increasingly confused Hardy.

"The French!" the sisters exclaim together.

Freda adds, "The French law courts make allowances for it apparently.

Well, they are supposed to be a very romantic lot, aren't they, the French?"

"But there again, Mr Henson isn't French, is he?" came Hardy's sarcastic response.

"Ooh no, you're right there," Freda agrees as Hardy shakes his head. She adds, "He doesn't strike me as romantic at all."

"And we don't like him," confirms Mary.

"No, we don't!" agrees Freda.

Pushing back his desire to stab himself in the eyeballs with a sharp pencil, Hardy takes in a long, controlled breath.

"Well ladies, as interesting as all this is, I need to draw this interview to a conclusion, unless you have anything further to share? No. Well we are very busy and as you may be aware, whilst the church may frown upon relationships between married members of the congregation and the clergy, there is not, as far as I am aware, any law against it. Detective Stanley here will show you out." He gives Stanley a curt nod to ensure he expedites their exit. As the twins are ushered out Hardy leans forward, putting his head in his cupped hands with elbows rested on his knees. Returning to the room Stanley tries to raise his boss's spirits.

"C'mon gaffer, you never know, it could be one of those *crime passionata's* they were on about."

"For fuck's sake Stanley it's called *crime passionnel*. And they are two frustrated spinsters with very little to occupy their minds or any other part of their body for that matter. You need to get a grip man."

To adding fuel to the fire of his boss's temper Stanley holds in his itching desire to comment further. But he did wonder about the Sherlock Holmes film he had recently seen. With great wisdom the fictional detective talked about eliminating the impossible as the key to solving any case. To be fair to the sisters their theory could be categorised as possible and therefore not be eliminated. Not only that, but they had also very little else to go on. A few leads but no firm suspects with motive. In fact, when he thought about it, they had nothing much at all.

7

THE LOCAL GP surgery almost half a mile beyond the western edge of Ayton's High Street used to be a double fronted Georgian mansion, situated on two acres of neatly kept ground and set back from the main through road into the Dales. Patients access the surgery from the main road by the gravelled driveway that stretches almost one hundred metres. The sympathetic internal conversion, from an industrialist's country retreat to a working surgery was not noticeable from the outside, which retained all the original features. Inside the building Dr Kamau practised medicine, assisted by his team comprising an office manager, a part-time receptionist, and a semi-retired practice nurse. The receptionist and nurse had left for the day leaving Stella, the office manager to multitask, which she always did with great efficiency. Fielding a call, she buzzed through to the doctor's extension.

"Dr Kamau, your father is on the line," she announced.

"Thank you, Stella, put him through please and feel free to lock up for the day."

"Thank you doctor, I will; putting you through now."

Kamau steeled himself. It was a call he was expecting but not one he had looked forward to.

"Father! How lovely to hear from you. How are you?"

"I am well Peter, and everything is fine, which is more than can be said for your current circumstances. Your mother has spoken with me."

Deflated, Kamau struggled to keep the cheery tone. "Yes father, but it is a mountain being made from a molehill. There's really nothing to worry about."

"On the contrary Peter, there is a lot to worry about. I did not pay for your expensive education at the University College London for some local cleric to flush it down the toilet. And if you do not have concerns about your own career and freedom, then consider the impact on the family."

"Father, I think you are overreacting." Kamau inwardly winced, realising he had lit the fuse.

"Do not — do not . . . speak to me in this disrespectful way boy. How dare you treat the family name with such disregard! What do you think the press will make of this? I can read the headlines now. The son of the vice president jailed for paedophilia! Shame on the Kamau family! Geoffrey Kamau must resign!" Kamau's father lapsed into heavy breathing after the outburst leaving the doctor with the dilemma of deciding whether to speak or to wait for his father to compose himself. He wisely chose the latter option.

"And, Peter, who is this priest? Who does he think he is making such accusations about the son of the vice president? Does this man have no respect?"

"He is a vicar father, not a priest." Kamau immediately regretted his response.

His father's voice almost reached through the receiver and grabbed him by the throat. "Do not dare to patronise me! I was raised in the country on my father's farm, everything I have — I worked for. You have been given everything! Including the house you are now sitting in. I may have not had your Queen's English education but clearly, they did not teach you respect nor gratitude in the schools over there. You think you are better than me? You think you know best?"

"No father. I am sorry, I did not mean to be disrespectful."

The apology fell on deaf ears.

"I told your mother that sending you away was a bad idea. We have educated you, financed your practice even though you chose to work in the middle of nowhere when all the best doctors are in London. You are the son of the vice president; you should be in Harley Street where all the real doctors are! We have pandered to you and your principles, yet all you do is bring ingratitude and shame on your family. This vicar dares to suggest that you acted inappropriately with a teenage boy just because the child goes to him complaining like some weak old woman. And you do nothing but tell your mother of this outrage. You could not even speak to me directly like a man. I had to learn about this from your mother!"

Hesitating to ensure his father had finished Kamau ventured a response. "I understand father, but the vicar is duty bound to report the incident, even if he does not believe it. At least he has come to me first to let me know what he will have to do. There is likely to be an investigation, but this is a normal process. Of course, I am worried, but I did not do what this boy claims and there is no evidence against me but the child's word. I have since found out that he has a long medical history of mental illness and self-harm. It was the first time he visited me because his family had just moved into the village. It will be clear that I am innocent."

"Why did this boy do this to you?"

"He is not mentally stable or well father. I was treating injuries to his arm after his mother had brought him into the surgery and I asked him questions about the cuts. His arm was covered in slashes. Although his mother was with him, she had left the room to take a call from her husband who was concerned at what had happened. He then just started screaming as soon as I asked him what caused the cuts. Two days later he had apparently visited the vicar who was counselling him. His parents are members of the local congregation, and this is when it all started."

"This vicar should have known better if the child is ill. Accusations such as these damage the reputation of the family. You may not be bothered by this but the damage to my reputation if this becomes public would finish me. Your mother would walk around our community with her head bowed in shame. You must stop this vicar from reporting it further."

"But I can't father. I have no authority."

"Well, if you cannot, or will not, then I will send over Joshua, he will deal with the matter."

"Joshua Kariuki? Father, you cannot do that. This is England."

"And we are in Kenya and will have to deal with the backlash. I clearly cannot expect you to resolve the matter. Do not tell me what I can or cannot do. You continue to show me disrespect and you refuse to do as I ask. The matter is closed. Expect Joshua in the next two days. Make him welcome and give him all the information he requires."

Left alone holding the receiver with no one at the other end of the line, Kamau's mind drifted back to his teenage days in Mombasa. His father had an ocean-side property on the island city, linked by a causeway to the mainland. He rarely saw his father, who went about his political duties in Nairobi. When he was at home he would spend most days in his large office at the front of the house, holding court to a steady stream of visitors. Always present and stood quietly in the back corner of the room was his bodyguard, Joshua Kariuki. Tall and thin in stature, Kariuki projected a menacing demeanour and when he stared at the younger Kamau it sent shivers down his spine.

Having served seven years in the 20th Parachute Battalion of the Kenyan Army, Kariuki was recommended to Kamau's father when he gained his first ministerial appointment. Kariuki quickly became a trusted employee after thwarting an attempt on his father's life during a short holiday at Samburu National Park. His father was driving the open topped jeep with his son in the passenger seat and Kariuki behind him, silently perched in the back seat with a rifle resting across his lap. They had spent two hours in the park and had seen elephants, buffalo, impala, and a herd of reticulated giraffe. Kamau was urging his father to take him to the leopards. With parental indulgence, his father explained that he could not guarantee they would see any of the notoriously solitary animals.

Located in the north of Kenya on the banks of the Ewaso Ng'iro river, the park was a popular target for Somali poachers. And so it proved when Kamau's father drove the jeep straight to the top of a ridge, where they were confronted with a dead elephant surrounded by three armed men. Two sustained fatal headshots within seconds whilst the third fled into the bush. Kamau covered his ears in fright at the noise of the rifle just behind his head until his father grabbed hold of him. With his father hugging him tightly, Kamau watched wide eyed as Kariuki leapt off the jeep and pursued the third poacher. Barely two minutes passed when he heard three more shots, shortly followed by the sight of Kariuki emerging from the bushland. Two images remained burnt into Kamau's mind. One was the dead elephant with its severed tusks laid beside it. The other was the expression of Kariuki returning from the bush. It was blank and emotionless as that of the giant dead animal. The bodyguard could just have easily been returning from a short stroll to fill his water bottle from the river without a care in the world.

"Everything okay, Dr Kamau?" inquired Stella, who stood in the doorway. Shaking him from his daydream, he smiled at her.

"Oh. . . oh yes, thank you, Stella. Sorry, was miles away, I thought that you had already left and I was here alone. You need to get yourself off now, it's been a long day."

"Will do," replied the office manager. "Was just dealing with an email that came in whilst you were on the phone with your father. Won't bother you with it now, but it was from Vicar Dibley. He is wanting to meet up with you again and he indicated that you would know what it was about, so I put one in the calendar for next Tuesday when you have a free time at 4pm. Hope that's okay?"

It took a few seconds for the distracted doctor to process what he had been told. "The vicar? Yeah, that's fine."

Stella had not waited for the reply, and he heard the front door close with a cheery "goodbye" shouted back to him.

"That's all I need . . . a meeting with Dibley and Kariuki turning up on my front door." The doctor muttered to himself, "How on earth am I going to manage this? It is not going to end well."

8

SINGING ALONG TO Duran Duran on the radio which she had turned up loud, Dolly Wilkes, the local landlady, goes about her morning routine preparing the pub for opening. Her rendition becomes louder and more confident as the song hits a verse that she is more familiar with.

". . . smell like I sound, I'm lost in a crowd and I'm hungry like the wolf, straddle the line . . ."

Convinced she hears a noise, she pauses and turns down the volume of the radio using the remote control. As the music subsides, she hears a distinct banging on the front door.

"We're closed," she shouts but the banging persists, so she goes to investigate. Unlocking the top bolt, she sees two men through the window. They look official and she has an immediate fleeting worry that Ken has been hurt. Smiling at them through the window she opens the door and greets them.

"Yes gentlemen, I am sorry, but we are closed."

"I realise that madam. Sorry to disturb you, are you by chance Mrs Wilkes?" Dolly nods in confirmation and her heart rate increases. The shorter man of the pair continues to address her.

"I am DS Len Hardy," holding up his identification card and nodding in the direction of the man next to him he adds, "And this is DC Keith Stanley. I wondered if you could spare a few minutes to help us with our enquiries."

Squinting at the card she responds hesitantly, "Well yes, but what is it? It's not about Ken is it? He's not hurt or anything?"

Confused, Hardy asks, "Sorry, who is Ken, Mrs Wilkes?"

"He's my husband, but he's not here. He went to Scarborough yesterday and is staying over with a friend whilst they sort out a business matter."

"No, please don't concern yourself Mrs Wilkes but I have to say we are here on a serious matter. We are making enquiries about the shooting yesterday. I am sure you have heard about what happened and hoped you could be of help."

"Thank God, I thought you were going to tell me Ken had been in an accident or something. Oh, I'm sorry that sounds very callous, doesn't it? The shooting . . . Oh, aye a real rum do that is. Yes, officer it was dreadful, I can't believe it. It's blooming awful. The poor vicar, such a nice man. But I am not sure how I can help you?"

Stanley intervenes to the mild annoyance of Hardy who was about to respond himself. "Please do not concern yourself Mrs Wilkes. It's not about your husband. We wondered if you had seen or heard anything?"

Irritated Hardy snaps at his colleague, "Thank you DC Stanley. I'll handle this," and turns to the landlady. "Do you mind if we come in rather than trying to conduct our chat on the High Street?"

Dolly gestures them in and sits them at a table she had just finished cleaning. As they settle into their chairs Dolly offers them a drink which they politely decline. Hardy resumes the questioning.

"So, Mrs Wilkes, did you see or hear anything unusual?"

"Not really, but I was telling Chris yesterday . . ."

Hardy interrupts, "Chris?"

"Yes, Chris Ashton, he was in 'ere yesterday lunchtime. Anyway, I was telling him that I did hear a gunshot but didn't think much of it at the time."

Eyes narrowing Hardy pushes for clarification, "And didn't this concern you?"

"Well not really, I thought it was those 'orrible Messruther boys shooting rabbits in Higginbottom's field." She begins to get upset adding, "But I guess I was wrong. Oh my, that poor vicar."

"Sorry Mrs Wilkes. We don't mean to upset you, but we need to get as much information as we can," assures Stanley.

Pressing his point Hardy continues. "Mrs Wilkes you said you were not concerned but you thought it might have been some locals. But how can you be sure what you heard was a gunshot and not something else?"

"Oh, I know what a gun sounds like. Ken 'as one which he uses regularly."

"So, your husband has a rifle and, I presume, a license for it?"

"Oh yes, but I assure you, he is very particular he is an' keeps it locked in a safe in the back room."

"Can we see it please?"

"What, his gun? Sorry luv you can't. Ken is not here and only he knows the combination t'safe."

"So, you don't know if he took the rifle with him?"

"No idea. He left early before I got out of bed. I don't know what he took with him. His briefcase and laptop I assume. May have taken the gun if he wanted to do a little bit of 'unting as well but I really have no idea. Early morning is the best time for it he says."

"But you do not know, and you cannot get into the safe?"

"That's right officer. But you are beginning to worry me. All these questions about Ken and his gun. What is it you are suggesting? What are you accusing my Ken of?"

Holding up his hands in a placating manner Hardy attempts to reassure the landlady. "No, no, Mrs Wilkes, we are not suggesting anything. A lot of police work of this nature is about eliminating possibilities so we can then focus on the things that are far more likely."

Dolly shakes her head; her expression indicates that she was far from convinced. "You both seem very bloody interested in 'is gun, pardon my French 'an I'm 'fraid I can't 'elp you. So, if there is nothing else other than your insinuations I need to get on. With Ken not here I am single handed and 'ave the place to get ready and a business to run."

Taking umbrage at the turn in the mood of the landlady, Hardy proffers his business card which she takes. His tone becomes more formal than previously. "When your husband gets back, please tell him to call me. We have a few questions for him, and, also, we would like to see his rifle and confirm his whereabouts at the time of the shooting. Good day Mrs Wilkes."

"Let yerselves out," she snaps and watches their exit through the front door muttering to herself, "Good day 'an good riddance." Grabbing her mobile phone off the top of the bar, she presses the screen a few times and puts the device to her ear.

"Ken is that you?"

"Yes luv, what's wrong? You sound angry," replies her husband.

"Where the bloody hell are you? I've 'ad the police around 'ere asking questions about you, and yer gun?"

"What! Why? What's happened?"

Exhaling with irritation Dolly tries to calm herself. "Haven't you seen the news? Don't you know about the vicar?"

"Dibley? What about him?"

"For God's sake Ken are you living in a bubble? He has been shot."

"What? Is he okay?"

"No, he is dead you idiot. The way they were talking to me it sounded as if they thought you did it."

"Are you joking woman? Jesus H. Christ."

"Don't effing blaspheme Ken—it *was* the vicar who was killed. I know you didn't see eye to eye with 'im but he is dead."

"What do they think I have to do with it?"

"I have no idea, but they want to see you and the gun. Where is it?"

"Locked in the car boot, I was going use it on the way back. Higginbottom asked me to join him to get rid of a load of foxes causing havoc on his land."

Dolly explodes. "Locked in the car boot! For God's sake Ken, I told them how careful you are with the gun. Safety 'an all."

"Sorry Dolly, you're right. To be honest I'd forgotten all about it. Was concentrating on the business with Steve here. I'll tell him I need to leave after lunch. We should be done by then anyway. I'll be back at the pub before 3pm."

"Good, 'an make sure you go and get that gun out of your car. Do it now. If it goes missing the police will think all sorts of bad stuff about you."

"Okay Dolly, but there is bugger all for them to think. I know I didn't like him with his perpetual bloody noise and nuisance complaints, not to mention threats to get our license taken away, but they can't possibly think it was us. As if I would bloody shoot Dibley."

"Ken, your temper is well known round 'ere. I wouldn't trust what anyone may or may not think. Or, for that matter, trust what ideas some of the local gossips like those silly old spinsters the Addinalls and the rest of the bloody congregation may put into the heads of the coppers. You just need to get back 'ere sharpish, talk to them 'an sort it owt."

"See yer later then," responds Ken, but the line was already dead.

Back in Ayton, the two detectives sit in their car discussing the next steps of their investigation whilst munching on pork pies from the local butcher, Proudfoot's. Stan Proudfoot took over the butcher's shop from his father who had inherited the business from his grandfather. The two detectives went through the motions of questioning the butcher but the affable rotund man with the bowling ball shaped head devoid of any hair could not offer any useful information. He had not heard or seen anything unusual, in fact at the time of the shooting he was at the local abattoir ten miles away in Malton collecting supplies for the coming week. Proudfoot's shop walls were adorned with a variety of prize-winning certificates attesting to the quality of his pies and these were the only positive outcome of their brief meeting,

"Bloody delicious," enthuses Hardy, not noticing the crumbs cascading down his shirt front and the tiny stain caused by a rogue globule of jelly.

"Yep," agreed Stanley, who was making a far more efficient and tidier assault on his pie, maintaining a stain and crumb free shirt. "What next boss?" asks Stanley as he pops the final piece in his mouth.

Struggling to cope with an overly ambitious bite of his own pie, Hardy eventually mumbles an answer. "We'll continue to interview the locals, particularly those living on or near the High Street, and the church. We already put out requests to the public to come forward. How are you going with the visuals?"

"We appear to be in a technology black hole here in bumpkin land. The only CCTV in the area is at the local petrol station and they have agreed to send though the electronic files covering the day of the shooting, as well as the day before. I checked my emails on my mobile and I can see that they came through a couple of hours ago, so I will go through them when we are back at the station. I did notice that the pub has security cameras at the front and back, but it slipped my mind to ask Mrs Wilkes when she got all angst. "

"Okay, call her when we get back to the station. Let's head back now."

Twenty minutes later the two detectives enter the reception greeted by the desk sergeant's regular rendition of their theme song.

"Give it a bloody resr Sergeant and get on with your paperwork so we can get on with proper policing," snaps Hardy.

Smirking, the desk Sergeant replies, "Did you get my text? You have two witnesses in Interview Room Three, responding to your call for information during your five minutes of fame on the telly. They have been waiting for over half an hour."

Barely acknowledging the desk Sergeant who buzzes them through the security door, they head straight to the interview room. Anticipation quickly turns to disappointment as they find themselves once more in the company of the Addinall sisters awaiting them at the table.

Blowing his cheeks out Hardy addresses them as he sits down. "Yes ladies, what can we do for you this time?"

Freda speaks first. "Well, on the TV you asked for people to come forward with any information that may be relevant, and, well, we thought of something else."

Hardy can barely muster any enthusiasm and expecting a fruitless exchange he indicates for his colleague to take the lead with a nudge of his elbow. Stanley gratefully and enthusiastically takes up the baton. "Tell me what you know ladies."

Freda taps the recording device, but Stanley shakes his head. "Not needed at this stage, Miss Addinall. Let's hear from you first," he encourages her.

'Well, it's the local publican, isn't it Mary?" Mary nods in agreement.

"What about him?" asks Stanley.

"He and Vicar Dibley didn't get on."

"How so?" replies Hardy on Stanley's behalf through a resigned exhalation.

"It was all the noise and trouble that happened when Mr Wilkes started having live music bands on a Friday night," chips in Mary.

"And what's that got to do with the vicar, didn't he like heavy metal?" suggests Hardy, his humour washing straight over the heads of the sisters.

"Oh no, it wasn't the type of music, it was the volume and the drunkenness of the young louts who spill out of the pub at the end of the evening. It's a regular thing now every Friday night. We hate it."

"And the vicar?" encourages Stanley.

"Well, he complained on behalf of his congregation"

"Including you?"

"Well yes but it wasn't just that," replies Freda looking towards Mary for elaboration which was enthusiastically taken up by her sister.

"It is disgusting, the noise is bad enough as they shout and scream at each other, but I have lost count of the number of times that one of them has vomited in our front garden, and last Friday Freda looked out of her bedroom window to see one actually urinating."

Good for the roses at least. Hardy muses but elects not to share his thoughts.

"That is indeed disgusting," agrees Stanley. "Have you reported this before?"

Mary once more took up the mantle. "Oh no, Peter addressed it directly with Mr Wilkes who turned up at one of our church meetings, at our invitation. Peter thought that it was best to talk directly and face to face. It was very acrimonious, and Mr Wilkes refused to stop the Friday night music as he said it was the most profitable session of the week; very popular amongst the young villagers and those from Malton, and even Scarborough."

Rapidly catching up with his boss's level of impatience Stanley attempts to get to the crux of the matter. "Okay Miss Addinall, I get what you are saying but it does not strike me as something that would lead a man to commit murder. Wouldn't you agree?"

"Yes, but we heard him as clear as day," offers Freda in support.

"Yes, we did." agrees Mary.

"Heard what exactly?" snarls Hardy as he grips the side of his uncomfortable chair with enough force to make his knuckles turn white.

"Heard what he said to his wife, that nice Dolly Wilkes, as they left the room."

"Yes?" queries Stanley. "Go on, what did he say? Just please — tell us what he said exactly."

The sisters look at each other and say in unison, "He said that he, 'Could bloody well murder that vicar if he ruins the Friday nights.'"

"Is that it?" snaps Stanley.

"Oh yes, we heard it as clear as day because we were at the back of the room, and Mr Wilkes spoke to his wife as he left the room," explains Mary.

"As clear as day," announces Freda, nodding in confirmation and support of her sister.

"For fuck's sake . . ." Hardy mutters, almost inaudibly.

9

RESTING ON HIS bed against the padded headboard, Joshua Kariuki mindlessly surfs channels on the TV in his hotel room. He barely glances at the young woman stood at the side of the bed pulling up her g-string followed by her short skirt. Hooking up her black lacy bra and pulling on her woollen crop top, she adjusts her hair in the mirror and pouts in satisfaction. Once she finishes dressing, she scoops up the notes on the side table, silently mouthing the numbers as she counts them. When she is satisfied, she pushes them into her mock leather handbag.

"See yer around," she calls back as a click of the door punctuates her exit from the room. Ignoring her, Kariuki continues to channel surf. Minutes later a knock on the door interrupts his peace and he is greeted by a cheery hotel staff member wheeling in his dinner and placing various items on the desk next to the TV screen. Despite a calculated short pause at the door there was no tip forthcoming, and the hotel employee gives a polite goodbye and leaves. Kariuki goes over to the desk, lifts the warming lids on the plates and methodically works his way through the meal with his eyes glued to the sports channel he'd settled on. Egypt was beating Gambia in the African Cup of Nations.

Kariuki has a love of football, despite the fact his own country was not even taking part in the competition. He tuts in disgust at the score, having adopted Gambia as his team for the tournament. It was a country which had given him very happy and profitable memories during his time there as a mercenary. Gambia is two nil down. A whirring sound on the side table draws his attention away from the screen and he notices his mobile, which he had left on silent, vibrating. Seeing the name of the caller he quickly snatches up the phone, swipes the screen and speaks.

"Hello, Mr Kamau, how are you?"

"I am well, Joshua, but where are you? Are you with my son yet?"

"No sir, I am in London in a hotel near Kings Cross . . . The Megaro. It's a small place, discrete."

"Why are you not in Yorkshire?" snaps Kamau.

"There was a long delay on the flight, I only just arrived at the hotel an hour ago," lies Kariuki. "I plan to take the train tomorrow and should be there around midday."

"Make sure you do. Time is of the essence, Joshua. Was there any issue at the airport?"

"None, just as you told me. I am liking this diplomatic immunity you arranged and everything in the luggage got through without question or examination. There is nothing to worry about. I am all set and ready to go sir." replies Kariuki.

"Delay or not, I am very surprised you could not get to my son today."

"Apologies, Mr Kamau, it was too late to get a train and I want to travel as invisibly as possible. No hire car records with my name. Just trains, buses, and taxis. Cash payments. You understand?"

"Point taken, Joshua. Call me when the matter is resolved."

Before he could respond further the line goes silent, Kariuki gives a sly smile, his employer seemed to want him to work on London time; a far faster beast than Kenyan. Urgent or not he intended to stick to Kenyan time, much more relaxing. Did he need to get the job done only to rush back? To do what? Spend days endlessly minding an overfed, overly demanding politician whose days in power were probably numbered anyway? Elections in May were going to bring change. What difference would a day make? Or two? Or even three if he felt like it.

Opportunities like this were rare, he wanted to make the most of it and taste what London and England had to offer. Yes, and he liked what he had sampled so far. From his conversation with Kamau's son earlier, Kariuki got the distinct impression that his presence was neither appreciated nor welcome. Despite the demands of Kamau senior, Kamau junior was in no hurry to see him, so he had a day or so to kill before he made an appearance to sort out the young doctor's mess. Mild disgust coloured Kariuki's attitude towards Kamau's son once he had heard the nature of the accusations. Maybe he deserved what he got if what was being said was true. Back in Kariuki's hometown Kamau would be lucky to get away with castration, let alone jail. His life, if he survived that local justice, would not be worth living.

Kariuki hops off the bed, undresses and takes a shower. It was settled in his mind, a couple more days in the capital was what the doctor ordered, even if the doctor's father did not agree. Fully spruced up, he leaves his room and takes the stairs to the reception area. Approaching the desk, he notices there is a new receptionist and a pretty one at that. Her tied-back hair accentuates her fine bone structure, and she smiles at him with perfect white teeth giving a startling contrast to her flawless dark blue-black skin. Summoning up his most charming smile he asks her if she could recommend a local pub with a bit of life.

"I am so sorry, I am new here and have only been in London for a week."

Drinking in her beauty he holds her gaze, "That's okay," then adopting an exaggerated quizzical look, he stares at her. She is drawn in by both his charm and his looks.

"Is everything okay?"

Eyes smiling, he speaks slowly to hold her attention. "Yes, all is well. I was just wondering if you are Kenyan? I thought I recognised the way you talk."

"Yes, you are right. I am staying here with my cousin until I find a place of my own. It's very difficult in such a strange and large city and I am finding it expensive here."

Holding his smile but narrowing his eyes to project empathy he asks, "Where are you from . . . the west perhaps?"

"Yes, Eldoret. What about you?"

"Practically your neighbour. I am originally from Kisumu. But I now spend my time between Nairobi and Mombasa mostly."

"So, you are Luo like me?"

"Absolutely," he beams. "Listen please, you are new here and I am just a visitor, how do you feel about coming for a drink with me? Perhaps show me around?"

"Thank you, I would like that, but I do not finish my shift for another three hours. And, as I said, I am new here myself."

Kariuki reads the name badge on her lapel, "That's no problem Rosemary, I'll go out and explore then pick you up back here when your shift finishes, if that's okay with you.?"

"Yes, of course, thank you, that would be nice," she replies. She tracks his exit from the hotel and although he has his back to her, she has the feeling he is aware she is watching him. His senses are honed from years hunting in the African bush and without turning around he raises his hand in acknowledgement, this makes her smile again before he disappears out of sight into the grime and bustle of the city.

The jarring cacophony of street activity rankles Kariuki and he stops suddenly on the pavement to gather his thoughts amidst the blaring horns, distant sirens and the roar of the traffic. A suited twenty something who was walking closely behind almost collides into him. Ignoring the loud tut and angry glance of the young man as he passes him, Kariuki tries to take in the scene. His attention is drawn by the voice of a Big Issue vendor calling almost tunefully for attention and trying to penetrate the guilty consciences of office workers racing to get home through the rush hour. The buffeting presence of a helicopter above takes his attention. He can see nothing in the sky other than an unrelenting blanket of gun metal grey which merges, as his eyes scan back towards the ground, into a slate grey cityscape. Shades of grey abound, including the complexions of the people rushing past him in all directions.

Momentarily, he takes himself back to the vibrant colour and smells of the African savannah and has a fleeting pang of homesickness. *How can people live in this?* For all the noise and movement, the city and its inhabitants seem to be devoid of vitality.

Wandering slowly, he meanders down the Euston Road, leaving the homebound commuters to dodge past him in both directions. Eventually he comes to a large intersection and stands in wonder looking across the road at a thirty three floor building towering in front of him. He notices the signage, Euston Tower, above the ground floor entrance. It too has a greyness which melts into the sky as, once more, he peers upwards. Turning left into Warren Street, he walks until he comes across a pub which looks inviting.

The black Victorian frontage is dominated by the name stencilled across its frontage above the door and bay window. Golden letters spell out Smugglers Tavern. The windows have painted offerings and enticements, including the finest rum and seasonal English food. He enters. Whilst the owners of the pub have attempted to create the atmosphere of a cosy almost conspiratorial haven engendered by the pub's name, the staff do not seem to have got the owners memo. A thin, blond, barmaid with a sallow complexion and an accent of indeterminate eastern European origin greets Kariuki. Her facial expression oozes boredom and the tone of her voice skirts somewhere between disinterest and rudeness. Kariuki's charm does nothing to melt her icy demeanour and he orders a pint of lager which is mechanically served to him with the merest glimpse of a possible smile.

He had just settled himself in the window bench and rested his drink on the table opposite two lonely stools when his phone starts vibrating.

"Hello Peter, what can I do for you?" Sipping his beer, he awaits a response from the doctor.

"Hello Joshua, my father called me a few minutes ago and was wondering where you are. I told him we had spoken on the phone, but you were not here yet. I'm just calling because when we talked earlier today, I thought you were on your way. What are your plans?"

"I am not sure yet as something came up. I was planning to be there either tomorrow or the day after. Why do you ask, has this vicar been back in touch with you? Are things getting urgent?"

"No, he hasn't and no, there is not really anything urgent. As I told my father he is simply following protocols, there is nothing in this and it could take weeks."

Smiling Kariuki responds, "Your father thinks otherwise. He wants the matter dealt with quickly."

"I know but he is overreacting and—"

Kariuki interrupted, " . . . and Peter, he is acutely aware of the elections and the damage this may cause him. That is why he sent me."

Scratching at a stress induced rash over his left eyebrow, Kamau is becoming increasingly agitated. "That may be the case, but we are unlikely to get any bad publicity once the process is completed and I am exonerated. It certainly will not reach Kenya from here. Anyway, the matter remains confidential unless the police decide to lay charges, which is never going to happen. I am more worried about what it is that you intend to do."

Pausing, Kariuki carefully considers his next words before speaking. The silence escalates Kamau's stress levels as he awaits a response until it finally comes. "I will talk to this vicar, explain the sensitivity of the family's circumstances and hopefully he will see reason."

"But it's not about seeing reason. Don't you understand? It is a process that he must follow. It doesn't mean he thinks I am guilty. The boy involved has a bagful of mental health issues which are well documented."

"Well hopefully he will also understand that there is a need for discretion, particularly if the accusations are, how can I put it . . ." Kariuki pauses once more and then adds in a tone which portrays self-doubt as to the veracity of what he is about to say, ". . . unfounded."

"No disrespect Joshua but you are turning up out of the blue from Kenya and having this sort of conversation with him could work the other way. It smacks of guilt and a fear of consequence, rather than my innocence. If I am right and it makes matters worse . . . where does that leave us?"

Once again Kariuki pauses for consideration, Kamau asks if he was still there.

"Yes, Peter, I am still on the line. If the vicar is unable to meet our polite requests, then perhaps a stronger approach may be required."

Kamau shouts into his phone "Good God, Joseph! You are not in Nairobi now, this is England!"

"It is but we are Kenyans, not English, and if the English approach does not satisfy an Englishman, then perhaps the Kenyan way will." Kamau sits in his office speechless. Kariuki adds, "I will be at your home in two days when my other business is finished. In the meantime, do not say anything to the vicar or anybody else on this matter. And do not mention that you will be having a visitor from your homeland. Think of me as one of your favourite animals, the leopard. I want to remain out of sight, unnoticed, shy, retiring, nocturnal." Kariuki swipes his screen and closes the call leaving Kamau open mouthed at the other end of the line.

"Nocturnal, yes because leopards, like you Kariuki, hunt in the night," Kamau mutters to himself.

10

DRIVING THROUGH THE centre of Scarborough, Chris Ashton ponders the potential outcome of his meeting. Approaching the junction where the main thoroughfare becomes pedestrianised, he takes a sharp left onto the road that leads directly to the police station. An architectural monstrosity built in the 1980s, the grey building with rendered orange panels looks more like a badly designed cinema than the headquarters of the guardians of law and order. Taking the advice that the station sergeant gave him on the phone, Ashton pulls into the back of the building and parks in a space allocated for official visitors.

Pressing his fob as he walks away from the car, a loud beep heralds the arming of the alarm. This prompts a comment from one of the two officers leaning against the station wall having a cigarette.

"Well done lad. Can't be too careful 'ere. A lot of dodgy types. Don't want some thieving bugger to take it do yer?"

"Too right officers," Ashton smiles back, acknowledging their humour. They point to a small alleyway and tell him he can take a short cut through it to get to the main entrance at the front. They turn back to speak to each other as Ashton waves in thanks and makes his way into the station. In contrast to the external garish design the internal décor of the building is neutral, the colour was probably beige when originally painted but now has a dirtier, yellowed brownish hue which is singularly uninviting. The desk sergeant greets him as he approaches the desk.

"Yes sir, how can we be of assistance?"

"Hello officer, my name is Chris Ashton. I got a call yesterday asking if I was able to come in to talk to some detectives. As I was coming to Scarborough anyway, I told the officer I spoke to that I could come in today at around eleven."

As if to make a point the sergeant glances at the wall clock and Ashton mirrors him noting he is late, it's 11:40 a.m.

"Yes Mr Ashton it was me that called you. Thank you for coming, the 'detectives' are already here. I will get my colleague here to escort you through." Gesturing to an officer behind him, the sergeant exchanges a smirk with the other officer. Ashton, perceives a disguised tone of sarcasm with the undue emphasis on the word 'detectives'. The officer disappears into the back and then reappears, opening a door to the side of the desk, he gestures for Ashton to come through. No words are exchanged until the officer stops abruptly and announces to Ashton that they are to go into Interview Room 3. After knocking on the door, the officer stands aside allowing Ashton to pass. With the door closing behind him Ashton sees two officers sitting at a table. He makes eye contact with a taller thin man and then an older one with a little too much middle-aged spread who addresses him.

"Come in Mr Ashton and take a seat. I am DS Hardy, and this is DC Stanley," says Hardy gesturing to a seat at the opposite side of the small table. An absence of natural light makes the room look even grubbier than the rest of the station. The lack of furniture other than the table, four chairs and the recording device add little to improve the ambience. Hardy attempts a welcoming smile which seems more strained than genuine. "Once again, thank you for agreeing to come in Mr Ashton. I recognise that it is a bit of drive from Ayton, and we appreciate your time."

Observing what looks like a small tomato sauce stain on the detective's tie, Ashton battles to resume eye contact but Hardy had already looked down reflexively at his front. A passing frown indicates that he could not see what Ashton had been looking at. Composing himself and meeting the gaze of Ashton he opens his mouth to speak but his thought process is immediately interrupted when he sees Ashton point to the recording device.

"Er, before we start, Detective Hardy, I just want some clarity. Is this an official interview and is it being recorded?"

"Why? Is there a problem Mr Ashton?" interrupts Stanley, "Is there something that is concerning you? We just want to clarify a few facts." Intentional or otherwise, the lines are drawn and from that point on

Ashton and Stanley take an instant mutual dislike for each other. Bristling, Ashton slightly shuffles in his chair, betraying his annoyance.

"Thank you, DC Stanley, I will handle it," interjects Hardy.

"Please do DS Hardy. I am not sure I appreciate the attitude of your colleague here. I was asked to come in and talk to you which I have done freely. I was marched into an interview room when I arrived and now it all looks a lot more formal than was implied on the phone." Whilst Ashton addresses Hardy he maintains a cold stare at Stanley who is itching to respond at the jibe but fears the wrath of his boss.

Hardy, annoyed that Stanley has immediately got Ashton offside and on the defensive, gives his partner a warning glance to be quiet. "Look Mr Ashton, we just have a few questions we would like to clear up. And no, we are only information gathering at this stage. It is not a formal interview nor is it being recorded."

"That's fine DS Hardy, but you haven't yet told me what this is about. I am sure my road tax disc is up to date."

"It's not a laughing matter Mr Ashton. It is concerning the shooting of Reverend Peter Dibley, of which I am sure you are aware given you live in the village and near the church."

"Of course I am, it is truly a terrible business . . . but what is it you want from me? How can I help?"

"Our enquiries have brought up a couple of issues which relate to you and are of interest. There is a possibility that they have some bearing on this case." Hardy sits back in his chair and awaits a response from Ashton. Thinking that Ashton has been cornered, Stanley smirks in satisfaction but he is only greeted by a neutral, calm expression. Mildly disappointed at the lack of any reaction from the interviewee, Hardy presses on with his questioning.

"The first matter relates to CCTV footage we have on the morning of the shooting." Pausing for effect, Hardy raises his eyebrows to indicate he expects some sort of comment but Ashton is unresponsive to the point of disinterest. If he is guilty of anything it is not showing thinks Hardy. With a mixture of frustration and anticipation Stanley fidgets in his seat crossing and re-crossing his legs. No response, no emotion from Ashton. Even when Stanley leans forward expectantly to encourage a reply, none was forthcoming.

"You have gone quiet Mr Ashton," Hardy breaks the silence, "Are you not interested in what was on the footage?"

"Look DS Hardy, I have not got all day. I came in here at your request and I really don't have time to take part in what looks like a very badly written episode of Columbo. So rather than leave me to guess so you can make some sort of big reveal, why don't you just ask me what is on your mind. It may be impressing your trainee here," he nods in Stanley's direction without looking at him, "But I have better things to do." Pausing and observing Hardy's complexion turn a deeper shade of red, he adds, "Of course, I am upset about Reverend Dibley, but I don't think there is much I can do to help."

Composing himself, Hardy endeavours to regain control of the interview which has not gone as planned so far. "You may or may not be aware but although there is not a lot in terms of CCTV in the village the local petrol station is an exception. DC Stanley here obtained the footage from the evening before, and from the morning hours of the shooting. You were caught on camera during that period."

"So?"

Stanley, despite the earlier warning, involuntarily spits out a comment. "So, Mr Ashton, it is clear and evident that you were there around the time of the shooting and, what's more, heading in the direction of the church."

"To be clear, you are asking me if I shot Reverend Dibley? Did it look as though I was carrying a gun?" asks Ashton sarcastically. Stanley wriggles in his chair and blushes at the dismissive nature of Ashton's attitude. Angry red fireworks burst in his brain as he struggles to find a riposte.

"Please leave this to me DC Stanley," snaps Hardy. Ashton smirks at Stanley and turns his attention to Hardy, raising his eyebrows to prompt an answer to his question. Taking this cue Hardy responds. "At this stage we are not accusing anybody of anything. We are trying to ascertain the whereabouts of everybody in the vicinity to both eliminate people from our enquiries and gather information on what people in the area may have seen or heard."

"Okay, so what would you like to know?"

"Firstly, Mr Ashton, what were you doing in that area alone at that time of the morning?"

"Well, first of all, I wasn't alone."

Taking a deep breath Hardy asks, "Well okay Mr Ashton, let's address that comment first. Who were you with?"

With his pen poised over his notepad Stanley once more interrupts, to Hardy's annoyance. "There was no other person on the CCTV footage!"

Ignoring the interruption Ashton continues to look directly at Hardy and answers. "I was with Barry."

"Barry who?" asks Stanley with now barely concealed exasperation.

"Barry the Beagle, my dog; it alliterates," replies Ashton He purposely maintains eye contact with Hardy whilst answering Stanley's question which winds up both the detectives in equal measure.

"Who are you calling illiterate?" snaps Stanley with his pen still poised above his notebook.

"Alliterate, it is spelt with an A. You know, words that begin with the same letter constable. If you were illiterate then there would be no point in you having that pen and notebook, would there? Though now I think about it . . ." Ashton leaves the last thought buzzing around like an annoying fly.

Desperately searching for a rejoinder Stanley settles on, "You seem to think you are very clever Mr Ashton."

Responding instantly Ashton replies, "Well only relative to those in the room."

Hardy had lost patience. "Okay leave it DC Stanley. I will conduct the rest of this interview and I would appreciate it, Mr Ashton, if you could just answer our questions directly. It will save your time and ours."

"Look, you two started the Columbo routine. The bottom line is I was out that morning jogging with my dog, judging by the timing of that CCTV footage. I suspect if you check it for the whole week, I will appear around that time most days. It's quiet, relatively little traffic and Barry can have a run around in the woods in peace. Why you think there is anything more sinister I have no idea. But on the day you are talking about I did not see or hear anything that I imagine could be connected to the 'vicar's murder. Or at least nothing unusual. I think I may have heard a shot or two in the distance at some point, but this is not uncommon with the local unlicensed sport of rabbit shooting that seems to go on, unfettered by any intervention by the local constabulary. Perhaps this is something you ought to get your colleagues to address. It's bloody dangerous with people in the vicinity." Pausing for a response Ashton sits back into his chair looking at the two detectives who are trying to process what he had just said.

Leaning forward, Hardy clasps his hands and rests his elbows on the table, causing Stanley to shuffle upright with a look of expectancy. Stanley knows the next query his boss is about to raise and smells blood. Ashton remains relaxed leaning back in his chair.

"Well, I said there were a couple of issues. During our enquiries we happened to come across something of interest. When DC Stanley here entered your name into our system it appears that you were red flagged.

This caused us to look into your history, which I have to say is impressive and unusual for a man who just appears to make pottery."

"Sculpture," corrects Ashton.

"Whatever! The point is Mr Ashton, that setting aside all the impressive military stuff we subsequently found about your past, you are also retained as a person of interest in a now ageing and unsolved inquiry into the death of a woman in North London. You can therefore see why we thought it was worth talking to you after the shooting of a local inhabitant, in a village where the most exciting event to ever occur was the building of a small tower."

Holding a steady gaze into Hardy's eyes, Ashton carefully processes what had been said and constructs his response before speaking.

"Whether or not I am considered a person of interest by the police, I have no idea. I also have no idea what information you may or may not have in your system, but I am sure it does not say that I was convicted of any offence. In fact, I was not even charged because I am innocent and clearly was nowhere near the area where the murder took place. My only connection was that I was employed as a bodyguard to the unfortunate victim."

"Looks like you did a great job there," mocks Stanley with a snide remark, trying to regain ground lost in his previous exchanges.

"Well looks can be deceiving DC Stanley. Here we are in a police station, and it looks as if you are a detective. What can I say?"

Jumping in before the exchange could further deteriorate, Hardy sought to regain control. "If you have nothing you can further add Mr Ashton, I think we are done. Thank you for your time and DC Stanley will show you out. We may be in touch again in due course, I take it you are not planning to leave the area?"

"Not at the moment but who knows," replies Ashton as he gets up and follows Stanley out of the room. When Stanley returns, he is greeted by a scowl.

"Stanley, I know you want to impress but you need to do less talking and more listening. It's bad enough making yourself look a fool but when you make me look an idiot as well, then I have a real problem. You did not tell me that the record you pulled indicated he had a cast iron alibi. In future you need to shut the fuck up and leave the talking to me until I say you are ready to do otherwise." Hardy pauses to gather his thoughts then resumes. "You also need to read the room. Clearly, he is not someone who can be intimidated, so we need to tread carefully and be smarter. Let's leave

Ashton for now . . . though I've got to say he does seem way too cocky for my liking. That, itself makes me suspicious. Anyway, we need to check out Wilkes. He'll probably be back from his trip by now." Chastised, Stanley remains silent and makes no attempt to move until Hardy barks at him, "Now bugger off and do some police work."

Resentful, Stanley gives a grunt of consent and walks towards the door but is brought to a halt when his boss speaks. Surfing his phone whilst sat slumped in his chair, Hardy shouts over to him without looking up. "And another thing, Stanley, do not try to engage in banter with people like Ashton. You'll always come off second best and end up looking like a clown."

Driving back to Ayton, Ashton calls out a series of instructions in his car and the ringtone surges from the speakers, blocking out the hum of the engine. The tone stops abruptly, and a familiar voice greets him. "Hi Chris, long time no hear, how's life on the farm?"

"It's a village mate, not everything outside London is a farm," laughs Ashton in response. His voice turns serious. "Listen mate, have you heard from Hoskins or Fraser?"

"No mate, what's happening? I've kept clear from those two since it all went pear shaped with you."

"Not sure, maybe nothing, it's just things up here in sleepy rural Yorkshire have gone a little off-piste."

"Why, have you seen either of them up there or, at least any of their apes?"

"No, but I would appreciate it if you made a few inquiries. It's probably nothing mate but just want to be sure."

"Okay Chris, I can come up if you want. I still owe you for what happened."

"Appreciated but no need . . . at least not now. Just see what you can find out."

"I'll be in touch Chris, but for the time being just keep vigilant and be careful."

Music from the radio replaces his friend's voice, signalling the end of the call. Dire Straits are telling him that it was money for nothing, and the chicks were free.

11

PERSISTENT FINE RAIN had silently trespassed into the very fabric of the capital. Everything was saturated and even the brickwork of the nightclub looked as though water would ooze out if you leant against the wall. There was nothing inviting about the night, the club, and particularly the two bouncers at the door. Two drunken youths approach the door but are stopped in their tracks by an extended arm from the larger of the two doormen. A brief exchange of words sends them packing, with the most resistance offered being a sulky backwards glance from the braver of the pair. Minutes later three more approach the club and, outwardly at least, they did not look as though they would be as compliant as the others.

The shorter of the two bouncers takes charge this time, stepping forward into the drizzle to appraise what is in front of him. Two had neck tattoos and a swastika on their forearms and the third had more metal in his head than London Bridge. Triple trouble. The shorter bouncer addresses them. "Sorry lads, you can't come in." There was nothing about his tone or demeanour that indicated he was genuinely apologetic. Metalhead appraises the bouncer by dismissively looking him up and down with exaggerated movements. He then glances at the taller bouncer. His erroneous conclusion is that he has the firepower to take the matter further and not lose face. Encouraged particularly by the short stature of the bouncer directly in front of him and buoyed by their reputation at the nearby housing estate where they lived, he fancied their chances.

"What the fuck mate, just let us in."

"Sorry, no can do. Just leave. You can't come in," replies the shorter

69

bouncer evenly. His taller colleague remains motionless and expressionless in the shadow of the door.

"Why the fuck not?" asks Metalhead with a challenging snort.

"Two reasons: one, you are not dressed appropriately."

"What the hell are you talking about! Eh . . .? Well, bollocks to that . . . 'an what's the other reason?" snarls Metalhead, looking back at his mates with a mean looking grin.

"I said so," replies the bouncer flatly.

The taller bouncer spoke from the shadows. "Lads, for your own health and safety I suggest you bugger off. Wouldn't want to lose your earrings on the dance floor. Wouldn't want your pretty little face jewellery to get ripped out of your itty, bitty, luverly ears, eyebrows and lips, would we?"

"Do you know who we fucking are?" shouts one of Metalhead's mates from behind him.

"I don't care if you are the three little pigs come to blow our house down. Just jog on; it's way past your bedtime and mummy will have your cocoa ready," said the shorter bouncer with a smile that could freeze the flame of a candle. Bursting into a bizarre bobbing movement to deliver a head butt, Metalhead never even looked like connecting with the shorter bouncer who eases back to a safe distance.

Without comment, the taller one takes three long purposeful strides from the doorway and catches the youth directly on his left temple with a short jab. Seeing their mate in a crumpled heap on the pavement the other two take flight, while the shorter bouncer drags him five yards into the doorway of a nearby bank and turns him on his side in case he vomits. Pointing to their unconscious friend he shouts for them to come back and take him home.

Once at a safe distance they stop, turn around and bob hesitantly on the spot while deciding their next move. Cautiously, they edge back towards the nightclub but take a wide arc to avoid the risk that their movements may be construed as attempting to gain entry. With a struggle they lift their friend upright and, holding him steady between them, awkwardly make their way up the street. All the while they keep a wary eye on the bouncers, now both in the doorway of the club and chatting casually, oblivious of the threesome making their ignominious journey home.

The atmosphere inside the club is marginally more convivial. It is dark and noisy but Fraser, the owner, had not pushed the boat out when investing in the décor. In the main area of the club the bar occupies one corner and in another a small platform houses the DJ. A half-hearted attempt at a dance floor in the centre of the room has seen better days, with the wood varnish mostly worn away. It is surrounded by a few tables and booths with cushioned red velour seats occupying the surrounding wall. The DJ is pumping out techno music, merging seamlessly into a new track every few minutes to become one continuous pumping beat.

With the beat intensifying after a lull, a group of arm waving youths become human pistons on the dance floor, moving in unison with the pounding bass. All the first timers in the club had lost their MDMA tablets due to the vigilance of the bouncers on the door. Their booty was dutifully passed to the barmaid, who resells them to the clueless punters in the toilets at inflated prices. Regulars are wise to this and take their fill just before going into the club. Nevertheless, there are enough mugs new to the scene to provide a good source of supplementary income to the security and bar staff involved in the scam. Those not dancing are sitting at the tables or standing against the wall, supping from plastic bottles of water, a few others are sipping on bottles of warm overpriced beer.

Adjacent to the bar, a door with a Staff Only sign leads into a small corridor, another heavier metal door at the end of which marks the entrance into a comparatively luxurious office, carpeted in light grey and tastefully decorated with a modern desk in the corner. A seating area in front of the desk comprises an expensive glass coffee table and a handmade flat weave ivory rug bordered by a light grey linen sofa and matching chairs. A small built-in unit with a bar and fridge stocked with spirits and mixers rests against the wall. Sound proofing ensures that the thumping bass from the club could only be heard when the office door was opened.

Fraser uses the office as his nerve centre and a place to retreat from the constant hassle of needy employees, clients and other losers who couldn't think for themselves. The club itself is a mere pimple on the face of his empire, it serves his purpose to remain low key with an air of mediocrity, neither a popular fashionable destination for night time revellers nor a highly visible nightspot. It is the only licensed premises in what is a borderline derelict area which would only be frequented by council tenants from the nearby estate or middleclass youths wanting to be edgy and check out the other side. Time Out characterised the club as "unremarkable" which is just the way Fraser wants it. Many a deal is done in the office away from the prying eyes and ears of the law, his competitors, and his enemies, of which he had a few. The office is constructed to be a safe room and at the flick of a button underneath his desk the solid steel door would lock shut, converting it into an impenetrable haven. Even if the club was set on fire and burnt down, the office with its fire and bomb proof shell would remain unscathed in the surrounding ashes.

Reclining behind his desk, Fraser extends his arm out to a colossus of a bodyguard who passes him a generous glass of whisky engulfed in his massive hand. Trent McCarthy who is sitting in a chair next to the coffee table receives a second glass which appears from the other hand of the man mountain. The bodyguard leaves the room having been dismissed with a flick of his boss's fingers. A pounding techno beat to temporarily sneaks into the room but is quickly exorcised when the door closes behind him.

McCarthy takes a sip of his whisky and nods appreciatively.

"Whaddya think?" asks Fraser.

"Nice drop, Edward," replies McCarthy

"Convalmore, thirty-six years; it's a beauty."

"Is it now? Yep, nice scotch."

"I'll give you a bottle to take back with you, make the journey back to Yorkshire a bit smoother." Fraser rests back into his chair, allowing them both to savour the drink in silence.

McCarthy drains his glass and puts it on the coffee table, oblivious to Fraser's annoyance that the glass has not been placed on the coaster provided. Fraser gets out of his seat and picks up the glass. Offering a refill, he pours it along with his own and pointedly places the glass back down on the coaster. Taking the hint in silence, McCarthy picks up the glass, takes a sip, and sets it down in the appropriate place. Fraser relaxes and returns to his seat behind his desk. McCarthy breaks the silence.

"So how is business Edward?"

"Good, and you?" replies Fraser.

"Going well . . . going well. Having to deal with a few muppets but nothing major. How is Hoskins? Not seen him around, isn't he usually attached to you like a limpet?"

"He's around. Just needs to keep low for a while after a bit of trouble."

"Is that to do with what happened to your bird?"

"You could say that."

McCarthy notes slight irritation in Fraser's tone of voice and wisely elects not to probe any further. So, he changes the subject on to the more neutral ground of business and upcoming opportunities. Their friendship is based on a symbiotic relationship where their business interests overlap, and the ledger of who owes the other a favour swings like a pendulum.

In every meeting the conversation always inevitably gravitates toward the ledger and this one is no different.

"Let's talk about the business up North. Where the hell is Ayton? Is that the place with the public school full of privileged puffs?" asks Fraser.

"It's only a few miles from Leeds. And no, it's not got a public school, yer probably thinking of Eton. It's just a pointless nondescript village where bugger-all happens."

"Well, something is going to happen now, isn't it?" snarls Fraser.

"Looks like it," replied McCarthy. Draining his glass he adds, "Right I'll be off. Great to catch up and by my reckoning once this is sorted, we'll be even. The job's best done by someone who's not local, so you made a wise choice there." Fraser nods in agreement and presses a button on his intercom to speak to his bodyguard.

"Mr McCarthy is leaving now. Take him to where he wants to go."

After McCarthy left, Fraser sat alone in his office pondering over their discussion. Was the irritating northern monkey getting above himself? It was not for McCarthy to decide when everything was evened out and sorted. Things were sorted when he said they were and not before. His musings were interrupted by a the return of the bodyguard. It seems that McCarthy didn't want a lift and said he would make his own way to the hotel. Fraser asks after Hoskins and frowns when the bodyguard confirms that there was still no sign of him. Sensing his boss's irritation, he assures him that they would continue to keep looking and asking questions around his normal haunts. Refilling his glass, Fraser takes a long sip. *Where has the dickhead disappeared to?*

12

NEATLY PARKED IN his designated space, Mandelson switches off the ignition with an audible sigh at the prospect of the evening ahead spent wading through the tedious mire of local government decision making. As the chair of the Scarborough Council Planning Committee he had reaped a healthy income in backhanders from local business owners keen to stretch the limits of the planning guidelines and regulations. Nevertheless, the meetings were laborious and time seemed to slow as they idled through protocols and endless bureaucratic procedures, punctuated by the ponderous mind-numbing deliberations of the other councillors on the committee. Tonight however, promised much more giving him a frisson of anticipation when he had read the agenda which included the application for a hotel development next to Ayton Church. It would yield a good pay day — if he could just get it past the committee.

Sunlight bathing the town hall building enhanced its grandeur, as it held court over the town centre to the west and the glistening bay to the east. The red brick Jacobean Revival mansion had been built in the nineteenth century as a home for a prominent businessman but was then converted and extended for municipal use in 1903. Mandelson marches into the lobby of the Grade II listed building, and, giving a cursory nod to the receptionist, he makes his way through the main corridor to the committee meeting room. He is purposely late, as always, and the fifteen committee members and officials are already seated round the long oak table, each chatting with their respective neighbour. Nodding to those who catch his eye as he strides to his seat at the head of the table, Mandelson sits down and brings the meeting to order. With robotic efficiency he speeds through the meeting items which lead to the real business. Officers are welcomed, previous meeting minutes approved, and agreed action items ticked off as completed. Of course, for the last agenda item before the main business he remains silent when committee members are asked to declare any conflicts of interest. There are none.

Thirty minutes passes as committee members quibble over points of detail for each application presented. Eventually, one by one, shop front facades, building extensions and a range of items are either approved, or rejected with requests for more information. Mandelson's eyes, which had begun to glaze over some time ago suddenly widen when application SBC/2021/0174/AHOT comes to the table.

The senior planning officer stands up to introduce the item. He has thinning, greying hair, a beard and a slight physical build that made his well-worn navy suit sit almost apologetically on his thin frame. Mandelson eyes him with barely disguised disdain as he nods to the officer to begin his presentation to the committee. "Please proceed, Mr Prendergast," orders Mandelson. The officer smiles weakly and starts the briefing.

"Thank you, chair. To remind the committee, this item relates to a proposal to build a hotel in Ayton on the land next to the local church. We have completed stage one involving pre-application advice where several concerns have arisen before we proceed to stage two, which is the validation of the formal application. So now, I propose—"

Mandelson interrupts. "Hold on, Mr Prendergast, what are the concerns?"

"We were contacted by the local vicar, a Mr Peter Dibley, who raised a number of concerns. He claimed to be representing his whole congregation, so we suspect that these may be well supported."

"We are only now at stage two of the planning process, Mr Prendergast, so I am at a loss to understand why these objections are being entertained, or even raised to the committee at this point? You know as well as the committee, that the consultation and publicity stage will follow once the application has been validated. We have a process, and it seems that you are circumventing this because a vicar has raised some concerns. Are you a religious man yourself?" Mandelson makes his irritation very evident to put psychological pressure on the officer.

Shuffling in discomfort, Prendergast starts to mutter a response but Mandelson speaks over him.

"The local vicar could barely field a football team with the number he has in his congregation. Let's not exaggerate the level of potential objection here, particularly as we are not at that point yet. We must follow procedures and if there are objections then these will be submitted as per due process, at the appropriate time. In the meantime, can we see a written copy of these objections?" which Mandelson knew was a rhetorical rather than genuine question.

With a look of contrite mortification, the council officer responds in a barely audible voice. "Er, I am afraid there is nothing in writing."

With inward relish, Mandelson launches into another verbal battery. "Nothing in writing, Mr Prendergast! Nothing in writing. So let me be clear. You are pre-empting process, potentially exaggerating the degree of opposition, and essentially bringing gossip and hearsay to the committee. This is highly inappropriate and unacceptable."

Most of the committee members began to shift uncomfortably in their chairs, choosing not to raise their heads above the parapet. There is one exception.

"Yes, Councillor Fosdyke." Mandelson acknowledges the committee member with her hand up.

"I agree, chair, that we must follow process, but I do think that Mr Prendergast should be heard on this matter."

Staring the councillor straight in the eye, Mandelson inwardly fumes but disguises his ire well and maintains his composure. He was not used to being challenged by the committee, who were generally happy to turn up, do as they were told and collect their attendance allowances.

"It is against process, Councillor Fosdyke, and therefore should not even be entertained as a discussion point. However, as a matter of goodwill and in recognition of your request, the committee will accept a full written submission at the appropriate time. And in this case the committee would be willing to see an early written submission at the next meeting if all members agree." Mandelson looks around the table and notes the assenting nods. He graces the councillor with a reptilian smile.

"But that is impossible, chair," announces Fosdyke, addressing the whole committee and seeking indications of support. Although appearing to remain forthright, her resolve was beginning to weaken; Mandelson looks at her with the eyes of a predator about to pounce on its prey. "How so, Councillor Fosdyke? But before you answer, let me clarify one point: Are you not a member of the congregation? If so, is this not a conflict of interest, I wonder?"

Deflated, the councillor responds, "Well yes, I am a member of the congregation, but surely you know the vicar has been murdered. It has been dominating the news for the last few days. A written submission from him is obviously impossible."

Devoid of any evidence of sympathy, the tone of Mandelson's reply is cold and businesslike. "I am sure we are all shocked at the news of the vicar. Mr Prendergast seemed to indicate, in his own inappropriate repetition of what amounts to hearsay, that several people in the congregation apparently objected. I am sure one of them must be literate." He looks over at Prendergast who sits in contrite silence, now reticent to answer in case he digs himself deeper into a hole. Mandelson turns back to the councillor, "Returning to your own contribution, Councillor Fosdyke, I think what has been revealed is a conflict of interest. Wouldn't you agree? Is it not best that you absent yourself from discussions on this application in the future?"

Several committee members sitting in a row nod their heads in agreement, like a bizarre fairground attraction. Mandelson sees that Fosdyke had noticed them and smiles at her. Fosdyke tuts but indicates her acceptance that protocol demands she should not be involved in future decision making on the proposal.

She replies curtly, "Yes."

"Well, if everyone is in agreement, I propose we approve the application which can proceed to the consultation stage. Are there any final comments?"

Prendergast considers reminding the committee that the process of application and validation was not yet complete. His mouth opens hesitantly but closes as he thinks better of it given the mood of the Chairperson. With a final shout of "Approved" from Mandelson, the committee moves on to the next item and the secretary records the decision in the minutes. For all the talk of process, very little has, in fact, been followed. There ended the interest of Mandelson in the meeting, and he sits through the final hour in a semi soporific stupor, created by a combination of rambling deliberations of the other members in between the monotone of Prendergast.

Once the Kafkaesque nightmare of small-town bureaucracy finally stutters to a halt, Mandelson quickly gathers his papers and leaves. He brushes aside the requests by various members for "a quick word" with a brusque semi-apology that he was late for another meeting. They did not know that the other meeting involved a half bottle of scotch in the quiet serenity of his living room, with the calming influence of Chopin flowing out of his Bang and Olufsen Beosound speaker. He marches down the corridor and through reception quicker than he arrived and ignores the cheery goodbye from the receptionist. Out of Mandelson's earshot the receptionist mutters, "Rude bastard," to herself as he turns left out of the main door and into the car park.

Driving through the exit of the council premises, Mandelson barks instructions and the ring tone fills the car followed by the voice of Neaves.

"Hi, Jeffrey, how'd ya go?"

"I'll tell you how I went, I went very well in trying to drag you out of this bloody mess."

"I'm telling you, Jeffrey, I haven't made any mess. Nothing is my fault."

Mandelson lost his already fragile composure. "What the hell is wrong with you? Your cowboys have practically brought the church building close to collapse, you got Dibley and his bloody flock offside — and you've got them gunning for your blood . . . God knows what else. At the meeting tonight some emaciated bearded council planning idiot wearing his father's suit starts to witter on about objections, and all the rest of the council puppets start nodding in sympathy. And that interfering cow Fosdyke then goes on about it, until I cut her off at the legs."

Years of friendship had taught Neaves that when Mandelson was in these moods it was best to keep his opinions to himself. "What's more, dear Ronald, I not only managed to shut her up, but she now cannot be party to any future consideration of the scheme. So, with the mood of the committee under my tutelage, plus those we already have on our side busily counting their cash incentives, it has a good chance of going through in the coming weeks. But hey — no need to thank me, but do not bloody tell me that you haven't made any mess. I am up to my knees in the shit you have created."

"Look, Jeffrey, thanks. I really appreciate it. We should both do well out of this. Just think about the money."

"I do not want to be counting my money behind bars. I concede that the death of Dibley has been a convenient turn of events, but if I find out that this was your doing and that you've got that psycho mate McCarthy involved in all of this then you and I have a major problem. Even I draw the line at killing anyone, let alone topping a bloody vicar. If that is the case, then I am well and truly out."

"I have told you, Jeffrey, I had nothing to do with it. I don't get why you don't believe me."

"I don't believe you because you are an idiot, you're impulsive, and the people you mix with are not exactly church goers themselves, are they? Once we introduce bloody gangsters into the mix everything can get out of control. We are not living in a bloody documentary about the Krays, are we?"

"No, Jeffery."

Mandelson's anger is spent. "Just tell me Ronald, one more time, that you did not have Dibley killed."

"No, Jeffrey. I did not kill Dibley, nor did I have anyone else do it."

As Mandelson ends the call and the line goes dead, Neaves mutters, "Bugger," and starts to key a number into his mobile. He gets no answer and leaves a message.

Back in the car, Mandelson makes another call which is answered immediately.

"Hello, is that you, Mandelson?"

"It's me. Just wanting to check in after tonight's meeting, Councillor Roberts"

"I'm not entirely happy," came back the terse reply.

"Well, councillor, you were happy enough to take the money, weren't you?" retorts Mandelson.

"First of all, Councillor Mandelson, I wasn't expecting someone to get shot, it's not worth the money to get involved in murder. If so, I'm out."

"Look here, Roberts, you are already in; like it or not. You were quick to take the money and you need to hold your nerve. No one's involved in murder for God's sake, you don't know what the hell you are talking about. And, my friend, if you start throwing about accusations like that you need to look out, that's a far more serious allegation than the exchange of a little cash between friends."

"What are you saying, Mandelson? Are you threatening me now? If you start that shit, I am straight off to the police, and I'll take what's coming to me. I am not a murderer."

Mandelson breathes deeply. A small red ball of fury inside him begins to expand. Rubbing his temple, he tries to follow the exercise that his psychiatrist taught him for anger management and mentally bursts the balloon with a pin. Redness subsides and his voice calms. "Listen, Councillor Roberts . . . just listen to me. It is all under control, and I can give you my word that I had nothing to do with the shooting. It was just a happy coincidence."

"Happy! . . . Not for the vicar," snaps Roberts.

"No . . . absolutely not for the vicar, an unhappy coincidence, but helpful all the same. I repeat, I — rather we, had nothing to do with it. Who the hell do you think I am? What the hell do you think I am? I am not a bloody gangster. Do you think I am some sort of psychopath?" Roberts chose not to answer, allowing Mandelson to continue. "We just need to stay calm and the whole thing will be done in a few weeks, and everyone involved is a winner, including Ayton, which will have a nice hotel to attract tourists and business to the area. It was a bonus tonight, because now we have Fosdyke well and truly out of the picture, and she was always going to be the one most vehemently opposed to our little venture. Just . . . stay . . . calm . . . and stop reading too much into everything."

"Okay, Mandelson. I'm with you, I am now calm, it just spooked me. I mean, who shoots a bloody vicar? We are not in America. I must admit . . . you bloody well handled it brilliantly tonight. You made her look a real fool. *Conflict of interest*. Genius. Brilliant!" Roberts chuckles "As long as you are sure you weren't involved in the death of Dibley."

"Scout's honour," replies Mandelson and presses a button on his steering wheel, terminating the call. "Piss weak idiot," he mutters to himself as he subconsciously accelerates to get home quickly. It had been a long day.

Mandelson's call ends.

Five miles away Neaves answers his mobile immediately recognising the voice of the caller.

"Hi, Neaves, you rang a few minutes ago."

"Why didn't you pick up?"

"Because I was busy, I am talking to you now. What is it?"

"I just want to check that everything is on track, and no one suspects anything. That there were no loose ends or anything I need to worry about."

"Like what?"

"Mandelson, for one."

"It's all been cleaned up. You now owe me the balance."

"Cash, at the same drop off point?" asks Neaves.

"That'll do nicely. Let's say eight p.m. tomorrow."

Neaves murmurs his agreement, and the line goes silent as he sits in his home office trying to process the events of the last few days. "Everything okay love?" calls his wife from their living room.

"Yeah fine," he replies whilst opening the small safe concealed underneath his desk. He reaches for a large tightly packed envelope.

13

GREETED BY THE merry tinkle of the bell above the shop door, Hayes and Hendricks make their way into Betty's grocery store. With no sign of the owner, Hayes calls out as he approaches the cash register and then jumps back startled when Betty's head pops up above the counter.

"Jeez, Betty! You frightened me," complains Hayes while Hendricks giggles in the background.

"Ooh sorry, luv — I was just cleaning the bottom shelves, 'ad to, they're right mucky. Anyway, luv, what can I do for you?"

"A pouch of tobacco and two packs of Rizlas please, Betty." The shop owner turns her back to them whilst she reaches into a cupboard behind the counter where the cigarettes are kept. Another tinkle of the shop doorbell marks the entrance of Jenny Wicker.

"Hi, Betty, hi, boys, how are you all?"

"Good," replies Hendricks who was nearest to her just inside the door, "And how are you, Jenny?"

"Great, Colin, I'm glad I've caught you . . . I've run out of those *special* mushrooms you get me." She winks as she puts an emphasises on the word. "Any chance you could drop a few over to me when you have time?"

"No worries," replied Hendricks.

Hayes adds, "We can bring a bag round this afternoon if you're in?"

"Great," confirms Jenny.

"Don't know why you want what these two have to offer, Jenny," chides Betty with a mild tone of complaint. Pointing to the corner of the store where she stocks the fresh produce, she adds "I've got some lovely mushies, fresh in today." All three customers exchange smirks, not noticing, Betty continues her sales pitch, "They are tasty, really tasty — just pan fry them with a knob of butter and a twist of black pepper. Lovely."

Hayes pays Betty and taps Hendricks on the shoulder, "Come on mate, we need to get going." As they turn to leave, the shop doorbell chimes once more, and in walks DC Stanley, who immediately puts out his arm to halt the progress of the two men.

"Aaah, gentlemen, I thought I saw you come in here. Wondered if we could have a quick chat?"

"What about?" asks Hayes suspiciously, he didn't like the look of the calculated smile he was getting from the detective.

"How about we get out of Mrs Jackson's hair and go outside? We could sit at the park bench across the road'; lovely day for it. Just want an informal chat if that's okay with you?" Clearly more a command than a request. Stanley ushers them through the door whilst a giving a nod of acknowledgement to Betty and Jenny.

As the shop bell tinkles into silence, Jenny, tracks the progress of the three men across the road. "Never really warmed to him. Gives me the creeps," she confides.

"Who, Phil and Colin? They're harmless, luv."

"No, Betty, that policeman . . . there's just something about him I can't put my finger on."

"Are you 'aving one of your psychic turns?"

"No, nothing like that, just a feeling."

"Couldn't agree more, luv," confirms Betty. "Now, what can I do for you? I know you don't want my mushies, apparently, they're not good enough for you, are they?" she jokes. "Well how about my brussels, they're fresh in?"

Dodging traffic, the three men cross the road and settle into the benches attached to the wooden park table. Stanley sits opposite the men, stares for a moment and pauses before he speaks; an attempt at unsettling them. Sunlight warms the three men, and a light breeze causes the leaves of a nearby elm tree to rustle punctuating the uncomfortable silence.

"So, what is it you want to talk about?" asks Hayes, opening what he hopes will be a brief conversation.

"As you probably can guess, I am investigating the shooting of Vicar Dibley, and thought you two might be able to help." Stanley shifts his eye contact from Hayes to Hendricks and back again, trying to read any reaction.

"Not sure we can," suggests Hendricks, and Hayes nods in support. Again, Stanley pauses for effect, causing the two men to shuffle on the wooden bench.

"Well maybe — or maybe not. I understand that you two spend a lot of time around here, including in that copse behind the Old Plough. The one in Higginbottom's field," Stanley elaborates to avoid any doubt. Keeping them on their toes, he pointedly looks at the worn khaki satchel resting on Hendricks' right shoulder. Both men shift uncomfortably on the bench; Stanley grins, relishing their reaction. "I mention this, gentlemen, because I thought you may have seen, or heard something on the morning that the vicar was killed?"

Both pretend to give serious and deep thought to the detective's assertion and eventually confirm they had not, and on reflection — they were not even in the area that day. They explain their movements to Stanley who listens and takes notes as they speak. When they finish, Stanley completes the sentence he is writing and raises his eyes from the notepad. Screwing his eyes as he looks at them directly Stanley asks if they were certain of all their facts. Were they sure they had told him everything?

"So, you say you were both in your flat that day doing some DIY. Was anyone else there who could corroborate this?" The two friends shake their heads. Stanley makes his scepticism evident with a *harrumph*. He feels they are holding something back, but realising he won't get any further he changes his approach. "Look, lads, I am just after information. We three all know you've had your collars felt for petty stuff, and shooting the vicar is a whole different ball game. No one is accusing you of murder . . . but if you remember anything at all — I need you to give me a call." Swinging his legs around the bench, Stanley rises then leans over to hand them his business card. After walking a couple of paces, he turns back to them adding, "Have a think lads, and bear in mind I didn't ask to look in that satchel of yours . . . so perhaps you can return the favour if you do remember anything else."

Their shared glance of relief is short-lived when the detective stops once more and turns back to address them.

"Oh! One more thing — there's been complaints from a few locals that some idiots have been firing weapons in the area. Apparently, they are shooting rabbits. Someone could get killed. You don't know anything about that do you?" Seeing the two men shake their heads in response, Stanley adds, "Do either of you own a rifle — or air gun, or something like that?"

"No officer, that's not our scene," answers Hayes. With a doubtful frown Stanley turns back and walks to his car, not noticing the exhalation of relief from the two men. When the detective is safely out of the way the two friends start to chatter nervously until Hayes almost jumps out of his skin at the sound of a disembodied voice coming out of thin air.

"What did he want, lads?" asks the voice.

Yelping in surprise, Hayes swings round to face a slightly dishevelled bearded figure wearing an army jacket and tatty grey cargo pants. He was barely a yard behind them, holding them in a penetrating blue-eyed stare.

"Jeeeeezz Bob! Where the hell did you spring from?" Hendricks shouts. "You nearly gave us a heart attack. Yer like some bloody ninja hobo."

Apologetically Bob replies "Take it easy, lads,"

"Are you bleeding ex-special forces or summat?" adds Hayes. Bob just looks at him sheepishly. "What're you after Bob? D'yer want a roll-up?" Hayes holds up the pouch of tobacco.

"No thanks, mate — not good for your health. Was just wondering what that copper wanted."

"He was just asking us where we were when the vicar was shot and if we had seen or heard anything," says Hayes absent-mindedly as he focussed on his cigarette rolling.

"Had you?"

"Had we what?"

"Had you seen or heard anything?"

"No, mate," chuckles Hendricks, now recovered from the shock. "He sounds a bit desperate to me, like they don't have a clue who shot him and why or anything. Clutching at straws hassling us I reckon. Why der yer ask? Did you see something?"

"No, mate. Anyway, I'm off to the pub." Bob marches off down the road towards the Old Plough without so much as a backward glance.

"Wonder why he is so interested . . ." muses Hayes.

"Not sure he is. Seems to live in a different world. How the hell did he creep up on us like that? I didn't hear a thing. He's like a blooming ghost."

"Never mind. Come on Col, we need to go mushroom picking for our Jenny. She's got her potions to brew, and we could do with some cash."

"Hang on mate, aren't you worried about the copper? I reckon he knows we have a gun, or why would he be asking us any questions?"

"I doubt he knows anything, and anyway, what's to know?"

"Mate, you were off your face when you were shooting that gun. 'Av you forgotten what I told you? You were all over the place and shooting everything — except the bloody rabbits. We need to take it easy and get rid of the bloody thing before you take somebody's head off and we get in more trouble than we can handle."

Across the road Bob's progress towards the Old Plough comes to an abrupt halt when he is stopped in his tracks by Betty, who appears in front of him from her shop door. He manages to swerve slightly to avoid bowling her over.

"Ow do Bob, saw you over there talking to the lads. I've got something for you. 'Ere you go." She hands over a neatly squared package of greaseproof paper packed with sandwiches. Bob's melts her heart, as it always does with his striking eyes and the genuine gratitude he shows her. She gives him a hug and he sets off on his way towards the pub, putting the package into his rucksack.

"Enjoy yer Guinness Bob, and say hi to Dolly from me."

Raising his hand in acknowledgement he disappears into the pub and out of sight. Betty keeps staring down the road with a fond smile. She often wondered what had gone on in his past that left him where he was now. He had been around the village for almost a year now but despite many conversations she never quite managed to break through his shell. She was perceptive enough to realise that, despite his appearance, he was a man of discipline who made the best of what he had to look presentable. But he was clearly a tortured soul. Maybe one day he would tell her.

Dolly gives Bob a warm greeting as he enters the pub. Making a joke about him being late, she points to his seat in the corner where a pint of Guinness is already waiting for him on the table. Ken Wilkes had returned from his business trip and was busy emptying the dishwasher and placing the glasses on the shelves above and around the bar. He looks over and nods to Bob who raises his glass in cheers. A customer, who had told Ken he was just travelling through, is at the end of the bar with half a pint of beer, working his way through one of Dolly's homemade pasties. Two labourers from Higginbottom's farm are having a liquid lunch and feeding coins into the jukebox spouting chords from Led Zeppelin. They laugh and joke, rocking their heads to the beat. The pub phone behind the bar rings and Ken Wilkes picks up the receiver. After a short conversation he hangs up and looks over to Dolly whose expectant stare tells him she wants to know who the caller was. Not wishing to shout across and share their business with the customers he walks over and whispers in her ear.

"It was DS Hardy, he said he was passing through Ayton and rang the pub on the off chance I was back. He asked to come over for a chat, so I told him it was okay. Best to get it over with I reckon."

Dolly nods in agreement, "Ken luv, I told you to call them. You should've done it when I asked you."

On his way to Ayton, Hardy makes a call as he drives out of the police station car park.

"DC Stanley, how can I help?"

"It's me," shouts Hardy, as he does whenever he uses the car speaker phone. "Where are you?"

"Heading back to the station, why?"

"Doesn't matter, thought you might still be in Ayton. Any luck with the locals?"

"None really, I talked to a couple of the local druggie losers. They looked nervous and I thought that maybe they knew something. But then again, they were probably more worried I would search them and confiscate whatever they had in their bag. I also talked again to the garage owner who gave me the CCTV recording the other day, says he hadn't seen or noticed anything that morning. A few customers went through but nothing out of the ordinary. Do you want me to do something?"

"Nah, I am on my way to see Wilkes. If you were still in the village you could've joined me, but it doesn't matter. I called the pub on the off chance, he answered so he is obviously back from his business. Told him I wanted a word and he said to come over now."

"Interesting that he didn't rush to call us then, after we talked to his wife."

"Nope, he didn't, did he . . . anyway, speak later." Hardy terminates the call. Ten minutes later he pulls into the car park of the Old Plough and walks into the main bar.

Ken Wilkes sees him come in and motions him into a small square backroom. Walls adorned with beige wood chip and a poor-quality print of a matador avoiding a charging bull, the room is stuck in a 1970's time warp. They bothl sit at the Formica topped table where Hardy declines the offer of a drink and gets straight to the point.

"I understand, Mr Wilkes that on the day Mr Dibley was shot and killed you were travelling to Scarborough on business? Your wife said you left quite early which, by the sound of it, would have been around the time of the shooting. Is that correct?'

"Yes, Detective Hardy. Well at least it's correct that I left early that morning. No idea if it was around the time the vicar was killed."

"Well, did you see or hear anything unusual?"

"Not really, nothing that sticks to mind. There was hardly anyone around at that time . . . I vaguely recall I may have seen Peter Dibley near the church entrance as I passed it on the way to Scarborough. To be honest I'm not sure — and it may not even have been the vicar."

"So why did you think it was him?"

"No reason really, it was a glimpse and I guess I assumed it was him because the figure was standing near the front of the church."

Hardy pauses to consider his next question. "Okay, Mr Wilkes, so you are not certain it was Dibley, but you did see somebody, and you did not hear a shot, I take it. Do you recall anyone else in the area?"

With a wrinkled forehead Wilkes trawls his memory and eventually shakes his head. "No detective, I was pretty much concentrating on the road. I think I saw a couple of people in the petrol station forecourt but couldn't in all honesty identify them or even be sure of how many were there."

Hardy waits to see if any more information is forthcoming, but Wilkes remains silent. "Okay, Mr Wilkes, let me move on to another matter. I understand you have a rifle that you use for hunting. Did you have the rifle with you?"

"Yes, I did . . . I intended to do some hunting with a friend after finishing my business in Scarborough."

"I take it the rifle is back in your gun safe. I would like to take it back to the station for examination."

A fleeting expression of anger floats across the publican's face. "Actually, you cannot have it at the moment, and I would like to know why you want to take it. I have a licence. . . don't you need a warrant or something?"

Remaining calm, Hardy responds. "All we are doing is eliminating people from our enquiries, and as the vicar was shot with a rifle and you are one of the few local people who own one, it is probably best for all concerned that we get you out of the picture. No one is accusing you of anything. If we didn't ask for it, we would not be doing our job, Mr Wilkes. I could get a warrant of course but I assumed you have nothing to hide and therefore would be willing to help." Wilkes just glares at him without response. Hardy presses him further. "Is there any reason why you will not hand over the weapon so we can get all the formalities done?"

"As I said, you cannot have it at the moment. I took it to Sanders and Co. They're local gunsmiths. Based in Malton. I use them to professionally clean and maintain it every few months — and they're recalibrating the scope."

Hiding his irritation and feeling out manoeuvred Hardy concedes, "I see, Mr Wilkes. Let's leave it for the time being but when you get the rifle back would you be willing to bring it to the station so we can get it examined and remove it from our investigation?"

Wilkes confirms that he would have the rifle back by the end of the week and tells the detective that he would bring it in to the station personally. After a polite but slightly tense exchange of goodbyes Hardy makes his way back through the main bar. Dolly turns to her husband as he leaves. "Everything okay luv? Thought you were a bit harsh with that detective . . ."

"Yeah fine, just don't like them coming in here giving orders," Ken replies as he acknowledges a customer at the bar holding up his pint glass for a refill.

14

BEHIND THE VILLAGE church is a small property locally referred to as the vicarage. Built in the 1930's, as vicarages go it was modest in size and amounts to no more than a small two bedroom cottage. The bedrooms and bathroom are upstairs whilst the ground floor comprises a small kitchen, a toilet, and a bay windowed living room overlooking a small garden hemmed in by woodland. Although not particularly small, the living room skirts a fine line between cosy and claustrophobic. It is covered in vintage delicate floral wallpaper and cluttered by shelves of books occupying two of the four walls. A comfortable light-brown three piece suite surrounds a worn Persian rug which had been donated by a parishioner many years ago. The furniture frames an original coal fireplace, now occupied by a gas flame-effect fire set underneath a flat screened television. Dibley sits relaxed with a gin and tonic in one hand, his other arm rests on the back of the sofa as he turns to face his guest.

Sipping from her own drink, Julia Henson sits in one of the chairs, smiling in the relaxed manner of a frequent visitor. Music is playing through the TV screen at a low volume allowing for easy conversation.

"Oh, Peter this is so lovely," Julia purrs as she re-crosses her slender legs into a more comfortable position. Noticing where the vicar's eyes were focussed as she did this, she inwardly glows with satisfaction at the effect she has on him.

"It is, Julia, and I want to thank you again for all the support you have given me this year. The Whist Drive was very successful and the funds you helped to raise for the church renovation have been nothing short of amazing."

"Thank you, Peter, it's just a shame that the builders owned by that awful man Neaves are doing such a dreadfully poor job. It is nothing short of scandalous."

"Don't worry, Julia. I am getting on to it and the Bishop is giving me his full support — not to mention our solicitors are working pro bono."

"That's good but Neaves is such a pig of a man. I doubt if he will be a pushover. He scares me a little I have to say."

"I wouldn't worry about it. Men like him are just bullies. I see them every weekend on the rugby field. If you stand your ground, they eventually cave in. We've got a growing army behind us. As we say in the business, *Onward Christian Soldiers*."

They both giggle as they drain their glasses. Dibley gets off the sofa and takes the glass from her hand, offering a refill, which she happily accepts. The brief brush of his hand with hers sends a little shiver of pleasure through her and he smiles with affection. After preparing the drinks he returns her replenished glass before sinking back down into the sofa. They lock eyes as Peter lifts his tumbler saying cheers and after a brief sip they resume their conversation. Two hours later Julia returns home leaving Dibley slouching on his sofa, listening to music with a satisfying soporific heaviness; a by-product of the alcohol and his time with her. Sleep was gradually taking hold until the jarring beep of his mobile phone rips him from his stupor. Glancing at the screen, his brow furrows as he realises the caller has withheld their number.

"Heeeello, Peter Dibley speaking."

"You need to back off, Dibley." The male voice has a flat accent — not local, but there was no mistaking the menace in the tone. Anger wells up in Dibley's chest like heartburn.

"Who is this?" asks Dibley, feeling himself quickly sobering up.

"It does not matter who it is. You know what I am talking about. You need to back off — or people could get hurt."

Righteous outrage grips Dibley, "I don't know who the hell you are! Or what you are even talking about but —" he is interrupted by the calm steely voice.

"But nothing, Dibley. You haven't exactly been acting like the model Christian, have you? You're not in a position to make pronouncements and judgements, are you? Not taking proper care of your flock, not exactly respecting, and loving your neighbour how you should be. Are you? Back. Off. Now."

Before Dibley could reply the line went dead. Double checking the call details, he found no clue as to who had made it, the number had been withheld. He dials Julia; she answers immediately.

"Oh, hello, Peter, are you missing me already? I've only been gone five minutes."

Trying to maintain a calm voice, Dibley replies. "No Julia, well yes — of course I am missing you but seriously, I just wanted to check you're okay."

"Of course I am, Peter, why wouldn't I be?"

"No reason really . . . it's just shortly after you left the vicarage I had this odd call. My mind went racing everywhere . . . and I wondered if it was a stalker, or someone who may have seen you leave and followed you home?"

"No, Peter, I'm fine, it's a lovely evening, I'm just walking up my drive now. The only person I saw on my way home was Chris Ashton taking Barry for a walk. He was actually just outside the vicarage when I saw him . . . is everything okay?"

"Strange place to take the dog. But are you sure you didn't see anyone suspicious? A stranger hanging around?"

"Yes, I am certain, Peter." Julia grills Dibley for the next few minutes, as it is her turn to fear for his safety. He eventually sets her mind at ease and assures her that it may have been a wrong number. Though he omits that the mystery caller had referred to him by name, or that the tone of the call was far from friendly.

"Okay Julia, see you on Tuesday, glad you're home safe. Look after yourself."

"You too, Peter. I had a lovely evening, see you Tuesday."

Pouring himself another gin, Dibley decides he needs to think this through. He's made a couple of enemies and matters are likely to get worse. *Threatening phone calls though . . . that's a whole new ball game.* It didn't sound as though it was something he should take lightly. Then again, perhaps it was just some gorilla, maybe one of Neaves' rugby mates trying to sound scary to encourage him to back off the complaint he was making about the mess of the church renovation? But that did not seem credible. Not convinced it had anything to do with Neaves, he starts to explore other possibilities, but the caller hadn't really left any clues. Just a direct threat from someone who sounded neither familiar nor local.

Dragging himself off the sofa he makes his way to bed, double checking that all the doors and windows were locked along the way. Whoever made the call had succeeded in putting him on edge. He switches all the lights off on the ground floor and, with a little trepidation, he climbs the stairs to the bathroom. Washing his face in the basin he glances out of the window overlooking the back garden and the edge of the woods. His gaze becomes fixed on a small clump of trees at the western edge of the garden. *Was that some movement over there?* Staring hard he couldn't see any further activity. Probably his overactive imagination, perhaps that call had got to him. Just trees, silent, motionless on a still summer night. The logical side of his brain wrestles with the emotional. *Calm down, Peter, you're just a bit spooked ... there is nothing out there.* A final visual sweep of the garden reveals nothing but trees and still shadows; a solitary hoot of an owl, but no movement. He berates himself as he switches off the bathroom light and minutes later, he is asleep in bed without any apparent care in the world.

In the woods, Hairy Bob settles himself in one of his favourite little clearings behind the vicarage. He stares at the clear summer sky, alight with a myriad of stars, until sleep creeps over him. His body twitches as his nightmares begin to take hold.

In his dream he immediately recognises the smell and heat of Afghanistan. Back in base camp his mates are letting their hair down with a squad of Australian SAS soldiers operating in the same region. After a gruelling four day mission patrolling an area where Taliban activity was reported by local farmers, there was a lot of steam to let off. Bob is sat in the corner of the tent, separating himself from the group but staring in disgust at the Australian squad leader who had produced a prosthetic leg from his pack. Laughing whilst he poured beer into the leg, the squad cheered as their leader drank from it. It was rumoured that an unarmed and disabled farm labourer had been shot in the back while trying to flee when the patrol appeared, shouting orders and gesticulating aggressively. When questioned, the farmer told the squad that the man had lost his leg under torture by the Taliban, loud noises had triggered him ever since causing anxiety which grew into panic. The helicopter and all the soldiers shouting were too much for him. Horrified, the farmer explained that the man tried to run, or rather, hobble away because he was frightened and didn't understand what was happening.

Bob begins to kick in his sleeping bag, struggling himself free as that word bubbles from his lips. "... wa-da ..." A barely audible mutter before he startles awake, sitting bolt upright he shouts, "Wadarega! —" But there is only the woods, and the silence. "He scans his surroundings and wipes away the sweat dripping profusely from his forehead. Unaware of what woke him, he listens intently and seconds later hears the grating shriek bark of a fox.

Bob sits forwards, shaking.

In the vicarage Dibley had also woken, although he was unsure of the cause. Sleepily dragging his feet to the bedroom window, he looks outside for some clues. There is no movement, but he hears the fox barking. To him this was a familiar, almost comforting sound confirming all was alive and well in the woods. Once disturbed from slumber, he knows it will be a while before he can get back to sleep, so he makes his way downstairs to pour himself a nightcap to help him reset. He sits on the sofa with a small schooner of sherry and his mind returns to the strange phone call, until he is disturbed by the slightest of breezes caressing his face. Placing the schooner on the side table he gets up to explore until he finds the source. The kitchen window above the sink is open, which perplexes him as he was sure he'd checked all the locks. He pulls the window shut and twists the lever down to lock it, then gives it a shake to ensure it's secure. Warily searching the rooms downstairs, he finds no sign of an intruder nor any evidence of anything missing. After re-checking that all the other windows and doors are secure, he climbs stealthily up the stairs, straining to hear any noise or movement. Tentatively, he checks the spare bedroom, the bathroom, then finally his own bedroom — nothing. All clear. It takes a further two hours for sleep to claim him.

Still shaking, Bob sits, listens, and strains his eyes to make sense of the darkness. Rustling. A thump. Bob tenses. It sounds heavy, far too heavy for a rabbit or a fox. Once more he strains his eyes and gradually lowers himself until he is lying flat on the ground, belly down, head raised. His eyes fix on the direction from where he heard the noise. Just trees, nothing moves. More rustling, then more thumping. Whatever or whoever it is, it moves with speed in the opposite direction. Bob remains prone, motionless until he can no longer hear the animal — or person — retreating in the distance. Five more minutes pass and Bob remains still, listening intently, his eyes are locked into a fixed stare. Satisfied he is alone, he speedily rolls up his sleeping bag, grabs his other belongings, and moves swiftly in the opposite direction.

15

THE SATURDAY BEFORE THE SHOOTING

ALANIS MORRISETTE WARBLES out of the jukebox in the Old Plough.

"I bloody hate this."

"What are you on about, Purple?" asks Hendricks while rolling a cigarette, ready for his next trip to the garden area at the back of the pub. They are sitting at the table next to Hairy Bob, who was occupying his normal seat in the corner.

Hayes clarifies whilst Hendricks takes a long deep pull of his pint. The glass is now a third empty. "This song, it winds me up. I hate this bloody song. It's called *Ironic*."

"And . . .?" Hendricks responds with an accompanying belch.

"It isn't."

"Isn't what?" asks Hendricks, taking another drag of his lager.

"Ironic, mate. There's nothing in the song that is ironic," explains Hayes.

"Whaddya mean, mate?" Hendricks drains the last drop of liquid from his glass, sets it back down and waits for Hayes to explain.

"Well for example, she calls raining on her wedding day ironic. It ain't mate. It is not ironic. The definition of ironic is something that happens unexpectedly and because of this is mildly amusing. Well, I doubt the bride and groom are amused. At best it's unlucky and at worst it is simply poor wedding planning. Plan your wedding in summer or something. Another bloke in the song goes on his first ever flight and the plane crashes, leaving a widow and kids without a dad. That's not amusing, is it? It is bloody tragic

95

— not ironic." Hayes pauses and waits for a comment from Hendricks but there was nothing forthcoming. He presses his point home.

"Having, 'A fly land in your drink,' she whinges in that yank voice. Annoying, even vaguely disgusting. But not ironic. And I don't think some poor bugger on Death Row getting a pardon after they've already flicked the switch on the electric chair is particularly ironic either. He ain't gonna be thinking as he shuffles of his mortal coil that, '*Oooooh looky looky here, I got a pardon but they fried me already, isn't that ironic?*' If he got a pardon, he was probably innocent, so it's tragic, isn't it? Morissette . . . she's just a stupid annoying yank who can't speak proper English, just like the rest of them."

"She's Canadian. Not American. Anyway, it might not be tragic either."

Hayes scratches his eyebrow. "What are you on about?"

Hendricks sits up to emphasise the point he is about to make. "He may have been a serial killer, and although he never got convicted of the other crimes and was innocent of the one that put him on death row, he may have deserved it anyway. He was actually guilty but not convicted of those crimes and ironically, he was convicted of a crime he did not commit." Hayes tries to respond but Hendricks cuts him off and continues, ". . . Aannd the irony is he was convicted of a crime that he did not commit — got a pardon which was too late and so was unjustly executed, but deserved it anyway. Maybe that's what she meant?"

"Mate, none of that shit is in the song."

Hendricks had confused himself, let alone Hayes, so he decides to bring the debate to a close. "Mate, you need to lay off those mushrooms for a bit. Never mind the bloke in the song who got electrocuted, it's your brain that's getting fried."

Having listened with interest to the conversation, Hairy Bob spots a gap and uses the opportunity to lean over, conspiratorially giving a nod towards the corner of the pub. In response to their shrug of confusion Bob points to a man who looks like someone to avoid in an argument. Lean and very mean. He has a crew cut and is dressed in a navy polo shirt, neat jeans and black trainers. Sitting alone, taking the occasional sip from his half pint, he surreptitiously scans the pub. "See him over there?" whispers Bob. The two friends nod, indicating they have. "Look at his eyes." They look but cannot understand the point Bob is trying to make. Bob explains. "Those eyes are killer's eyes. I've seen them time and time again. They are killer's eyes. Steer clear boys. Steer clear."

The two friends smirk and roll their eyes at each other. They resume their conversation. "I think maybe Bob needs to lay off the mushrooms as well. Anyway, your round Purple," Hendricks punctuates his statement by placing his empty glass in front of his friend. Taking the hint, Hayes goes to the bar. As he is about to place his order with Dolly, he is beaten to the punch by another villager sitting on a stool at the end of the bar.

"Nurse, nurse, medication please." A middle-aged man with immaculate grooming waves his glass with a grin.

Dolly looks over, "Be right there, Donald, another G and T is it?" He waves in acknowledgement, and she prepares the drink and takes it over to him. "You on yer own tonight, Donald?"

"You know me, Dolly love, the only gay in the village."

Dolly tuts, "You need to get yerself a new script luv, and not one nicked from the telly." They laugh together before Dolly turns to Hayes, takes his order, and pulls two pints of lager. "There you go, Purple." Hayes hands over a tenner and Dolly, as the cash register rings open triumphantly, puts the cash in the till and gives him change.

At the other end of the bar, Ken Wilkes is serving Sebastian Henson. "Here you are, Sebastian. A bottle of your favourite wine, which I ordered in specially, and here are two glasses for you and your lovely wife."

Henson looks back at the table where his wife is sitting and sees that, to his annoyance, Peter Dibley had just walked into the pub and was settling himself down beside Julia, in Henson's chair. They immediately engage in deep conversation. Turning back to the landlord, he tells him, "Better make that three glasses, Ken." The landlord puts a third glass on the counter and swipes Henson's credit card to take payment. Henson returns to the table, struggling to carry the bottle and three glasses. Just managing to place all the items on the table without any toppling over, he takes the seat opposite his wife and the vicar who are sat cosily together. He pointedly stares at the seat the vicar is now occupying. The gesture goes unnoticed, and his irritation is compounded by the fact that Julia had not felt moved to tell Dibley that the seat was taken by her husband. Breaking from her conversation with Dibley, Julia looks over at her husband, oblivious of his irritation.

"Oh! How sweet, darling," she purrs, "You got an extra glass for Peter, I knew you wouldn't mind if he joined us." Smiling, Dibley goes through the pleasantries with Henson, who reciprocates whilst inwardly fuming and wishing the vicar would just bugger off. He realises as Julia pours Dibley a full glass of wine, this was not going to happen any time soon.

Every Saturday evening is busy at the Old Plough, and this Saturday is no different. Buzzing conversation with background music from the jukebox fills the air and creates a genial atmosphere. Chris Ashton comes through the door and gives a few hellos to various locals on his journey to the bar. He pretty much knows everybody, except for the man with the crew cut sat alone in the corner. His military training was too deeply ingrained in him not to notice an unfamiliar face in familiar surroundings. He looks over to the stranger and their eyes meet. Ashton maintains eye contact for a few seconds. Intuition honed from his army days rings a few alarm bells, but his attention is diverted by a friendly voice from behind the bar. "Ow do Chris luv, what can I get yer?" Dolly smiles at him with an expectant expression as she waits for his order.

"Hi Dolly, I think I fancy trying that local cider you just got in."

"Good choice." Dolly turns to the glass cabinet behind her and takes out a bottle.

"Don't need a glass, the bottle will do." Ashton settles onto a stool at the bar and takes a swig of his drink. He raises his bottle to say cheers and hello to Donald, who smiles back, returning a friendly wave. The musical mood of the jukebox takes a dramatic turn as Alanis Morissette is evicted in favour of Def Leppard. Out of the corner of his eye Ashton is conscious of a large figure looming up to the bar. The figure addresses Dolly.

"Ay Dolly, can yer turn up the jukebox, I can hardly hear it." Ashton looks over; it was the local bully who'd landed on the wrong end of an altercation with him some weeks ago.

Dolly smiles, "Sorry, Dave, luv, but the rest of the customers don't like it too loud, they want to talk. That's why we have the live music on a Friday, so the youngsters get a turn."

"They're just a bunch of old farts. I've put in good money into that machine, so turn it up," demands the bully. Dolly smiles and looks around for her husband, but Ken had disappeared into the cellar to change a barrel.

"Sorry luv, can't do that. I'll give you yer money back if that helps?" Dave is two pints above the limit of good behaviour.

"Turn . . . it . . . up," he demands.

Donald, who is nearest to the bully, goes to Dolly's aid. "Now look here young man, the landlady has told you she can't turn up the music and she has offered you your money back. Stop making a fuss and causing trouble." The bully looks over to the slightly built Donald and smells blood. Sensing an easy target, he turns towards Donald, whose facial expression transforms from irritation to mild concern.

"Mate, I think you need to leave it."

Dave springs round aggressively but his confidence drains as he confronts the man addressing him. Self-justification had gone some way to repairing the dent to his ego. He had been paralytic, so not able to defend himself and, on top of that, Ashton had started it by pestering his girlfriend. It was a lucky punch. Glaring at Ashton, he starts to weigh the odds. He has four inches and fifty pounds on him. Yeah — he could take him. He takes a step towards his nemesis. Ashton tenses but remains on his stool. A voice booms from behind the bar.

"That'll do Dave. Let's not spoil the mood tonight. If you are going to cause trouble you are going to have to leave, and this time you'll be barred."

Dave knew only too well that the landlord of no mean size himself had a long history of dealing with troublemakers. He had witnessed Wilkes at his most ruthless, and, with Ashton also next to him, his cause was lost. Trying not to lose face, he continues to stare down Ashton whilst speaking to Wilkes.

"Okay Ken, sorry mate, but this place needs livening up. Don't worry about it. I'm off t'Scarborough anyway — to somewhere the locals have a pulse."

"Don't be angry, Dave luv," says Dolly in a conciliatory tone, but it washes over him.

Satisfied he has come out of the situation with honour, he stares at Ashton as he marches out, waving away Dolly who holds out her hand with some coins for the jukebox. The pub door slams, marking his exit. Ashton relaxes and orders another cider, and a gin and tonic for Donald, who smiles in gratitude.

Neaves sits at a table with Mandelson, observing the scene. He had considered getting up and intervening himself. He was itching to return the favour to the bully who had taken a cheap shot at him in a rugby scrum during a local match some weeks ago. No one would have shed any tears if he had approached him from behind and taken him out with a haymaker. He might have been the local hero and even got a round of applause. The bloke had it long coming to him. Shame Ashton, then Wilkes had dealt with the situation so quickly. And, to Neaves' disappointment, so peacefully.

"If I can wrestle back your attention, Ronald," snaps Mandelson. "We have a matter to resolve." Neaves turns back round to face his friend.

"Sorry Jeff, was waiting for Round Two of the Ayton Heavyweight Championship bout over there, but Wilkes stopped it before it got interesting."

With a look of irritation borne from his friend's low attention span, Mandelson continues. "I noticed Dibley walked in a few minutes ago. Don't look round now, but he is at the table with the Hensons near the far wall." It takes willpower, but Neaves maintains eye contact with Mandelson, who proceeds to make his point. "I have a council meeting coming up which will make or break our little hotel venture. Dibley is getting very vocal, and the odds are, with the interfering flock of Christian do-gooders behind him, that the proposal could be stymied. We need find a way to shut him up. Cut off the head of the snake so to speak."

"I know, Jeff and I have it under control."

"Well, it doesn't look very under control at the moment Ronald. In fact, it is gradually getting more and more out of control. It would also help if you got that bunch of cowboys from the 'Bodge It Corral' to fix the mess. Or should I say the, ludicrously entitled, church renovation. It is beginning to look in a worse state than when you started. You are meant to be renovating the bloody thing not demolishing it. It is being called the leaning tower of Yorkshire."

"It's under control, Jeff."

"Unfortunately, when you mutter those words, they do not inspire confidence in me. Quite the opposite. However, I'll try to take your word for it but do not wish to know what you are doing; or what you have in mind. The less I know, the better for both of us. I just hope it doesn't involve anybody from your more dubious circle of acquaintances." Mandelson gives a pointed stare and Neaves chooses not to respond and turns around to check out Dibley.

At that table the mood had an outward appearance of conviviality but — on Sebastian's part at least — underlying tension. An outsider looking in would assume Julia and Dibley were the couple, and Sebastian the gooseberry. A striking-looking couple with the overweight, balding, sorry 'plus one' who couldn't get a date.

"Well," announces Sebastian when there is a lull in the conversation. "You two are spending a lot of time together. You'd better be careful because people might start to talk. You know what gossips there are in the village."

Dibley smiles, not recognising the bitter undercurrent of Sebastian's mood. "We are, Sebastian; indeed, we are spending a lot of time together.

Julia is doing an amazing job in the parish. I don't know what I would do without her. She is an absolute star. You must be very proud of her." He winks at Sebastian and adds, "You are a very lucky man, which I am sure you know." Julia simpers in embarrassment at all the praise as she shuffles beside Dibley. *Perhaps a little closer to him than decorum might expect*, thinks Sebastian.

"I don't want you overworking her Peter, she seems to come home exhausted and these meetings seem to get later and later." comes the curt response which sails over the top of Dibley's head.

Julia takes up the mantle on Dibley's behalf. *Yet again taking his side*, thinks Sebastian with irritation. She addresses her husband. "Oh, don't be so silly Sebastian, you'll make Peter feel guilty. It's all for the good of the village. I can't just sit in the house all day whilst you work and have all these late business meetings, can I? I get so bored."

"Suppose so," replies Sebastian with a touch of petulance.

Now sensing the mood and its undercurrent, Dibley gets up to leave. "Right, I will leave you two lovebirds to it. I must go."

"Oh, *must* you Peter?" Julia expresses her disappointment with a pout.

"Fraid so. Thanks again for the drink, and see you Tuesday."

Sebastian tries to hide his pleasure as he watches the vicar leave. He is not the only person who seems to note Dibley's departure. The stranger in the corner drains his glass and gets up to leave. As he walks towards the door hairy Bob leans over to Hayes and whispers. "There he goes. Mr Killer eyes."

Hayes ignores the comment. "I'm off back up to the bar, Bob, fancy a pint?"

"A Guinness mate, cheers."

Hayes smiles, scoops up the empty glasses and takes them to the bar. He waves them at Dolly to get her attention and she smiles at him, waiting for the order.

"Two lagers and a Guinness, Dolly, please."

"Yer a good lad, Purple, getting Bob a drink an' all."

Hayes beams at the compliment. "He's a nice bloke, Dolly. Just feel a bit sorry for him. Don't reckon he's all there. You seem quite close to him. Any idea what happened to him?"

Dolly busies herself filling the glasses and talks to Hayes as she works. "Don't really know, luv. I think he was in the army and something happened to him which sent him over the edge. He's not told me much — but I think, between the lines, that he got a medical discharge of some sort.

He did a few postings abroad — in the Middle East I think, but I am not sure where he was and what he was doing. Whatever it was, he came out damaged. All that said he is a lovely fella, underneath the beard and grimy clothes. A heart of gold I reckon, and he keeps pretty clean, considering he is homeless 'n all. I guess it's his time in the army."

"I know, Dolly, but he says some strange stuff. He reckons that bloke who just left was a bloody murderer or something."

"What, the one who left just after Peter?" asks Dolly

"Yep."

"I have to say, he didn't look particularly friendly, barely said a word when I served him. No thank you nor nothing."

"Maybe so, Dolly but that doesn't exactly make him a murderer, does it?" laughs Hayes as he pays Dolly and gathers up the glasses.

"Nurse, nurse," shouts Donald.

"Be with you in a second, luv," replies Dolly.

Balancing the glasses in his two hands, Hayes carefully makes his way back to the table, not noticing a sideways glance from Neaves as he passes by him.

"He's a fucking loser," sneers Neaves to Mandelson.

"Maybe so, but your job my friend is to be everybody's friend. If we are to get this planning through, we need as many people on our side as possible. Or, at least as few against us as possible. So, you need to change a habit of a lifetime and be nice." Neaves has little to say and just absorbs himself in the activity of drinking his beer.

"One thing you can do, Ronald." Mandelson pauses until Neaves looks up as he sups. "One thing you can do is to try to schmooze the locals. I know that schmoozing isn't your thing but at least try to be nice, try to be reassuring to the busy bodies like the Fosdyke bitch. She's a big fan of Dibley, another religious nutter — and she is on the planning council. There's no way of getting her on our side, but equally we do not need to antagonise the woman. I need to work out a way of shutting her up at least."

"How do you plan to do that?" asks Neaves.

"Governance, my dear Ronald. Good governance."

"Haven't a clue what you are talking about Jeffrey, but I am sure in your good hands it will do the business."

"Let's hope so," replied Mandelson. "Let us hope so."

At the bar, Donald had exceeded his limit by at least two gins and, as was his nature, he became increasingly indiscrete. He calls Dolly over and, after checking there are no other customers waiting to be served, she goes over to the end of the bar for a chat.

"Yes Donald, what can I do for you?"

Slurring a little, Donald whispers conspiratorially. "My dear Dolly, I may be the only gay in the village, but check out the good doctor sat on his lonesome over there. He's the only black in the village."

"Behave Donald, you can't say stuff like that anymore," chides Dolly.

Ignoring her he continues to gossip. "There is a rumour around the place that our dear black doctor may have been indiscrete with a local teenager."

"Stop it, Donald. Yer just being racist."

"No, I am not, how dare you!" slurs Donald. "I am telling you, I have it on good authority."

Dolly looks over to Kamau. He is staring over at them, but she is not convinced that he can hear Donald. Hoping he cannot, she smiles at him, gesturing if he wants a refill. He shakes his head with what looks like a forced smile and then gets up and leaves. Turning to Donald she says in an exasperated tone, "Seriously, you really need to keep those sorts of opinions to yerself. The doctor seems a nice man, I hear he comes from African royalty. He wouldn't do anything like that."

"Not sure coming from royalty is a guarantee of good behaviour. Look at our own lot," sneers Donald.

"Really Donald, you are terrible. You've had enough. Time for bed for you. It's almost closing time anyway." Dolly ushers Donald out of the pub, accompanying him all the way to the door. When she was satisfied he was on his way home, she turns around with hands on her hips, exasperated, looking directly at Ashton who had turned in his stool to watch Donald's walk of shame.

"Deary me, Chris, that man, he is an absolute bugger; but I do love him."

Ashton smiles in response, "Takes all sorts, Dolly."

Ken Wilkes walks around the bar to the jukebox and puts in a coin. It is a ritual that all the locals love. With about five minutes to closing time he would always put the same track on. Elvis Presley and his version of "My Way." Those left in the pub always sang along to the bits that they knew. Ken booms out the first line,

"And now, the end is near. And so I face the final curtain ..." Others join in sporadically. Hayes, Hendricks and Hairy Bob link arms and sway in time with the music, then join in with the second verse. They are a bit

less tuneful than Ken and a lot less tuneful than Elvis, but no one cares. *"Regrets, I've had a few. But then again, too few to mention. I did what I . . ."* Everyone in the bar joins in on the bits they can remember, except Ken who knows it word for word, and he closes off the song with a rousing final refrain. *"The record shows, I took the blows but,"* and the whole pub sings, *"I did it mmmyyyyyy waaaay."*

Everybody claps, drains their glasses and Dolly slowly ushers them all off the premises. With an audible sigh she bolts the pub doors after the last customer leaves. "What a bloody night Ken, I am totally pooped. So busy."

"Don't moan, luv, busy is good, and if it keeps this way we can get out of our debt. Hopefully that bloody vicar who had the cheek to come in tonight will keep his trap shut about the noise and supposed disturbance on Fridays. The live music night is a blooming goldmine."

"He's okay," yawns Dolly. "And before you come up make sure you put that rifle back in the gun safe. You've left it out. It's in the corner of the living room."

"Will do," replies Ken. They finish locking up and go straight to bed, leaving the mess to wait until the morning.

16

MCCARTHY LOUNGES IN a booth at the back of his favourite haunt. He'd purchased a small church some years ago, renovated it, and redesigned the building into what his architect had told him would be a *bijou* entertainment space. Unlike the other clubs he owned, which were run for the sole purpose of making money, this was more of a hobby: a passion, rather than a business venture. Dukes was established as the only venue in town devoted to live Jazz, and it was one of McCarthy's happy places where he could live his passion and relax. An homage to an earlier era where political correctness, hip hop and shell suited idiots calling themselves 'gangsta rappers' had not yet reared their ugly heads. Every second Friday the local musicians surrendered the small stage to old school acts, which McCarthy also loved. Magicians, comedians, burlesque dancers and impressionists regularly featured on the bill. Time had marched on and acts like these were increasingly hard to find as most local artists were either knocking on death's door, retired or riddled with dementia.

He settles back with a glass of whisky and the half empty bottle placed in front of him to enjoy one of his favourites, Benedict Bunton. Seventy-six years on earth had shrunk Bunton's body and the audience was presented with a thin old man in a suit that probably once fitted perfectly but now looked a couple of sizes too big. In the late 1970's he had a brief career on television hosting a game show that only lasted one season. In those days he had the stage name Benny B, but now he used his full name. He was a comedian of his time and his act had not evolved one iota, and that was just how McCarthy liked it. If any audience members went down the path of heckling Bunton thinking the old crock before them was an easy target, they soon found themselves on the wrong end of a verbal battering. Bunton's core audience knew him well and loved him; any retorts to hecklers were met with rapturous applause and laughter.

The crowd hush as the lights are lowered to signal the beginning of the next act. Shuffling onto the stage Bunton gives a quizzical look as if he does not know where he is, causing the audience to giggle in anticipation. He grabs the microphone and launches straight into his act.

"I met a good friend the other day and he told me he was depressed. I said, 'What's wrong?' He said, 'My second wife just died, so I am a bit down.' 'What happened to the first wife?' I asked, trying to change the subject and cheer him up. He said, 'She died also, she ate some mushrooms, they were poisonous.' I said to my friend, 'That is bloody unlucky, who would have believed it, poisonous mushrooms!'"

The audience giggles, Bunton pauses, and with perfect comic timing picks his moment to resume the story.

"So, I tried to change the subject again. 'Oh dear,' I said, 'So what happened to the second wife?' 'Well,' he told me, 'She died from a severe head injury, cracked her skull.'"

More giggles from the audience. Bunton pauses again, looking down from the stage he smirks at those nearest to him. He continues.

"I replied that this was really, really, really, unlucky. 'Cracked her skull you say, what happened?' He replied, 'She refused to eat the bloody mushrooms.'"

The audience bursts into laughter and applause; Bunton raises his hand in appreciation. A young woman sitting with her boyfriend does not laugh. They were wannabe hipsters and had come hoping to see a jazz act, thinking it would be retro and cool. She shouts out to him. "Disgusting! Making jokes about domestic violence and women being abused, haven't you heard of the Me Too movement, you old fart?"

McCarthy peers into the audience trying to see where the heckler was seated. He gesticulates to the manager of the club, who is standing nearby. Acknowledging his boss's request the manager nods and moves across the floor to deal with the young couple. Before he gets to the table, Bunton responds. "Oh aye, folks, we've got a live one here." Making eye contact with the woman he addresses her directly. "Hello, love, shouldn't you be doing yer homework or something? Your school bus leaves in ten minutes — be under it."

The audience bursts into laughter as the girl and her boyfriend get up and leave. Still three tables away the manager aborts his mission whilst Bunton continues his act without missing a beat. He picks out three men sitting at a nearby table, they all have long black hair, earrings, and tattoos. "Hey, are you boys gypsies?" They give him the thumbs up. "People look at me like that young lady over there, the one who's gone off to do her homework, they say I'm a dinosaur. I'm racist. I'm sexist. I'm this, I'm that. Blah, blah, blah — they're wrong. See lads, there's a lot of stereotypes about gypsies aren't there? I hate it, and I don't believe them either. I bet you three have never tarmacked the drive of an old lady in your whole life, have you?"

The audience giggles.

"No, mate," replies one of the gypsies, laughing and nudging his friends sat either side of him. "We don't do tarmac."

"See what I mean people? Stereotypes, laying the tarmac, it's all bollocks." He looks back at the young men with a mischievous grin. "Tarmac a drive. Course you haven't, mate, never laid any tarmac in yer life. Course you haven't. Just because you are gypsies doesn't mean you're labourers. You've all got brains 'aven't you?" A short pause and the comedian's now serious expression melts into a wry smile. "You just took her money and buggered off without doing it all."

The audience erupts into laughter, including the three men.

Engrossed in the act, McCarthy barely notices one of his bouncers escort a man towards his table. Both men were of similar size and build. It would have been hard for any stranger to identify which of the two was the bouncer. The pair stop at the side of McCarthy's table careful not to block his view of the stage. Eyes focussed on the comedian as he continues his act picking out a hapless looking bald man, McCarthy addresses the visitor.

"Mr Neaves, how nice of you to visit my club. I have to say that when you called, I thought to myself, 'Well, this man has bigger balls than I thought.' Take a seat." He pushes an empty glass and the bottle of whisky in front of Neaves who slowly squeezes his large frame between the fixed table and the red leather seat. "Pour yourself a drink, relax and just give me a few minutes whilst Benedict finishes his act. Don't worry, won't be long. Old Benny is getting on, he'll only be about five minutes. Any more than that and he'll pass out." Muttering a thanks, Neaves fills his glass and watches the act in silence as McCarthy chuckles and guffaws at the comedian. Seventy-six and the old fella still had it. On stage, the comedian closes his act ten minutes later and as he shuffles off McCarthy claps loudly, catching Bunton's eye who gives an appreciative wave. McCarthy smiles reflectively for a moment, but by the time he turns to face Neaves his expression is stoic.

Desperate to keep the meeting short, Neaves opens the conversation, "So, Mr McCarthy, thank you for seeing me. Have you given any thought to my proposal?"

Narrowing his eyes and tilting his head, McCarthy responds. "I have, Mr Neaves, but I like to look into the eyes of who I am going to do business with. It helps me assess commitment, so to speak. Especially given the sensitive nature of the proposal. Don't really trust phones, even my burner ones, never sure who is listening and what is being recorded. After the little lesson I gave to you it would not be out of the question that you held a grudge. Would it?" Sensing that the question was rhetorical Neaves doesn't respond, allowing McCarthy to continue. McCarthy chooses his words carefully, ensuring that vagueness and ambiguity keeps the conversation secure from uninvited ears. A day earlier he had cut Neaves short when he'd phoned with a proposal and the conversation started to cover uncomfortable ground. Couldn't be too careful. "My understanding is that if I do as you ask and the impediment to your little village project is removed, then in recompense for my, how shall we say, 'business consultancy', I have a small share in the ownership of the project, plus a substantial fee for services to facilitate its progress. Is that correct?"

"That's it," confirms Neaves, then adds with a small degree of bravado to regain a tiny portion of lost ground, "Providing everything is done satisfactorily."

McCarthy's smile was as cold as packed ice. "We have a deal."

"Great, Mr McCarthy . . . when will it be done?" urges Neaves.

"When the time is right and not before. But within the timeline you indicated. You'll know. Let's face it, when it is done you're going to know about it before I tell you anyway." McCarthy turns back towards the stage, indicating the meeting was over.

Neaves struggles out of the booth, and after an ungraceful ejection from its confines he stands up straight and offers his hand to McCarthy. Ignoring the gesture, McCarthy picks up his re-filled whisky glass, "Goodbye Neaves," he says, "I assume you remember from your experience in the past that it would be unwise not to hold up your part of the bargain?" Withdrawing his outstretched hand, Neaves nods uncertainly until he is ushered out of the club by the bouncer who had maintained a respectful distance.

McCarthy turns back to the entertainment to see the three gypsies in front of the audience making clucking sounds and goose-stepping around the stage. The young hypnotist, Trancemaster Flash, was shouting a series of instructions to the three men who were being told to find the rooster in the farmyard, who had a special surprise for them. Bawling with laughter, the audience is gasping as the three men desperately run around the stage, bumping into each other with lascivious expressions. As he watches the scene play out, McCarthy muses over the outcome of the brief meeting. He has Neaves where he wants him, and there was the extra bonus of a nice earner. Possibly even a favour for his most valued employee, Sebastian Henson.

17

WITH NO SMALL degree of trepidation, Hardy and Stanley sit in the office of Detective Inspector Parkins. DI Parkins had just switched on the TV screen after his secretary informed him that there was about to be a news item reporting on the case in Ayton. It was fortuitous timing, as he had already called a meeting with the two detectives to discuss their progress. Flicking through the channels Parkins found the news just as the headlines had been read. All eyes were glued to the screen.

"Thank you, Simon, let's hope the crisis at Scarborough Hospital will be resolved quickly. Now over to Sue, who is on location in Ayton to give us an update of the investigation following the dreadful shooting of the local vicar: the Reverend Peter Dibley. Can you hear me, Sue?"

"Loud and clear, Warren, thank you. To remind viewers, the shooting was just over a week ago, tragically killing Reverend Dibley outside the front entrance of the local church. He was a much-loved member of the community and the shock of this event hangs over the village. Local people have many questions but so far very few answers have been provided. Many I have talked to, believe the police investigation has stalled and others have gone so far as to say the police seem to have lost interest. No tangible progress has been reported and the police continue to ask for anybody to come forward with information no matter how trivial it may seem. The police are emphasising that any information is welcomed, anything at all."

"Sue, can I ask whether the police have indicated any possible motive for the killing?"

"Very little has been revealed, hence the scepticism of local people. That said, Warren, we know that the police often must keep their cards close to their chest, so that

the investigation is not compromised. Also, they will not reveal potential suspects for similar reasons, as well as the risk of compromising the legal process."

"Yes, Sue, but often we learn of individuals helping them with their enquiries, so to speak, or persons of interest they would like to talk to."

"None that I am aware of, Warren. It really does seem that the investigation so far has stalled, and the police have encountered a series of dead ends. In conclusion, Warren, it is fair to conclude at this stage that the police are no closer to finding out who did this and why."

"Thank you, Sue." The host turns to face the camera and addresses the viewers. *"We will keep you posted on further developments on this terrible crime as soon as they occur. Now, to update viewers regarding local celebrity Jack O'Nelly, who became severely ill following his attempt on the world oyster eating record. He has now been discharged, and it appears that there were probably one or two oysters which had seen better days ..."*

Pointing the remote at the TV, Parkins switches it off with an accompanying hiss of dissatisfaction.

"So, Detectives, take me through what we have."

"We have learnt that Dibley was shot through the head by a rifle fired at some distance, probably in excess of three hundred metres," says Hardy, whose flow is abruptly halted by his boss.

"Well, that is an effing outstanding piece of police work, let's all go home now and open a bottle of champagne. Tell me, Detectives — and I use this title in the loosest meaning of the term — do you have anything at all that I couldn't just get off the damn news? Suspects perhaps? Or at a stretch, a prime suspect?"

Ignoring the sarcasm, Hardy continues. "We have footage of a local, Chris Ashton, around the church at the time of the shooting. He was caught on the CCTV at the local petrol station."

"Was he alone?"

"Except for his Beagle, yes, he was."

"Well, I suspect you can rule out the dog. What's the story with Ashton?"

"He's a local artist. A sculptor."

Parkins exhales loudly in frustration. "I don't care if he is effing Michelangelo, do you have anything on him?"

"Nothing concrete, but he was flagged on the system as a suspect in a murder case down south, in London. But he wasn't charged or anything, just remains a person *potentially* of interest in an open, but cold case," explains Hardy.

Parkin picks up his pen and starts tapping it on his desk. His frustration and irritation are growing, Stanley could see the inspector's temper shortening by the second, so he keeps quiet, leaving Hardy to take all the heat.

"Please, tell me you have some other ideas after a week on the case. Any other suspects?"

Hardy steels himself, knowing that all the available straws were being clutched. "There is a Sebastian Henson. He's a local accountant who has done very well for himself, has a trophy wife who was an ex-model. Punching above his weight, but money is the best aphrodisiac they say. Two locals, the Addinall sisters, came to the station following a request that we made for information from the local community. They told us that it was rumoured that Henson's wife was having an affair with Dibley, and we thought this could be a potential line of enquiry."

Pen tapping goes up a notch. "So, you are telling me some ugly little accountant took a high velocity rifle and shot the vicar right between the eyes? From a distance that an effing army marksmen would be proud of? And he did this, all because the vicar shagged his wife. Tell me. Tell me seriously, do you think this scenario is credible, you bloody idiot?"

"Well — no, sir, at least not with him doing the shooting. But he has money, and he could have hired a professional."

"Hired a professional. I think I'll bloody hire a professional. How about I hire Benny effing Bunton to take your place on the investigation? At least he is a professional comedian, because believe me, you two are not funny. Please tell me you have something else? Anything."

Stanley finally raises his head above the parapet and tries to regain some lost ground. "It appears, sir, that the vicar had got on the wrong side of a few other locals. He was complaining about the renovations on his church and threatening to take the builder to court. Also, he was becoming a vocal opponent of a proposed development next to the church as well."

"Anything else?" asks the inspector in a tone that made it clear he was rapidly giving up all hope.

"The local publican has a beef with the vicar, who is apparently complaining to the council about the noise and disturbance of youths coming out of the boozer on a Friday night."

"Why Friday?" utters Parkins, with little enthusiasm for the theory. He was resigned to the fact that he was not going to discover that they had some credible lead.

"Music night, sir."

112

"So, to summarise: you have a builder, an accountant and a publican with a possible motive. To which, you have an apparently motiveless dog-loving painter, who just happened to be somewhere near at the time he was shot." Stanley held himself from correcting the inspector that Ashton was in fact a sculptor. Parkins continues, "I don't suppose you two have found out who owns a rifle locally by any chance? Given that this was the murder weapon."

"It may not have been murder. sir, there are also stories of locals in the area being a bit reckless with guns and shooting rabbits. Theoretically it could have been an accident. This is another line of enquiry we are pursuing."

Parkins exploded. "It's not the bloody *O.K. Corral*, for God's sake! With everyone armed and itching at the trigger. It is a small Yorkshire village where the last known killing was probably about three hundred years ago with a bloody bow and arrow. Start doing some proper police work. Find out who has a registered rifle, cross check this with ballistics and see if anything matches."

"It is underway, sir, the only registered weapon we are aware of is the one owned by the pub landlord. He promised to bring it in by Friday."

"What the hell! Why didn't you get it off him when you interviewed him?" snaps Parkins.

"It was at the gunsmiths, sir, being cleaned and serviced," explains Stanley.

"For God's sake — so he has a freshly and professionally cleaned firearm? I'm sure that will be very useful to forensics, won't it? Get yourselves busy and make sure you interview everyone in the bloody village and beyond. Someone must know something. Now get out of my office before another murder is committed!"

The detectives leave with their tails between their legs and decide to regroup in the station canteen over a cup of coffee. They find a table in the corner to give them some privacy and start to discuss what the next steps would be.

"What do you reckon boss?" asks Stanley. Scratching his eyebrow Hardy is concentrating intensely. Stanley sips patiently on his coffee giving his boss the space of silence to work things through.

"Okay. The first thing we need to do is to tie up the loose ends so far. We need to get the ballistics report to identify the type of firearm and get hold of Wilkes's rifle. The likelihood is that he will be ruled out, because if he isn't, and there is a match, he will have a fair bit to answer for. So, you need to get on to these asap."

Stanley nods, "Anything else boss?"

"Yep, go back through the CCTV and see if we missed anything. Take your time, there may be something important, or someone else on the recording, even a partial image we can work on. Check the number plates of any cars going through the petrol station throughout the timeline of the recording and identify the owners and see if anything sticks out like punters with previous. If there is anybody worth questioning don't approach them until we have talked it through."

'Well, that should keep me busy," replies Stanley with a hint of complaint that goes unnoticed. Nor does Hardy fully grasp the implied criticism of Stanley's next comment. "So, what are you thinking of doing next yerself, boss?"

"Not that I have a great deal of hope, but a couple of names have come up which might be at least worth pursuing. Having a cosy chat with, so to speak. Seeing if they can account for their movements when the vicar took a bullet."

"Who are you talking about?"

"Ronald Neaves and Sebastian Henson. Neaves seemed to be at odds with Dibley over the church renovation. As for Henson, we ought to at least eliminate him, if possible. Though having seen him around he doesn't look as though he would harm a fly. But you never know, let's not entirely rule out the Addinalls' 'crime of passion' theory."

Widening his eyes Stanley responds. "You can't be serious boss."

Hardy snaps back, "At this point Stanley, we have something between zero and bugger all. Frankly I am willing to consider or try anything. In fact, if you think that is a long shot, wait until you hear this." Stanley waits with interest whilst Hardy wrestles with how he was going to explain his latest idea. "I was talking things through with DS Hocart."

Stanley could not stop himself interrupting. "Hocart — Hocart? You hate him, boss, you think he's an absolute wanker. What on earth are you talking to him for?"

Irritated that he must justify himself, Hardy raises his voice. "Yes, Stanley. He is a wanker, and he is arrogant, and he is a pain in the arse. But, my dear Stanley, he is an intelligent, successful, pain in the arse, so, for any ideas he can offer, I am willing to listen. He also was, as you know, a lead investigator on that murder case in Pontefract where they got the nutter who did it. What you probably don't know is that they were going nowhere as quickly as we are in this case, until he took the unusual step of involving a psychic."

"What, a bloody gypsy fortune teller?" scoffs Stanley, adding to Hardy's irritation.

"A clairsentient," declares Hardy. Seeing the blank, gormless expression of Stanley, he elucidates, "It's a person who can perceive things that the likes of you and me can't." He sees Stanley opening his mouth to speak and decides to cut him off before he is drawn into explaining a theory that, in all honesty, he did not really believe himself. "Before you go on at me, Stanley, the point is that whatever it is, it worked for Hocart. Not only that but the psychic we are talking about is right here on our doorstep. A Miss Jenny Wicker who lives in — would you believe — Ayton."

"No way, and she was the one who helped Hocart?" asks Stanley. Hardy nods in affirmation. Scratching his head, Stanley looks to the ground, "Well, boss I suppose we have nothing to lose."

"Actually, Stanley, we have a fair bit to lose. We're looking more Inspector Clouseau than Inspector Morse as far as the media is concerned, nor as far as Parkins is concerned for that matter. There's a lot of scope for ridicule from either party. I was thinking more of a private word with the woman, doing it all on the quiet, keeping it all hush-hush," says Hardy tapping the side of his nose.

"Fair enough, boss, let's give it a go."

18

ALTHOUGH THE MANAGERIAL style of DI Parkins was unlikely to be found in any modern human resources manual, his pep talk had the desired effect of spurring Hardy and Stanley into action.

Stanley had found a soulless, dark and windowless room in the station, ideal for giving him the peace and quiet he required as he undertook the laborious task of reviewing the CCTV footage. He stuttered through still frames, pausing intermittently, minute by minute, searching for anything that could be vaguely meaningful to the case. Hours passed slowly, and the task seemed fruitless. He had checked the number plates of all seventeen vehicles that appeared on the forecourt during the evening and early morning and had drawn nothing but blanks. The owners appeared to be very ordinary people; the motorists included a teacher, a social worker, an estate agent, three nurses, and six lorry drivers delivering their wares either eastwards towards Scarborough, or westwards, presumably to the more inland villages and towns. Other than the occasional minor offence, which was mostly traffic related, none looked like the sort of person whose hobby included shooting vicars at long range. That said, what would a long-distance sniper with a propensity for killing vicars look like? The social worker had a minor offence of shoplifting, they are usually atheists. And one of the lorry drivers had an assault charge, but other than that there was nothing, nada, zero, zilch. Not a sausage.

The one beacon of hope which lifted his spirits and provided psychological, if not actual relief to his tired, scratchy eyes, was a blurry image in the background at almost 2:00 a.m. on the morning of the shooting. There was also an image around 7.30 a.m. It was hard to make out the individual who appeared at the edge of the camera's field of vision. Both times the image was blurred and became even more indistinct when it was paused to allow him to examine it more carefully. As soon as he resumed the recording the man disappeared off camera. Stanley could make out a large figure, with baggy clothes, long unruly hair and a beard. There was no real definition in terms of facial features. Just a blob of a face which clearly had a lot of hair surrounding it top and bottom. He had not come across anyone in the village who fitted the description, so he drove to Ayton with the intention of asking around.

To his surprise, the mystery man was identified immediately at his first port of call. Using his logic that the village pub would be the centre of the Ayton universe, he went into the Old Plough. In fact, as it turned out, he had managed to kill two birds with one stone. Based on the description, Ken Wilkes immediately identified the man as Hairy Bob. Wilkes also confirmed he would be getting his gun back the next day and would bring it straight over to the station. When Stanley asked if he knew Bob's surname and address, the landlord drew a blank, but informed him that Bob was homeless and tended to spend a lot of his time in and around the village. Thinking he'd reached another dead end, he thanked Wilkes and turned to leave when the landlord added that the rumour was that Bob had PTSD from his time on tour in the Middle East. This peaked Stanley's interest, and keen to get hot on the trail, he rushed straight to his car. Consequently, he did not hear Wilkes shout another vital piece of information, which had occurred to him just as the detective was leaving the premises. Namely, the man he was looking for was likely to turn up at the pub in a matter of minutes. Had he heard this, Stanley would have saved himself a great deal of work.

The information that Stanley did take on board, set him on a journey of what could be possibly described as impressive detective work. He drove two hours to meet a friend in the local army base at Catterick Garrison, it was a good excuse to catch up. Over a beer in the local hostelry, he learnt that the central military records are kept in Glasgow so a bit of a dead end but the pub did an amazing lunch and was knocking on the door of a Michelin Star apparently.

Eventually, Stanley returned to the police station, where he spent most of the following day on the phone, being shifted from pillar to post by a steady stream of bureaucrats. Thinking his luck had run out, he was ebullient when he received a phone call out of the blue the next day. Apparently, the enquiry had shifted up the line from the Clerical Officer to Executive Officer, to Higher Executive Officer then to the Senior Executive Officer, and finally, to Miss Dunbar, who had obtained the lofty heights of Chief Executive Officer. For twenty-five minutes of the thirty-minute phone call, Stanley found himself tapping his feet, chewing his pen, and rubbing his forehead with impatience. Miss Dunbar was hell bent on explaining to him the process her section had gone through to potentially identify the person of interest. In the end, Stanley jubilantly threw his arms in the air when Miss Dunbar confirmed that a Robert Jenkins had served in the SAS, served three tours in Afghanistan and had been medically discharged with diagnosed PTSD. Address unknown. It did get better; Stanley fist pumped the air when Miss Dunbar added that Robert Jenkins was also a designated marksman spotter in his squad. Three days of quality dogged detective work yielded a result.

Or at least, so Stanley thought. Had he stayed in the Old Plough for ten more minutes with the landlord and not rushed off at such great speed, he would have encountered Hairy Bob and saved himself the round trip of North Yorkshire and the bureaucratic catacombs of military administration. Bob had walked into the pub for his daily Guinness, blissfully unaware that the police were looking for him, and as Dolly had taken over the bar from Ken, who was at a meeting with the bank, she was equally as unaware of the detective's visit.

Before he reported back to Hardy, Stanley wanted to see whether the laboratory boffins had completed their ballistics report. Here he hit a roadblock and got nowhere with the technicians, who seemed determined to frustrate him at every turn. He demanded to speak to the manager, who was already planning his retirement later in the year and wanted a hassle-free pathway to blissful peace. The likes of Stanley and their demands were an inconvenience he could do without. Stanley's call was put through, and the manager picked up.

"Yeeesss, Morgan here, I understand from my staff that you have insisted you want to speak to me. What can I do for you?"

"It is DC Stanley speaking; I am trying to follow up a report that is overdue from your team, and it is an urgent matter."

At that point Stanley did not know it but the battle was lost. Desmond Morgan was not a man to be challenged, and the implied criticism immediately rankled him.

"Really, DC Stanley. And which case are you referring to?"

After giving the case details, Stanley awaited a response, but all he got for two minutes was what sounded like papers shuffling, intermittent keyboard clicking and heavy breathing. Eventually Morgan came back on the line.

"Yes, I have it, test number A425/A/H. A shooting in some obscure little place in Yorkshire," came the deliberately pompous and sarcastic voice. "And what exactly do you want me to do?"

Stanley was equally as belligerent, having been given the run around. "I want you to do your job, how does that sound? We need the report."

"Listen laddie, you sound as though you are fresh out of kindergarten and have watched too many detective shows. You may be aware that the bullet entered the face of the victim directly through the *zygomaticus minor* and straight out of the back of his skull, leaving about half his brain intact and the other half decorating the church wall." Stanley winced at the graphic description, but Morgan was not to be deterred. "The bullet, DC Stanley, was pretty much destroyed when it made contact with the wall, which I suspect was crafted from Yorkshire granite, as there is barely anything left of the bullet to examine."

Struggling to regain the upper hand Stanley said, "So, you can't even tell me what the bullet was fired from then?"

"Laddie, my dear laddie, for all we know it could have been fired from an elephant's arse the morning after it had consumed an extra hot prawn vindaloo from the local curry house. There is nothing that is recognisable from the remains of the bullet. Get an education and don't waste our time in the future. This is not an episode of *CSI: Yorkshire Sheep Worriers.*" The line went dead, and Stanley was left hanging.

Chastised but not defeated, Stanley still thought he had a good lead and at least something to report to Hardy. This bloke Bob ticked a few boxes: a crack shot, and a nutter. Problem was, what could his motive have been? Perhaps there was no motive other than the fact that the bloke is clearly unstable, and possibly armed and dangerous. *It happens daily in good old gun-toting America, so why not here?*

Hardy had emailed Stanley earlier in the day suggesting a catch up and they met, as agreed, in the station canteen. Deciding to save the best until last, Stanley took Hardy through all the work he had done poring over the CCTV recording and following up the owners of number plates on the footage. He then took Hardy through the story of how he spotted a blurred image and tracked down, through insightful enquiries, who the image belonged to. Stanley allowed himself some dramatic licence and by the end of the story he could see that his boss was at least a little impressed.

"Righty-ho! Good work, young Stanley, so we may have a credible suspect. Now we just need to find the elusive bugger for questioning. Oh, hang on, what is the story with ballistics? Didn't you get it done?"

Stanley gave an edited version of the exchange, which in his world and in his report to Hardy, left him with the verbal upper hand. Hardy's outrage was eventually quelled, and Stanley persuaded him that there was nothing more to be gained by Hardy calling the useless sods and giving them a piece of his mind. Hardy told him to return Wilkes's rifle, as there was nothing much to gain by keeping it, on top of which it had been thoroughly serviced and cleaned since the time of the shooting. Anyway, they had what looked like a more promising line of inquiry.

"So, boss, how did you get on with Henson and Neaves?" asks Stanley.

"Spoke to Henson at his home. Bloke looks as though he wouldn't harm a fly. Hard to imagine him shooting anybody, or even having the balls to pay someone and give the order. That said, he did seem a bit nervous when I probed here and there, especially when I asked about his wife's relationship with Dibley. I didn't go in hard; I just explored round the edges. Y'know, along the lines of understanding that his wife knew the vicar well and perhaps she might have insights as to if he had any enemies. He blocked me off from speaking to her directly, saying the shooting had severely impacted her mental health and she was in no state to be questioned. It was, apparently, too soon."

"So, we will keep him in the picture then?"

Hardy nodded. "For the time being. As for Neaves, he has been away on business apparently, but I've arranged to see him at four p.m. He said he would come to the station."

An hour later Neaves walked through the reception area of the station greeted by the patiently waiting Hardy. The detective thanked Neaves for coming in and explained he just wanted an informal chat as part of the process of eliminating locals from the inquiry. He guided Neaves, who towered above him, through the corridor into Interview Room 3 and indicated for his guest to take a seat at the table. Hardy sat opposite.

"Once again, thank you for coming in, Mr Neaves I shouldn't take too much of your time."

"No problem," replied Neaves in an even, no-nonsense tone.

"Let me get straight to it, as I know you are a busy man. Do you know where you were on the morning of the shooting, Mr Neaves?"

Neaves made a show of thinking about the question and confirming the date and time so he could answer accurately. He surmised that it was likely he was still in bed. He was at a function the night before, the Yorkshire Concrete Awards. The function had run on late, and he had drunk a fair bit. He was short listed for best concrete structure but added, self-effacingly, that his company did not make the podium. Hardy jokingly commented that he hoped Neaves had not driven home drunk afterwards. Neaves confirmed the function was in the Royal Hotel and he had booked a room.

"Can anybody verify you stayed the night, Mr Neaves?"

"Dunno really. The wife can, I suppose, and the hotel."

"Of course they can, perhaps I can just explore your relationship with Peter Dibley?"

Neaves struggled to retain his nonchalant expression. He knew what was coming.

"Obviously, Mr Neaves, the shooting of a cleric is a very rare event, so we are just trying to piece together who could possibly have any conflict. I understand that your company was commissioned to undertake the church renovations and that not everything has gone as planned. Was your relationship with Peter Dibley rather strained because of these circumstances?"

"You could put it that way. But if you are suggesting I would shoot him because of a dodgy wall you must be clutching at straws. Is that what you are suggesting? Do I need to get a lawyer?"

"Not at all, Mr Neaves, just trying to get a complete picture of Reverend Dibley's life and understand where there is conflict. I appreciate you have been honest, and this is helpful. And for the record, I doubt anyone would shoot anybody over a botched wall." Hardy had purposely used the word 'botched' to get a reaction, but Neaves saw through it and remained calm.

"Unfortunately, detective, the vicar was not a builder and we warned him prior to when the project began that until we started to do our work, the full extent of repairs could not be known. That wall had been slowly shifting for years. It was lucky we got to it in time and put in supports. If we'd started a few weeks later there would be nothing there to hold up. I deal with clients who are disappointed all the time and they always look for someone to blame."

The interview continued skirting round several topics. Neaves confirmed he'd seen no one suspicious in the village on the days prior to the shooting, but if he had further information, he would contact the station. After Neaves was shown out, Hardy sought out Stanley, who was working at his desk.

"Any luck, boss?"

Shaking his head, Hardy replied, "Nothing much. Funny really, we seem to be able to account for the fact that he was not around at the time of the shooting, but like Henson there is something about him. He is definitely withholding something, but who knows what."

"Okay, boss, we'll keep him on the list for now then."

19

A SOMBRE MOOD had descended onto the Henson household; like a fire blanket extinguishing a flame, and with it, all light and warmth.

Following the news of the shooting, Julia had taken herself to bed for long periods during each day. She had retreated within herself, and Sebastian suspected she had some form of depression. A significant part of her normal week was tied up in church activities and she had developed a close friendship with Dibley. (This, of course, had been the source of village gossip). All that was gone, and grief now filled the hole in her life and her heart. He reminded her about the property he'd purchased in Biarritz and suggested that perhaps they should get away from the village for a break. She did her best to appear pleased and grateful, but he knew her heart was not in it; she was in no mood to travel. Dr Kamau was called and responded sympathetically, agreeing to make a house call after his daily surgery was finished and, true to his word, the Henson's doorbell rang in the late afternoon.

After a greeting and brief discussion, Kamau asks to see Julia and Henson tells him she is in the bedroom. At the foot of the stairs he calls out to his wife to make sure she is awake and ready for the doctor. Reluctantly and devoid of enthusiasm she responds and he ushers Kamau upstairs. When Henson tries to follow him, Kamau holds out his hand in a gesture requesting him to remain downstairs, so he can see Julia alone. Henson gives him the thumbs up and returns to the distraction of the spreadsheets in his office.

Kamau enters the bedroom with a token light knock on the open door and appraises Julia on the bed sitting upright against a bank of pillows. She smiles weakly as she greets him, which he acknowledges, walking over to sit beside her. He goes through all the usual doctorly motions, pulse, temperature and asking for symptoms but quickly concludes the issue is psychological, not physical. All he can really offer is compassion, empathy, a mild antidepressant and sleeping tablets. Try as he might, Kamau cannot dispel the conflicting emotions wrestling within his own mind. Yes, as a doctor he is concerned for his patient but equally he could not exorcise the little red demon of relief that his own personal problem had perished along with the life of Dibley. With a promise to come back to the house in a couple of days, Kamau leaves Julia and makes his way down the stairs. Seeing the light from the office and hearing the click of a keyboard, he knocks on the open door. The room is in semi-darkness, with the glow of the screen pushing away the creeping shadows. Engrossed in his spreadsheets, Henson does not hear the gentle tap. So Kamau knocks louder. Henson swings round in his chair with an apology; Kamau hands him a prescription and explains his opinion on Julia's condition, urging him to fill the script without delay and ensure that his wife takes the medication, at least for the next few days.

As Henson stands at his front door watching the doctor climb into his car, his mobile rings. He left his glasses on his desk and has to squint at the small screen as he walks quickly into the living room. It is a call he must take. The moment he picks up, McCarthy launches into several work-related problems and issues without any of the niceties such as enquiring after Julia's health, or his own for that matter. Henson systematically works his way through and resolves each financial dilemma presented to him. Now more relaxed and pleased at what he has been told, McCarthy's mood becomes less businesslike and more convivial.

"Seb, my old mate, you are a finance superstar. Thanks for all that. And how is your gorgeous wife?"

"Pretty down actually, Dibley's death has hit her hard." McCarthy tries to say the right things and respond sympathetically but he is fooling no one, particularly Henson. Continuing to describe the domestic situation in his household, Henson gets a few murmured 'Ohs' in response. On his part, McCarthy initially avoids the obvious implication of why Dibley's death may have hit Julia so hard. That is until the end of the conversation.

"She'll get over it, Seb, and let's face it, we got a result there, didn't we? It's turned out well for you, as I said it would. Trust your Uncle Trent: if he says it is going to be okay, then it is going to be okay — okay? Speak tomorrow." Before Henson has time to process the comment and respond, McCarthy terminates the call, and he hears the sound of his wife's footsteps as she comes down the stairs and joins him.

"Hi, darling, how are you doing?" asks Henson with a caring sigh.

"Okay, darling. I guess I cannot stay in bed all day, so I thought I would come down and we could have a glass of wine together. Who was that you were speaking to on the phone?"

"McCarthy, it was just business."

"Horrible man," says Julia as she opens the bottle of red which was resting on the sideboard.

As the Hensons settle down to their wine, Kamau enters his own driveway, parks his car and switches off the ignition. The sound of a dying engine marking the end of a long working day. Darkness creeps over the village and the fading light of early evening struggles to penetrate the windows of the doctor's surgery and home. After a momentary struggle with his keys, he unlocks the door and enters the house, heading straight to his living room to help himself to a stiff, well-earned drink. He fumbles for the light switch and quickly expunges the threatening darkness. Sitting down on the sofa with a well filled tumbler, he raises the glass to his lips and immediately spills half of its contents onto his white shirt when he hears a voice behind him at the doorway of the room.

"Hello, Peter, I let myself in. The front door was open, you really need to be more careful — anybody could walk in."

"JOSHUA! Good God, you frightened the life out of me. Where did you spring from? I didn't hear a car pull up."

"I like to travel on foot, Peter. Everyone in this country drives everywhere, or takes the bus, or the train. It's easy to get soft, no wonder most of the population here is overweight. I left my car parked in the village and I fancied a bit of a walk."

"Oh okay, so here you are, what are your plans now?"

"Just wanted to say hi, and goodbye, nothing left for me to do now. Problem is now solved. I am going to return to Nairobi after a couple of days' rest and recreation in London. Your father knows what has happened and he is pleased to learn about the unfortunate end of the vicar. We spoke earlier; he sends his regards, wanted me to tell you he will call you in a few days. So, goodbye, Peter. The matter is solved, and I have done my duty and can tell your father I have seen you, and you are well."

Conversation over, Kariuki turns and leaves.

Kamau, exhausted, tries to process everything. What could he say? Kariuki was right, the matter was resolved — but not how he would have wanted it.

He hears the door close. He does not know it, but this would be the last time he ever sees or speaks to his father's bodyguard.

20

SLIGHTLY BRUISED CLOUDS hover apologetically over the church, offering the mild threat that it may decide to rain on Jenny Wicker and the two detectives. They stand outside the front door of the church, close to the spot where Peter Dibley had gone to meet his maker, who he had faithfully — or some thought, not so faithfully — served all his adult life. Birds chirp happily from the parapet, a dog barks in the distance and the hum of traffic from the main road signifies that life goes on.

Jenny's eyes are clamped shut, creating wrinkles which betray the intensity of her concentration. Both Hardy and Stanley had each ventured a question earlier in the session but were quickly shushed, and now stand around rather awkwardly staring at the woman with freshly dyed light green hair. She had tired of mauve and decided it was time for a change of colour. Springtime, rebirth; felt like green was the way to go. Dressed like a refugee from a 1960's *kibbutz*, in a flowing Indian print skirt, a tie dye long sleeve blouse and head scarf, Jenny circles the ground where Dibley's body had fallen. Four cynical eyes stare at her in silence, as the minutes drag by without comment from the witch. The two detectives shuffle on the spot, eagerly waiting for something that may help them solve the case. Just about reaching the limit of his patience, Hardy was about to voice a complaint but it is pre-empted by the ringing tone of his mobile which, in turn, evokes a tut of annoyance from Jenny. Hardy silently mouths an apology and creeps away to a safe distance before answering the call. He instantly regrets taking it, when the agitated voice of DI Parkins assaults his ears.

"I've had that bloody woman from the news on the phone asking about further progress on the Ayton shooting. 'What have we found? When will we be making a further statement? What should she tell the viewers? Why aren't the police doing anything? Can you confirm that the *bloody* vicar was having an affair? Was it a crime of passion?' . . . and on and on she went. And of course, I had bugger all to tell the woman other than 'No comment', which makes me, and the force look like a bunch of clueless numpties."

Hardy, who had winced throughout the verbal barrage, spent the next few minutes trying to justify his existence, calm his boss down and explain the progress made. The inspector was calmer, but not appeased.

"So, you are telling me, DS Hardy, that the vicar wasn't shagging the Henson woman, but now some ex-military nut job shot him, with no clear motive other than he lives in La La Land?" Deciding the inspector was being deliberately obtuse, Hardy tries to avoid antagonising him.

"No, sir, we are just following various lines of inquiry, and this came up after we spent hours carefully examining the CCTV. We spotted a figure in the background which was too blurred to be identifiable. To Stanley's credit he has managed, after a lot of effort, to identify the man, who we believe merits further investigation. It is worth pursuing. Ballistics, I have to say, have been little help. Apparently, the bullet is too damaged to be of much use in identifying the exact model of the murder weapon. There is, to be fair, very little in the way of physical evidence or witnesses. We are still pursuing several angles, including an accidental killing, and the Henson theory."

Parkins ends the call shortly afterwards, with at least something that he could offer the press. They had a new person of interest who they would be keen to speak to. Satisfied he could at least make it look as though they were making progress, he had a few crumbs to give the reporter when — that was a 'when', not an 'if' — she called back. Hardy had also sent through a picture of the suspect that could be presented in the next news item. A critical fact that eluded both Hardy, and subsequently Parkins, was that the photograph of the person of interest was obtained from military records during Bobs service in the SAS. It would take an impressive feat of identification from any member of the public to connect the image of a clean-shaven, sharply dressed, smiling male, with cropped hair and fifteen kilograms less body weight, to what this man had now become: Hairy Bob.

Hardy sidles up to Stanley, who is still focussed on the local witch.

Whispering to avoid further angst from Jenny, he tells Stanley that Parkins is on the warpath, but he has, for the time being, headed him off at the pass. Jenny's right eye opens abruptly, and Hardy first thinks he had broken her mojo, so he shrugs apologetically, but it is clear she has finished doing whatever it was she was doing.

"I've got all I can," she announces, "It all happened so quickly here, so there aren't many psychic impressions."

The detectives nod sagely. Neither have a clue what she is talking about, and neither are going to vocalise an admission of ignorance. Spots of rain begin to fall. Holding out his hand and catching a couple of droplets to make his point, Hardy wants to get on with it and do some proper police work. He, of course, does not vocalise these thoughts.

"Thank you, Miss Wicker, please tell us what you heard."

"I am not schizophrenic, DS Hardy. I don't hear strange voices. I am clairsentient, as I explained previously."

Hardy mutters an apology despite still being unclear as to what she is or, for that matter, what is the difference. Stanley, with equal ignorance, wisely keeps his thoughts to himself. Feeling things, hearing things, seeing things, smelling things; call it what you want, they all sounded like a direct pathway to the looney bin.

Jenny continues. "I feel sadness, and I feel there was some sort of mistake. The vicar was certainly worried about something serious. He was in conflict and felt there may be some retribution coming, but he certainly was not expecting this. It is strange, but I get the overwhelming feeling of injustice, that it was not fair that he was shot, that he had made mistakes, but the reason he was shot is not clear."

Like the increasing number of droplets from the sky, questions rained down on Jenny, but she could not give the detectives anything more than she had already told them. It became a logical merry-go-round; her answers were unavoidably circular and repetitive. Making mistakes, but not fair. Does that mean he was somehow culpable of doing something wrong, and he expected some form of revenge? Whatever it was, it did not warrant getting a bullet in the head. Maybe it means he recognised that his behaviour — or even that of others — created animosity; but the shooting was accidental. Even unintentional. *Local hunters, maybe? Kids messing around? More likely someone, like Robert Jenkins, who wasn't quite right in the head,* Stanley muses, increasingly convincing himself that he is on the right track.

Slightly damp and none the wiser, they drop Jenny back at her home and drive back to the station. It is left unsaid but they both leave her cottage, after drinking the herbal tea she gave them, with a feeling of unease.

They are grown men, but both feel the place was a little scary, a bit creepy, and to cap it all — she *is* a bloody witch.

Engineers, sound assistants, cameramen, runners, floor managers, best boys, secretaries, and all other manner of other workers scoot around the studio like demented ants, scattered by a drop of boiling water. In the middle of the stage the morning show host sits serenely and patiently as the makeup artist applies the finishing touches. A calm voice purrs into his earpiece; it is the producer.

"Warren, lovey, it has been confirmed that a Detective Inspector Parkins has agreed to appear in person, and he will come on after the piece about the dog with one leg." Peering into a hand mirror held up by the assistant, the host adjusts his fringe, smiles with satisfaction, and gives the producer the thumbs up. His earpiece buzzes again. "And remember, Warren, love, this is *Daytime in the Dales* not *Question Time*. You don't need to go all Jeremy Paxman or Roger *bloody* Cook on me. If we upset him, he won't come back on, and a bit of crime makes a good filler for our demographic, lovey. It's all about pleasing the demographic. Listen, love, it's a welcome break from limbless animals, bread making tips and how to reuse and recycle ketchup bottles. Just go easy and let him say what he has come on to say."

Another thumbs up. The stage clears, theme music plays, and the floor manager points to the host, counts down and signals the start.

Direct smiles to camera, energetic hand waving. "Aaaand good morning viewers, have we got an interesting show this morning, so glad you could join us." The viewers are given a rundown of the goodies they can expect before he launches into the first item, which involves interviewing the owner of the unlucky canine. Guided by the host, the owner explains the unfortunate series of incidents that left the animal almost limbless. Conscious that the positive energy is being drained out of the whole program by the dour demeanour and laboured delivery of the dog owner, the host tries to close off on a positive note.

"He's a gorgeous little fella and seems quite happy laid there in his little basket. I know his name is George, but I heard your friend backstage call him St Andrew . . ."

"Yeah, that's the nickname my mates have given him." Sensing the hosts confusion, the owner elucidates. "It is after St Andrews, y'know, the famous golf course."

"Sorry, I still don't understand."

"It's a golf course, different types of holes, but only one dog leg," replies the owner, maintaining his gloomy expression.

Momentarily speechless, the host processes and recovers, "Ha, well, thank you for bringing little George into the studio and sharing your story." Smiling to camera the host introduces the next item with the dog owner still visible in the background, as he trudges off camera carrying the dog basket. During his introduction to camera, Parkins is guided into a chair and an engineer checks his microphone. Reminding the audience about the events in Ayton, the host eventually turns to the inspector and welcomes him to the show.

"Let me get straight into it, DI Parkins. It has been over a week since the shooting but no sign of an arrest, what can you tell the audience?"

"Er, thank you, Warren. It is certainly both an unusual and difficult case, despite the dedicated work of the team, we are hampered by the lack of witnesses and forensic evidence on the scene, because the killing was done from some distance." Warren nods sympathetically as Parkins describes the mountain of work involved in the case and, despite no arrests, their continued determination to bring the guilty party to justice.

Obsequious murmurs of appreciation and support from the host provide the appropriate accompaniment to Parkins's excuses and explanations. "That's very comforting, Inspector Parkins, and I am sure all the audience appreciate the work the boys in blue do to protect the community and keep us all safe. But I understand you have had a possible breakthrough, thanks to the skill and dedication of your team?"

A still image of a good-looking young man with piercing blue eyes and close-cropped hair fills the screen whilst Parkins explains it to viewers. "We believe this man, who goes by the name of Robert Jenkins, may be able to help us with our enquiries. If Mr Jenkins is watching or if anybody knows him or his whereabouts, I would ask them to contact the investigation team." The picture is replaced with a number for viewers to call. Warren thanks the inspector for the amazing work he is doing on behalf of the community and the program cuts to an ad break.

On York Talk radio, Hardy's contribution to the campaign to elicit information from the public is not going quite as smoothly as it had for Parkins. Upon arrival he had been ushered through a labyrinth of corridors and into a windowless, soundproofed studio room. He was unceremoniously dumped into a chair opposite a bank of equipment with the DJ's face peeping over the top, signalling, with his index finger, for him to put on the headphones. Ignoring Hardy, the DJ continues with his current caller.

Food poisoning had claimed the normal host of the morning talk-back radio slot and Neville Riders had been press ganged in as a substitute, both at short notice and much to his annoyance. When he received the call from the studio, Riders was deep in slumber land after his own late-night slot. Unlike the bland and inoffensive Mike Mills, who was the regular host, Riders modelled himself on the American shock jocks whom he'd admired in his youth and now sought to emulate. His show, *Riders Brings a Storm* always begins with the theme music taken from The Doors classic. Riders himself would sing the name of the show over the title lyrics of the song. Beggars could not be choosers, as far as the radio station was concerned. Only Riders was available at such short notice, who yawned through the briefing from the *Mills Show* producer and ultimately, half the directions he was given fell on deaf and disinterested ears. Faced with an option of one, the morning team were making the best of a bad job with the stand in jockey. With increasing horror, Mike Mills, the normal host, listened from his sick bed as Riders systematically insulted his regular callers who, generally, could be found sitting comfortably on the right of the political spectrum.

"Thank you for your opinion, Doris, and give my regards to the Harrogate National Socialists. I'll pass on your views when I talk to the health minister this morning. I am sure she would be happy to prioritise waiting lists based on those born in good old blighty. Never mind the poor traumatised Afghan refugees who, incidentally, are now British citizens."

The audience never heard Doris's complaint that she was not a socialist, nor a communist for that matter. Nor was he accurately reflecting what she had said. He was twisting her words, the horrible man, and when would Mike Mills be back?

Mike Mills had taken a turn for the worse. He groaned at the radio and then he groaned again as his stomach somersaulted and he leapt out of bed, rushing to the toilet for what felt like the twentieth time that morning. Bloody oysters.

Casting a mischievous glance over to Hardy, Riders introduces him to the listeners.

"Now we have, Deee . . . tect . . . tive . . . Haaaardy, who has kindly come in to update us on the awful shooting in sleepy old Ayton a few days ago. Sounds like an Agatha Christie novel, detective — tell me, who shot the vicar?"

Shuffling to find a comfortable position on the chair and adjusting the headphones, Hardy starts to speak but the DJ cuts him short.

"Whoooaaa, detective, you don't need to lean so close to the microphone, you'll deafen our listeners." Hardy tries again and gets the thumbs up.

"Thank you, Neville. At this stage we are still gathering the facts, but we would like the public to come forward with any information they have, no matter how trivial they may believe it to be."

Smelling blood, Riders threw Hardy a devilish glance. "I take it you have no suspects and, by the sound of it, no idea why he was shot."

"Well, that's not entirely true," replies Hardy with a little too much bluster and far too little conviction in his words.

"Righteo, then you do have an idea who did it?"

"Well, no," stutters Hardy.

"No — as in you *do* have an idea, or — no, as in you *don't* have an idea?" Riders lets the ultimate radio crime of dead air hang for a few uncomfortable seconds. To the producer, whose heart rate was climbing, seconds feel like minutes. Allowing enough time for listeners to draw their own conclusions, Riders changes tack and asks the detective why he came on the show. Hardy tries to repair the already damaged impression that the listeners had now been given and appeals to their better judgement, beseeching them for assistance. Explaining they had a person of interest, he holds up the photograph of the young Robert Jenkins.

A wicked grin replaces the look of boredom on Riders' face. "Well, thank you for your time, Detective Hardy. For the sake of the viewers, DS Hardy is holding up a photograph of a person of interest, which I realise is of little use to you, as we are on the radio." Hardy fumes with embarrassment. A blush of anger accompanies the scowl he gives the DJ who just responds with a smug smile. "However, *viewers* — or should I say listeners — ha ha, fear not, I'll make sure the ever-efficient, Tim, our glorious producer, will put it on our station website." After reading out the website address twice, Riders turns to Hardy, who is already rising from his seat to leave. "Well, thank you once again, detective and good luck." Throwing off the headphones, Hardy huffily marches out of the studio. Riders cannot resist a final dig, "Well, listeners it seems the thin blue line is a little too thin, not that you would think that, if you could see Detective Hardy. Ha ha, only joking, detective. Seriously listeners, we wish our boys in blue well, they do a great job . . . sometimes."

21

AN AMBER LIQUID swirled in a small cast iron pan, the centrifugal force causing it to climb the sides in deference to the vortex commanding the centre. Ripe with the aroma of oranges, the cottage is a welcome haven for Jenny, who stirs dreamily, conjuring memories of her time in Seville, Spain: orange groves and sunshine. Weeks of research on the internet and in the local library, gave her hope that she had she had found the right potion for Betty. Successful remedies had eluded her when she trawled her own esoteric journals, manuals and encyclopaedias, including her own personal bible, *The Witch's Book of Potions – Simmering Infusions and Magical Elixirs.*

Moussaka explodes from his doze into a cacophony of barking as he races to the window and stands up on his hind legs balancing his front paws on the windowsill. Spittle sprays the glass. Admonishing the dog she shoos him off the sill, and looks through the window which frames the scene before her like a work of living art. Eight ravens circle the rim of the bird bath at the bottom of her garden. Shushing Moussaka she begins to mull over the meaning of their gathering. Folklore interpretation of the presence of black birds was contradictory. Their collective nouns, an 'unkindness', or 'a conspiracy', tended to give them a negative connotation and could indicate death or misfortune. To others, their presence brought good fortune. Jenny had no firm opinion, but in that moment her clairsentience overcomes her, so much so that she has to switch off the gas flame, leave the pan on the stove and rest in her rocking chair. Betty's potion for her arthritis would just have to wait a little while longer. Sorry, Betty. Today was a day to be careful and look after yourself, felt Jenny.

She had not had a *turn* like this in a long while. Not since the horrific coach accident involving a school bus just outside Scarborough last summer. She had rung the police, but there was little they could do without specific information and probably placed her call in the "local nutcase" pile. Later that day, a coach accident involving school children on an outing to Helmsley castle resulted in fifteen children seriously injured and two dead.

By the end of the day there would be a series of unfortunate events, all connected to the village and its residents.

Due to popular demand, Chris Ashton ran a pottery workshop in the village hall and the locals had raised funds to buy a kiln, which was housed in a lean-to structure on the patio at the back of the hall. Clay work was not his forte, but his skills were serviceable. Other than Donald, all the class members were female. That did not surprise Donald, whose acerbic wit was matched equally by his perspicacity. When class members called for Ashton's assistance and he stood behind them assessing their hand skills on the potter's wheel, Donald would hum 'Unchained Melody' whilst picturing the scene in *Ghost* with Patrick Swayze and Demi Moore. Even Chris had enough self-awareness to laugh.

Today's class had gone well, and seven pots were being carried with great care to the kiln. Great care until, with untypical clumsiness, Julia trips slightly, and the work of the last hour falls to the ground. An elegantly thin flower vase ready for the kiln instantly transformed into a soggy splodge of mud. With clay covered hands placed on her cheeks in horror, Dolly neatly expresses the view of the room. That was a very unfortunate accident.

An hour later, Julia is sitting with Sebastian in their living room. Nursing a coffee, she is flicking through a copy of *Tatler* whilst Sebastian sits opposite, working his way through a pile of work correspondence. Paperwork had taken a back seat during a very busy client-facing week, mostly spent comforting those who were stressing about their tax returns. It was that time of the year.

Luckily, most of the correspondence requires nothing more than putting it into the bin, at least until he comes to one with the Inland Revenue logo, which brings a frown to his face even before he's opened the envelope. With a small degree of dread, he slashes the envelope top with a swift flick of his letter opener; a solid silver present from a very grateful overseas client. This time of the year it was all about sending stuff to the taxman, not receiving it. That came later when the assessments were being reported back. Receiving letters was usually bad news. Under a shadow of increasing scepticism, he reads the contents of the letter, which assures him it was routine but one of his client's companies was selected for a random audit. Immediately recognising it as the parent company of a group he'd set up for a client, his exclamation of "Bugger" causes Julia to look up from her magazine. Asking her husband what the matter was, he responds by telling her that he was going to be hassled by the taxman and the client would not be happy. That client was McCarthy. Not realising the implication but wanting to express support, Julia comments that it was unfortunate. Henson does not hear his wife's words of comfort as he is already on his mobile, walking out of the room to his study. It was a conversation that needed privacy.

Those ravens were stubborn, mused Jenny, staring through her window. They had remained in a circle, ignoring the rain, which was now falling heavily. Large droplets bouncing off their shiny black heads, were disregarded by the birds as they stared at each other with dark, cold glass eyes.

The heavens opened. The village became engulfed by a deluge. Later in the day, the weatherman would announce in his slot after the six o'clock news that Ayton and the surrounding area had witnessed its highest recorded inches of rainfall ever experienced in one day. Thunder boomed, lightning flashed, and the storm continued for several hours.

Desperately jamming spare planks of wood together, Ashton created a makeshift dam across the entrance of his back door. The pathway from his workshop at the back of the garden to the cottage had turned into a small stream. Luckily, he bought the wood for a project to build a small shed and had enough left over to do the same for his neighbours, the Addinall sisters. As he secures the last piece of wood, they thank him once again, returning the favour with a jar of their homemade green tomato relish.

Not all waterways could be contained so easily, and the river Derwent bulged and bulged, rising to the point where the overflow was washing over the banks onto the road and High Street. The church had been built on a slight rise, so flooding was not an issue. Well, it would not normally be an issue, except for the fact that the renovation works to the west wall required the contractor, Neaves, to sink deep holes next to it to provide an anchor point for the eight wooden struts installed to prevent the wall from collapsing. Each hole had quickly filled with water around the struts. Their surfaces were now bubbling as more rain tried to force its way into an already flooded space. Within two hours the mud became so saturated that it could no longer support the struts. The two nearest to the High Street gave way first and, like gigantic skittles, the other six followed. It did not take long for the west wall to follow suit. Stonework peeled apart, collapsing into the mud. Its already undermined foundations were further weakened by the flooded strut holes whose walls collapsed and washed down the small rise. The inevitable happened: it gave way, and the wall was history.

"That's bloody unfortunate," muttered the council engineer to his colleague, who had come to witness the carnage from the warmth of his van, following a call from a concerned local.

Sat in his living room having a civilised afternoon wine, Mandelson thought he heard a knock on the door and was presented with a man huddled in his raincoat. Water dripped down his face through channels created by his thinning hair. Mandelson ushered Councillor Roberts in but asked him to wait in the hall whilst he got a towel, so that his visitor could dry himself off before entering his living room. The sodden overcoat was placed on the hallway table, and he directed his now well-towelled visitor onto the living room sofa and handed him a glass of wine. Pleasantries were exchanged and Roberts was asked what it was that brought him out in such inclement weather.

Mandelson hated it when people began a sentence with, "We have a big problem." Acid reflux burnt his throat as he waited for his visitor to explain further. He was aware that Roberts sat on the Finance and Audit Committee of the council, as well as the Planning Committee. As soon as Roberts mentioned he had just had a meeting the previous evening, Mandelson realised that the problem may well be "big".

Remaining outwardly calm, Mandelson gave Roberts the space to speak. Rudyard Kipling came to mind; "If you can keep your head when all about you are losing theirs . . ." as the poem advises. Roberts went on to explain that the audit plan for the next financial year had been presented and approved. On grounds of financial materiality, the newly appointed Head of Audit had put forward the need for a review of the tendering processes, examining the effectiveness of controls in place. Not only this, but another focus of the plan was a specific examination of the decision-making process for selected planning approvals. Two tenders on that list were awarded to Neaves Construction and one of the planning approvals to come under scrutiny was the proposed hotel development in Ayton.

Roberts apologised, emphasising there was nothing he could do without raising suspicion. It was just unfortunate. Mandelson took a sip of wine and winced; another wave of reflux rose, he patted his chest, trying to knock it back down. *Unfortunate doesn't even come close.*

Soaked to the skin, Purple and Hendricks stood dripping in the flooded copse. Horrified, they stared wide eyed as most of their crop of magic mushrooms uprooted and washed away into oblivion. They salvaged what they could, clumsily scooping a muddy mess into their canvas satchel. Despondent and dripping, they trudged home. Hendricks was moved to declare the situation was unfortunate, but Hayes disagreed; unfortunate did not cover it — this was a bloody disaster. Neither saw that an edge of the previously buried holdall containing Hairy Bobs' rifle was now visible, as the rain continued to wash away the topsoil.

Hands on her hips with water up to her ankles, Betty surveyed the scene in her storeroom at the back of the shop. It had taken the brunt of the deluge and the main casualty was her delivery of fresh vegetables, which had arrived that morning. If she had underfloor heating, she could have prepared a giant-sized vegetable soup. Sprouts bobbed in the water, reminding her of the fairground game where the kids had to hook a plastic duck to get a prize. Carrots, mushrooms and parsnips jockeyed for position nudging each other. She set about shepherding the escaped veggies into a bucket to determine what could be dried and saved, and what was going to be consigned to feeding Higginbottom's pigs. It was unfortunate but could have been worse, which is more than could be said for Austen, the Addinalls' cat.

Austen had sought refuge from the rain underneath the rear wheel arch of Dr Kamau's car. In his rush to respond to a call from a local aged care facility in the nearby village of Snainton, he did not notice Austen, whose demise was masked by the crunch of the doctor's tyres on the gravel driveway. It was only when he returned to his surgery that he realised what had happened. Staring sorrowfully at the flattened cat, he now had some unfortunate news to pass on to the Addinalls. The hissing and spitting of the bad-tempered tortoiseshell cat that had made it notorious and generally disliked in the village, was now a thing of the past.

When Kariuki had left the village, he decided to spend a night in Leeds. He had read in a tourist guide that the rejuvenated city was pumping with a vibrant night life, and, after London, he had developed a taste for tripping the light fantastic. Far more interesting than Nairobi. Keeping to his mantra of a low profile, he used transport that left him untraceable. Train tickets paid for by cash took him on a journey from Scarborough to York, and then through to Leeds. A low rent hotel, cash again, provided his base, and with an air of expectancy he walked into the city centre. The tourist guide was not wrong, and bars everywhere were packed by revellers having a good time; the excessive use of alcohol by those who could not handle it created a few exceptions. Kariuki shook his head in amusement as he passed the odd fight and occasional drinker — usually a young woman — sat unceremoniously on a road curb, vomiting, with concerned friends looking on. Bar hopping, he eventually ended up in Fads, which as fate would have it, was a club owned by McCarthy.

Normally a straight beer drinker, he stuck to small bottles of Tuskers' lager back in Kenya. Not so this evening. Kariuki exceeded his limit by five Jägerbombs, four tequila shots and a *snow bomb*. A little packet of cocaine was given to him by his newfound friend, Tezza, who was one of a group of five Leeds United supporters on a night out celebrating a home win over the Wolves. The group had taken to him, thinking he looked like an old Leeds legend. *"Radebe, Radebe, Radebe,"* they cheered when he bought the group a round of beers and shots. One thing led to another, and with the room beginning to spin he told his new best friends that he was calling it a night. Their objections about the night still being young fell on deaf ears, as he unsteadily made his way out of the club and on to the main street.

Setting off in the direction of his hotel, he came to a halt after about fifty yards to adjust his now blurry and swirling vision. He swayed to the side and placed his foot on the edge of the curb, causing him to twist his ankle and fall into the road, directly in front of the passing number forty three bus. Distracted by two drunken youths stood at his cabin, the driver saw Kariuki, arms flailing, too late. Slamming his foot on the brake pedal, the bus screeched to a halt. The shocked passengers heard a sickening thud on the bus's undercarriage as the front wheels rolled over the Kenyan. *Whoooosssh*, the automatic doors flew open, spewing out the two youths who leapt onto the pavement and sprinted up the road. They had been berating the driver, who had refused to let them off half a mile up the road at an unscheduled stop. Passengers screamed, the driver leant forward with his face pressed against the windscreen. In shock, he stared in horror as blood slowly spread over the road and pooled. Fate was Atropos and Kariuki's mortal coil had been well and truly cut. It was an event that would later be described in the local paper as a tragic and unfortunate accident and a warning to all late-night revellers about the perils of excessive drinking.

22

LIKE TWO NAUGHTY schoolboys called in by the headmaster, Hayes and Hendricks sit in front of the two detectives in Interview Room 3. They are both looking down, hands clasped between their rocking knees. Stanley looks at them with mild contempt; a couple of scruffy losers with no purpose; a drain on society. Hardy opens the interview.

"Well, gentlemen — any idea why we called you in?" Shaking heads and still no eye contact. Renewed knee rocking. "Let me ask you a question then. What do you do up in that copse on the edge of the farm? You are there all the time, according to Higginbottom. Reckons he sees you just about every day."

"Nothing much, just chillin," replies Hayes.

"Really, just chillin?" scoffs Stanley.

"Yeah, just chillin," echoes Hendricks.

"Well, unfortunately for you two it seems that whilst out on a walk, Higginbottom's dog dug up this." Hardy reaches under the desk, drags out a large holdall and places it on the table in front of them. "Apparently it had been buried but was half uncovered by the downfall the other day." Their reaction is not encouraging to the detectives. All they get are two slightly puzzled expressions that neither indicates it was their bag, nor that they had ever seen it before now. Hope of a result dissipated in Hardy's mind. On the other hand, Stanley is less astute and far more convinced that he had them on the ropes.

"Are you telling me that you have never seen this large holdall, in the middle of the small copse that you both spend half your lives in? You're going to have to tell that to the judge. I assume you know what was in the bag?" snarls Stanley.

"Looks empty to me," replies Hayes as he leans forward for a closer look.

"Yeah, well, it wasn't when we found it, as I'm sure you know."

Taking back control before the interview disappears entirely down a rabbit hole, Hardy gestures for Stanley to back off. A change of tack is needed. It may not be their bag, but they may have seen it before, or seen someone in the woods who might have buried it.

"Okay, gentlemen, let's assume for the moment the bag is not yours, any idea whose it might be? Have you seen anyone else in that area who shouldn't be there?"

Both shake their heads.

"You are absolutely certain you have no idea?" presses Hardy.

"Nope," replies Hayes. "Unless it's *his*," he adds, pointing to the bag. It was the detectives turn to look puzzled and a little clueless. Fruitlessly, they look at each other for the clarification which neither of them can provide.

"Sorry, you said 'his', who are you talking about?" asks Hardy. Hayes does not answer but continues to point, shaking his index finger towards the bottom corner of the holdall. All eyes in the room focus on the bag and a small smudge that had previously gone unnoticed by the detectives jumps out at them like a beacon. Letters written with a black marker come into focus. Wear and tear — or the rains — had made the letters indistinct, faded and smudged, but still readable.

"Maybe it's RJ's," suggests Hayes. "Whoever RJ is."

Squinting, Hardy can now see the blurry black mark and it did indeed morph, under scrutiny, into the initials that Hayes identified. Blustering, Hardy turns on the defensive. The two men just shake their heads in denial as the detective begins to pose a string of hypotheticals. They could have stolen the bag; the letters may not be the initials of the owner; second-hand luggage from charity shops is a cheap option for losers like them. Neither Hardy nor Stanley really believes any of these theories have any legs. It was more face-saving damage limitation. Eventually the interview is terminated after Hendricks confirms that the detectives had their correct address, and that the two friends had no intention to travel away from the village. If anything came up, if anything else occurred to them, they agreed to call the station and inform the desk sergeant. Feeling cheated of an arrest, Stanley escorts them out and re-joins Hardy. Resignedly, he sits himself down opposite his boss across the table and waits for the onslaught.

"For fuck's sake, Stanley, I told you to examine the bag."

"I did, boss, but I concentrated on the inside and its contents. The rifle is now with forensics."

Hardy puffs his cheeks and blows out his breath in exasperation. "If you are going to succeed as a detective you need to have far more attention to detail and, for God's sake, much better powers of observation." Stanley tries his best to look contrite, even though it crosses his mind that his boss did not notice the letters either. Discretion in this case was the better part of valour.

"I take it you have worked out who is the number one candidate that owns the bag?" asks Hardy in a patronising tone.

"Yes, boss. RJ, Robert Jenkins, the sharp shooting nutter."

"Absolutely, Sherlock *bloody* Holmes. We had better get out there and find him."

Everything was going smoothly in the studio, all the guests had been punctual and everything was on schedule, though Edna was starting to ramble. The earpiece of the host buzzes with the voice of the producer. "Warren, love, we need to wrap up this item as we have Sue waiting with breaking news on the murder case." Warren does not miss a beat and touches his ear to signal that the message was received and understood.

"That was amazing, Edna. Thank you for coming into the studio and showing us all the amazing things that an egg box can be reused for. You are without a doubt the *'Repurpose Queen'* of Yorkshire." Gushing at the compliment, Edna is escorted off the stage struggling with her armful of tools and materials leaving the host to directly address the camera. His smile fades into a crafted expression of concern to signal the change of mood.

"You are watching *Daytime in the Dales,* loyal viewers, and now we are going to cut across to Sue, who has some breaking news." The screen splits into two halves, now revealing the young female reporter, microphone in hand, stood in the church grounds with the collapsed wall in the background. "Sue, what can you tell us?"

A slight transmission pause is filled by a nodding reporter, indicating she is listening to the question. "Yes, thank you, Warren. Well, the whole of Yorkshire is recovering from the aftermath of last night's storm, but Ayton has been hit harder than most." She looks back over her shoulder, directing viewers to the collapsed wall. "One of the worst casualties is the local church, as you can see over here, it now does not have a west wall, which was washed away by the intense flooding." The alliteration enables the reporter to give dramatic emphasis. "Despite the damage throughout the village, the storm has had an unexpected and welcome impact. Torrential rain carried away some topsoil in a nearby field, revealing a buried bag. The local farmer who owns the field found it whilst walking his dog." She pauses for dramatic effect, prompting the host to ask what the bag contained. "Amazingly, Warren, the bag contained a rifle, which the police believe could be, potentially, the weapon used to kill Peter Dibley, the local vicar shot dead just over a week ago. It must be said that the police have emphasised that this is not confirmed, and investigations continue. Nevertheless, it looks encouraging, and the police have again asked the public for information regarding the whereabouts of Robert Jenkins, whose image should be appearing on your screen now." The screen split into three, showing the host, the reporter, and the picture of the younger, clean shaven Hairy Bob.

"Well, Sue — it looks like progress is being made. Viewers will recall we had DI Parkins on this show just the other day. His team are certainly doing an exceptional job. Tell me, are they confirming that the rifle belongs to Mr Jenkins?"

"No, Warren, not at this stage, but they are saying that they have some promising lines of enquiry. They are encouraging the owner of the bag to come forward to help them with their enquiries. They also want anybody who knows the whereabouts of Robert Jenkins to come forward. Indeed, if, Mr Jenkins, you are watching *Daytime in the Dales*, the police are asking you to present yourself at the nearest police station."

"Well, thank you, Sue, be sure to keep us updated if anything further develops."

The image of the reporter disappears from the screen leaving the smiling host who addresses the camera. "Now here is an interesting item folks, our next guest is Emma Postlethwaite and her cat, Cosmo. Emma tells us that Cosmo here is psychic and has predicted who will be our next Prime Minister. Apparently photographs of all the party leaders are placed in front of him and he taps the photo of the winner. He successfully identified the winner of the Grand National last year . . ." The camera pans to a woman sat in the chair opposite the host mindlessly, stroking a white cat on her lap, both wearing a bored expression.

*

Dolly switches off the television in the Old Plough, having just seen the bulletin on *Daytime in the Dales*. She looks over to her first and currently only customer, Hairy Bob.

"Psychic cats, whatever next? It's a rum do isn't it, Bob? I've no idea what's going to be done with the church. Anyway, looks like the police are closing in on whoever killed poor old Peter."

Bob nods without comment and takes another sip of his beer.

"And that picture, Bob, of the fella they're looking for. He seems such a nice young lad. Doesn't look like a bad 'un at all, does he?"

Bob just stares in silence at the landlady.

"You okay today, Bob, yer even quieter than usual?"

The sound of traffic breaks the silence when the front door opens, followed by another customer. Bob welcomes the distraction as Dolly looks across the bar towards the door and smiles in recognition.

"Ow do Chris luv, what you doing 'ere? Thought it would be far too early for you."

"No, I don't want a drink, just a favour, can I borrow your mop and bucket? I don't have one and I am helping clean the Addinalls' kitchen, it's still a mess after the rains. Water leaked through the planks I put up for them."

"Ooh, you are an absolute gem, Chris, of course you can, I'll get it now."

Dolly disappears into the back, leaving Ashton alone with Bob. His attempts at small talk fall on stony ground. Bob is not being very responsive, barely offering up even single syllable answers. Screwing up his eyes slightly, there is something bothering Ashton as he assesses the man in the corner. There is something familiar about Bob, those eyes; has he seen him somewhere out of context. Maybe out of the village? Maybe he reminded him of someone on TV, or in the forces? Couldn't place it, couldn't pin it down. His mind was turning to mush; too many pottery classes and nothing to care about or stress him. *The simple life is catching up with me, I'm losing my edge.* Dolly breezes back into the bar with mop and bucket in hand, her friendly voice dragging him out of his thoughts. Thanking her, he looks over to Bob as he leaves, saying his goodbyes but getting barely a brief nod of acknowledgement in return.

'Yer in a funny mood today, our Bob," chides Dolly. Bob just grunts in reply.

23

BRACING THEMSELVES FOR the usual sarcastic greeting, the two detectives enter the reception area of the station. Maybe they were simply unlucky, but leads in the case were few and far between and those they had got, seemed to be fading away. Certainly, they could do without the morning wit in the shape of the forever smirking desk sergeant, who draws breath to address them as they walk past.

"You've got visitors. Interview Room Three. Been here for an hour, had six cups of tea between 'em."

Hardy raises his chin indicating more information would be welcomed.

"It's the *Marple* twins, they think they've blown your case wide open. I tried to get them to give me more details, but they insisted that they would only speak to you two."

Entering the room, they are greeted with the welcoming and excited smiles of the Addinall sisters. Light was finally about to be shed in the dark confines of Interview Room 3. Before the day was out the perpetrator would be in handcuffs. Television cameras like attentive robots and the camera flashlights of the adoring press would be surrounding the detectives who were being congratulated on solving the case.

None of these scenarios remotely entered the minds of Hardy or Stanley as they both took their seats opposite the sisters. Although nothing of this nature transpired, the interview did set the detectives on what appeared to be a promising path of investigation.

Freda taps the recording device. "You may want to switch this on this time."

Hardy stares at her wearily and then at Mary who is wearing her cardigan with a cat embroidered on it in deference to the recently deceased Austen. Shuffling and giggling, the sisters can barely contain their excitement. Sensing the resigned disinterest of his boss, Stanley takes charge.

"Hello, ladies. How about we wait to hear what you have to say before we go through the formalities of recording the interview. Whaddya know?"

"Well, we saw DI Parkins on our favourite show, *Daytime in the Dales*. He is such a lovely man, very clever, very distinguished," gushes Freda.

"He is," agrees Mary. "Very distinguished. And he said that if anyone had any information, no matter how unimportant it seemed to be, then they should come forward."

"So, we have . . . come forward that is," confirms Freda.

Hardy held his own counsel. Stanley followed suit.

Prompted by the silence, the sisters go on to describe several recent visitors to the village who had looked suspicious. Descriptions were given along with behaviours that would place most of them as potential murder suspects, to their eyes at least. Despite this telling information, they noticed that the detectives still had not switched on the recording device. *Disappointing*, thought Freda, but perhaps you need a good memory to be a policeman because they did not seem to be taking notes either.

Once more Freda taps the recording device, only to receive a dismissive shake of the head. She is undeterred. "But we think the most suspicious man was in the village a few days ago."

Without a speck of enthusiasm, Hardy asks for a description.

"Thin, tallish, short hair, and he is black," offers Freda thoughtfully.

"Yes, black," confirmed Mary. "Didn't like the look of him, and we don't get many blacks in the village."

"Except Dr Kamau," said Freda.

"Yes, but it wasn't him, Freda, was it? Although they do all look similar to me. To be honest, I don't think of Dr Kamau as black, because he's a doctor."

An annoying worm of irritation was now burying itself into the recess of Hardy's mind, and he could not get to it. Not painful, just irritating. He rubs his temples, searching for a way of extricating the worm and the two smiling worm farmers that were in front of him. Extricate them from the station that is. This was going nowhere, fast.

"What exactly did this 'black' man do that made you think he might be involved?" asks Stanley, oblivious of the sideways scowl of impatience being fired at him. Hardy is in no mood to encourage the gossip. He needs firm leads, firm facts.

"Well, he is a stranger, he is black, and I didn't like the way he looked. He seemed to sneak around the village as if he did not want to be noticed, like he was up to something," replies Freda.

"But we did," adds Mary. "We noticed him. He looked like a killer to us, those shifty yellowish eyes."

"Did you talk to him?"

Both sisters give Stanley a look of horror and tell him that there was nothing on earth that could persuade them to talk to a strange man, and a black one at that. They also confirm that they did not see him at the church, nor talking to the now deceased vicar. He was related to the doctor, mused the sisters, as he is also black. It was not their place to ask the doctor if he knew the man, but perhaps the police should ask. It is worth a try as they are both black, they could well be related. *Perhaps they should not*, thought Stanley, unless they wanted to find themselves subject to a racial harassment complaint.

Rapidly reaching the point of implosion, Hardy tries to bring the interview to a halt. "Thank you for your time, ladies, if there is anything else?" Rising from his chair, Hardy was sending a message, loud and clear, that there was — in his opinion — nothing else. But his hopes of terminating the discussion are quickly dashed.

Freda spoke. "Well, yes. That picture on the telly, the man who DI Parkins wants to talk to. We saw someone a bit like him in the village a few days ago. We saw him leaving the Old Plough. He was alone, but he came out shortly after Reverend Dibley." She leans forward conspiratorially, "Almost as if he was following him."

Hardy sits back down; his interest is piqued. "Can you describe the man you saw? How certain are you that he was the man that was shown on television?"

"Well, he had short hair like in the picture on the telly, but we only saw him briefly and we couldn't really remember enough to be certain he was the same man. The eyes looked the same. Maybe slightly older, but we assumed the picture may have been taken a while ago; it could be him. He was wearing a polo shirt — and jeans. And this was the Saturday before the poor vicar was shot, we were on our usual mid evening walk." Freda goes quiet and looks at the detectives expectantly.

"It was probably the last time we saw Reverend Dibley alive," blubbers Mary.

Reinvigorated, the detectives probe further, starting to take notes and, to the delight of the sisters, the recording device is switched on. Bubbling with excitement, the sisters recount the events of the evening in detail, the timing, a description of the mystery man, the direction they were walking and any other villagers they saw out at that time who may also be able to help. Were they now on to something? Were they getting close?

An hour later the sisters are being escorted out of the station with the status of VIPs. Hardy makes a point of loudly thanking the ladies for their helpful information in earshot of the desk sergeant. A sceptical expression comes from behind the desk. With the sisters successfully seen off the premises, Hardy passes by the sergeant, giving him the victory sign, making sure it was clear that the two women had, in fact, been helpful. The sergeant's sceptical facial expression goes unnoticed by Hardy, who re-joins Stanley in the interview room.

"Right, Stanley. You need to go back to the Old Plough, interview the landlord and landlady. Find out if they remember this *mystery man*. Description, his behaviour, where he was sat, anything unusual, anyone he talked to."

"Okay, boss."

"And get a list of all the punters from them. Those who they remember were in the bar that night, at least until the point where Dibley and this bloke left. We then need to interview every one of them. All the same questions, see if anyone talked to him and, if so, what was said. Was he acting suspiciously? Did he ask any unusual questions?" Looking slightly overwhelmed, Stanley remained rooted to the spot staring blankly. "Well, Stanley, don't just stand there — off you go. You wanted to be a detective. Real life isn't Poirot: you, stood in the manor house, leaning against the bloody fireplace slowly revealing facts and motives to an audience of suspects to eventually expose that the effing butler did it. Real policing is dogged, laborious work. Checking facts, taking statements, cross checking what we get told, finding physical evidence, getting it tested by forensics, hours watching CCTV, hours on stake outs, waiting . . . and on and on it goes. Often with no results. Welcome to the real world."

Stanley stares like a deer in headlights, but Hardy has not finished his list of tasks. "And while you are there, get yourself back to the petrol station and grab their CCTV of that Saturday evening. You never know, we may have him on camera. Parkins can put a picture of him on the telly as well; he's big mates with them all now."

*

The Old Plough is closed but Stanley is let in through the back entrance, having phoned Ken Wilkes in advance. He settles down in the back room, sitting opposite Ken and Dolly resting his elbows on the Formica table. With a freshly made cup of tea in front of him, pleasantries completed, he takes out his notebook and starts the interview.

"Taking you back to the Saturday evening before the shooting, do you remember a man in the bar? Short hair, polo shirt, jeans, probably drinking alone?" Both nod and Stanley's hopes rise immediately, he pursues his line of questioning with vigour. How they could be sure they remembered the customer? How he did he behave? What did he say?

Dolly responds.

"Well, he stuck out from the rest because he was not a local and he was sat alone, nursing a half pint for almost an hour. Other than ordering his drink he said very little. No small talk. Didn't offer up why he was in Ayton or anything. Just ordered his beer and went and sat on his own over there." Dolly points to the seat and asks her husband, "Did you notice anything strange about him Ken?"

"Didn't really take much notice, all I remember is him sitting there just staring around the place, sipping his beer. I didn't even notice him leave the pub to be honest. Had a mean look about him I thought at the time, there again maybe he was just a bit shy."

With that vein of enquiry exhausted, Stanley busies himself questioning them about the other customers present on the night. After a few minutes of prompting and probing the publicans, he has a list of fourteen people that could be identified as present. One person that could not be interviewed was Dibley, so he taps a little deeper into the memories of Ken and Dolly about his behaviour on the night. Nothing very fruitful seems to be offered up. As far as they could tell, Dibley seemed totally relaxed; not angry, not agitated, just his normal self. Dibley had stayed for less than an hour, he had sat with the Hensons and he left the bar unaccompanied. It was worth a chat with the Hensons. After some thought, Dolly mentions that Hayes and Hendricks were seated at the adjoining table next to the stranger. Maybe they talked to him? Stanley makes a note to talk with the local deadbeats.

Having got the address from Dolly, Stanley pulls into the driveway of the Hensons and, as luck would have it, they were both at home. His luck ended there, and a futile twenty minutes were spent learning that they had talked about nothing out of the ordinary or more controversial than the date of the next whist drive. Dibley seemed to be his normal self and, no, they did not recall seeing a stranger wearing a polo shirt and jeans with short hair. Disappointed, Stanley thanks them and leaves. A dead end, he is out of luck.

Lady Luck returns dramatically with aplomb. Driving down the High Street on his way back to Scarborough, he spots the pair of deadbeats, flicks on his indicators, and pulls alongside them. Pressing the button to wind down the front passenger window, he leans across and calls them over. About to tell the driver to bugger off and leave them alone, Hayes recognises the detective and complies reluctantly, gesturing for Hendricks to follow.

"Wonder if you two could spare me five minutes?" The question wasn't in contest, and sensing that they understood that, Stanley continued, "Jump in lads and I will park over there," he points to the car park of the Old Plough. Following instructions, they jump in the back seat and Stanley drives the short distance to the pub, the reluctant passengers exchanging worried glances. Stanley parks in the most remote space he could find; the detective decides a little privacy is needed. He twists round in his seat to face them and guides their minds back to the Saturday before the shooting, patiently easing their fuddled brains into gear. At first, he thought it was going nowhere. Yes, they remembered the man — no, they did not talk to him — yes, they could describe him — and no, he did not behave strangely, as far as they could tell.

"Except," announces Hendricks, "Hairy Bob reckoned the bloke had 'killer's eyes.'" It was at that very moment that the detective's stars aligned in the universe, and the fog of misdirection was lifted to reveal where they had gone wrong. Freda Addinall's comment started ringing in his ears, *We assumed the picture may have been taken a while ago.* The photo the Addinalls, and the rest of the viewing public had seen on the TV, was the younger, short haired Robert Jenkins. It was not the short haired stranger they should be focussing on; it was Hairy Bob. That *is* Bob; Robert, who was hairy. Long hair, beard, and all. The light bulb was on, enlightenment had dawned, an investigation epiphany. Forget the stranger, focus on Bob.

"Right lads. Change of tack. Do you know where this Hairy Bob hangs out?"

"I know exactly," replies Hayes, pointing to the stone wall. "He's over there."

"Yer right, Purple," said Hendricks pointing to the rear of the car park. "He's sat by the wall."

Heart racing, pushing the two friends out of the car, Stanley calls for backup. A local police car which was fortunately passing through the village responds immediately and pulls up behind Stanley's vehicle. Quizzically looking up at the approaching detective flanked by two burly looking constables, Bob gives a brief "Ow do" showing no visible sign of concern. Following the instructions barked at him, he springs to his feet, grabs his bag, and accompanies the detective to his car, seemingly without a care in the world. In a matter of minutes, Bob, compliant, is in custody. The two responding constables are left wondering what all the fuss was about. Stanley starts to wonder what the smell in his car is about. It had been a while since Bob had got to a shower and an underlying odour of vague, indeterminate origin and composition pervaded the car, as Stanley drives Bob, in silence, to Scarborough. Stanley sniffs involuntarily but audibly several times during the journey.

On arrival Bob is escorted through the back entrance of the station and into Interview Room Three. Sat opposite Hardy and Stanley, he regards them with surprising disinterest. It was not what the detectives expected, given the man before them had diagnosed PTSD and was, potentially, a murderer. They expected someone far more agitated, far less in control. Bob was calm, Bob was in his comfort zone. He could handle anything put in front of him with situations like this, situations he could control or — if not control — situations he was trained to handle. Nightmares could not be controlled. Cloying guilt, or rather, guilt by association, at the horrors he had witnessed are what had diminished him. Not direct military service. He was trained, willing and motivated to fight the Taliban. Innocent teenagers and farmers, murdered at the hands of those sent to protect them was too much for Bob. Two village coppers did not worry him at all.

Refusing the offer of legal aid, Bob told the detectives that he was willing to answer all their questions to the best of his ability and cooperate. Recording device switched on, with Bob's permission, Hardy and Stanley spent two hours throwing questions and veiled accusations, rewording and repeating questions to check for consistency in the answers they got first time around. Asking the same question in several different ways to try to trip him up also bore no fruit. It was all in vain. Every trick in their book was used. Unfortunately for them, Bob had a far bigger book of tricks, courtesy of his SAS training, which included RTI: Resistance to

Interrogation techniques. What the detectives had to offer was a cake walk. Subjected to the SAS training regime, Bob could handle things well outside the police manual; hooding, sleep deprivation, prolonged nakedness, sexual humiliation and deprivation of warmth, water and food. A couple of village coppers throwing a few questions at him over a nice cup of tea was a lovely way to spend an afternoon, compared to a six-hour spittle facial from two screaming trained killers in combat fatigues.

What about the initials on the bag? How could he explain that? Bob could not, primarily because he had no idea what they were talking about, he could not see any initials, it looked like a smudge to him. He did not own that bag and, if there was a rifle in it, as they said, it certainly was not his. In fact, he had never owned or even held a rifle since his discharge; that would have been against the law. What about his appearance on the CCTV late at night prior to the shooting? Conceding it was very possible he did appear on the CCTV at the petrol station, Bob queried why this should make him a murder suspect. He spent many hours wandering around the village and had difficulties sleeping because of his PTSD. Did the vision that they obtained show him committing an offence at the petrol station? Trespass maybe? If so, he apologised; it was unintentional. Both detectives sat in silent disappointment.

Another promising avenue of enquiry faded like a ship sailing into the mist.

Not that the detectives had dismissed the theory, more that the lack of evidence other than circumstantial — and tenuous at that — hampered their progress. At least for the time being. Connecting the rifle with Bob was inconclusive, despite the blurred initials on the bag, and fell far short of anything that would convince the Director of Public Prosecutions to take the matter further. An added complication was that even if the rifle could be connected to Bob, ballistics could not categorically, or otherwise, confirm that this was the murder weapon. A strategic but not permanent withdrawal was agreed between the detectives, who conspired outside the interview room, leaving Bob alone to finish his second cup of tea. They would have to let him go for the time being.

Reluctantly, Stanley agrees to Bob's request for a lift back to Ayton. After all, it was the least he could do as Bob had been cooperative and had not even demanded legal representation. Homeless, Bob could not offer any permanent contact address, but agreed to remain around the village and assured the detectives that Dolly, from the Old Plough, would be the best person to find him when needed. Failing Dolly, Betty from the village store saw him most days. *A veritable harem,* mused Stanley, involuntarily sniffing as he drives Bob back to the village. Bob is dropped off where he was picked up, in the car park of the Old Plough.

Returning to Scarborough, Stanley takes his car to a valet service run by a gang of Serbians operating from a disused garage forecourt. Serbians make him nervous, they were always busy but you got the impression it was all just a cover. They also sound like half the villains in Bond films. In fact, all Eastern Europeans make him nervous. Paying his tenner in advance for the Gold Star Cleanse, Stanley tells them he will return at the end of the day. He gets a curt but polite reply that it would be no problem. Looking to shake off the odour his clothes had acquired, this allows him the opportunity for a welcome a ten minute stroll in the fresh sea air back to the station as seagulls, squawk, mew and squeal overhead.

24

WEARING HIS BEST cloak of deference, Hardy decided to conduct a visit to the police laboratory in person, and without his junior partner. His phone call in advance to arrange the meeting revealed that Stanley had succeeded in irritating the admittedly irascible scientist within milliseconds of their previous interaction. He needed Desmond Morgan onside. As he walked through the laboratory carrying the rifle found in the copse, he could see Morgan through the glass panel of his office door vigorously tapping at his keyboard. He knocks on the door and waits whilst Morgan continues to tap away for a few seconds. Eventually, with a rising flourish of his right hand, indicating a completed sentence, Morgan pauses, turns from the screen to look through the glass panel, spots Hardy, and waves for him to enter.

"Hello, Desmond, nice to see you again and thank you for your time."

"I see you did not bring your pet monkey with you, but you do seem to have brought a very dangerous looking firearm," replies Morgan in a tone that was almost, but not quite welcoming.

Ignoring the insult to his partner, Hardy strikes the required level of deference mixed with conciliation.

"Look, Desmond, we are struggling in this case, you know, the Ayton shooting, and we need all the help we can get. I know what you told Stanley . . ."

"Who?" interrupts Morgan.

"The pet monkey," replies Hardy and moves on quickly, feeling he had been slightly disloyal to his young partner. "I know what you told us about the bullet, but this rifle is a potential candidate as the murder weapon. Is there anything from what you have seen from the bullet that can link it to this?"

Hardy waited in silence whilst Morgan scrabbled through his in-tray, eventually pulling out three photographs which he examines impassively, but for Hardy, who could not resist peeking at the photos, they were graphic to the point of making him nauseous. Putting the images down on his desk, Morgan takes the firearm from Hardy and carefully examines it, confirming out loud his understanding of the type and model. Hardy replies that this is what he had also been told. Snatching the images from his desk, Morgan holds them up for Hardy to examine more closely. Reluctantly he focusses on the gory images causing a small knot to begin forming in his stomach. Making a show of closely examining the pictures, he looks up expectantly for clarification.

"What I can tell you is that the entrance and exit wounds from the victim's head . . ." Morgan deems it necessary to point to the respective holes in the front and then back of Dibley's bloodied half destroyed skull. ". . . indicate that a weapon of this nature could have been used with appropriate ammunition." Observing Hardy's positive reaction, Morgan sought to dampen it.

"I am telling you, Len, that it *could* have been the weapon used, but there is nothing that I can confirm as absolute. When I stand in a courtroom faced with a smartarse defence lawyer who asks me in front of the jury whether I can say without doubt that this was the weapon used to kill the vicar, I will have to say I cannot be certain."

"But. . ."

"No 'buts', Len. I cannot be certain. In fact, I cannot be certain by a long shot . . . if you'll excuse the pun."

Hardy thanks Morgan, who assures him that he would send through a written report for the detective to use as he sees fit. It felt a bit like being told you have won the lottery, but instead of five million it was only five hundred pounds. But it was better than nothing and potentially of use if part of a longer string of evidence; one piece of the jigsaw, so to speak. Still not enough to convince the office of the Director of Public Prosecutions. Getting nearer at least, maybe. Problem was the lack of witnesses. Still a problem even if they could find someone who had seen Jenkins in the area at the time. A dearth of witnesses was only the beginning. What about motive? A convincing motive? Why would he shoot the vicar? Nobody is going to buy the PTSD loose cannon nut job theory if Jenkins performs as well in front of a jury as he did in the interview room. Perhaps there are too many eggs in one basket and maybe the stranger with the half pint holds the answer.

Whether or not the stranger nursing the half pint was the answer to cracking the case, it was not going to come easily. Stanley had been busy interviewing residents of the village to no avail. Neither did he have any success with the manager at the petrol station, who had long since wiped the recording of that evening as part of his usual cycle. All he could offer was the Saturday after the shooting with an apologetic shrug, recognising that it was probably a week too late.

In his workshop, Ashton puts down his phone, returning his attention to his latest project, an abstract stone piece which is not going as he had hoped. Too many distractions, not least the conversation with his friend and ex-employer in London. A long discussion revealed very little, other than that the security business was going gangbusters and if Chris wanted to return to the smoke he would be welcomed back with open arms, even as a director of the company. Both knew that this was of no interest to Ashton, but the gesture was made and was sincere. What about the affair with Fraser, Hoskins, and the deceased girlfriend? Everything quiet as far as Ashton's involvement was concerned, which was more than could be said for Hoskins, who had gone AWOL. Rumours abounded that Hoskins had screwed over Fraser and done a runner, or that Fraser had done over Hoskins because he had been screwed over. Murmurs that Fraser had not gotten over the death of his girlfriend and that Hoskins' culpability became evident also had a lot of legs. Hoskins did have a reputation of being handy with his fists when it came to women and Fraser was aware of this. Whatever the rumours, the only certainty is that Hoskins has gone underground, either figuratively — or literally.

His own training ensured that he neither relaxed nor took these matters for granted. Ashton had met too many 'Frasers'. With men like him everything was about reputation, respect, power. Weakness could not be tolerated; people could not be allowed to take liberties. If someone close to Fraser was disrespected or hurt, then someone else had to pay; otherwise, the name 'Fraser' meant nothing.

The short haired, polo shirted stranger in the pub that evening had not escaped Ashton's attention. What was evident from the man's body language was that he had not popped into the Old Plough for a quiet relaxing drink. There was a certain alertness about him, and it did not escape Ashton's attention that the stranger left as soon as Dibley had. It was the eyes: cold but active, taking in everything but giving out nothing. No one would have noticed that Ashton had surreptitiously taken a photo on his mobile phone as he sat at the bar, by pretending to drop it, then snapping a picture as he lifted it from the floor. Checking the photo in the toilet, he was pleased to see his handiwork had given him a usable image when zoomed and edited. He texted the image to his friend but enquiries in London drew a blank. No connection with Fraser as far as anyone could tell. No one knew the stranger — at least no one in London did. Ashton remained sceptical; the man was not good news. But if no one knew him then no one knew him. Sometimes it was about looking in the right place; after all, everyone was known by someone. You just had to ask the right someone.

Had someone looked two hundred and fifty miles north of London in a small bijou club called Dukes that night they would have seen the very same stranger sat with a half lager laughing at Benedict Bunton ripping shreds off a couple on holiday from Beijing who unfortunately, for them, had taken a seat at the front of the stage in his direct eyeline. McCarthy had tears running down his cheeks and was slapping the table so hard that the stranger's beer was spilling over the edge of his glass. But he did not seem to mind.

25

PRESSURE IS A downward movement in the police force. Recent media had highlighted the apparent lack of progress in the case and the concerns from the higher echelons were passed down the line and now sat heavily on the shoulders of DI Parkins. Seeking relief from the load by moving it even further down the line, Parkins had called in Hardy for an update: by God, it had better be a positive one. The briefing from Hardy and Stanley, who were currently sat opposite him in his office, was neither comforting nor promising. He had listened with as much patience as he could muster. Yes, he recognised the industry and toil they had been put in and were at pains to describe in excruciating detail, but he was not getting any indication that all this endeavour was leading to a tangible outcome. Namely, someone having their collar felt. Not even the green shoots of a credible theory as to why the vicar had ended up in the morgue. Blowing out his cheeks, he tried to make sense of what he was being told; there had been a lot of words but very little clarity.

"If I can summarise where I think you are. You are currently of the opinion that the most likely culprits are either this Robert Jenkins, who is homeless, a trained killer with PTSD and fully armed to boot. Or, failing that, some unidentified stranger. And to be clear, a stranger who appears to have been enjoying a quiet drink in the pub minding his own business, but a few locals did not like the look of him. Don't all village pubs in northern England have the reputation of being suspicious of strangers? Like that one in the film about the two young Americans and the werewolves?"

"You mean *An American Werewolf in London*?" offers Stanley.

"Was fully armed," corrected Hardy. "Jenkins *was* fully armed, but we now have what we believe is his weapon."

"I am aware of that from what you told me earlier. You also told me that you are struggling to prove that the weapon you found was his, and clearly you have fallen well short of satisfying the DPP that there is sufficient evidence to lay charges."

"We have not given up on this yet, boss," insists Hardy.

Waving away the remark, Parkins continues with his questions. "And what is this I hear that you have resorted to some bloody *witch* to try to solve the mystery for you?"

"Miss Wicker is a respectable psychic who has assisted the force on a number of cases, as I think you are aware," replies Hardy, attempting to hide the lack of conviction in his own voice.

"Personally, I wonder whether the handful of times she seems to have helped were more to do with luck and coincidence. My experience of these people, these so-called psychics, is that they spout such general nonsense that it can pretty much fit any set of circumstances. When genuine facts and events come to light, they can shoe horn them into their half-baked theories and their bloody visions. I understand this woman does not even get visions; she just *feels* things for God's sake. What the bloody hell has she been feeling? Please do tell me, what *does* she feel?"

Neither Hardy, nor Stanley was entirely clear as to what exactly Jenny Wicker did feel and their attempt to explain this fuelled the inspector's cynicism and bubbling anger in equal measure. She said it could be an accident, the vicar didn't expect to be shot. Who the hell expects to be shot going about their business in a village in England? It's not redneck, deep south, gun-toting America. The meeting descends into an outpouring of the inspector's angst, liberally sprayed over the two detectives. Once Parkins has run out of steam, he issues instructions.

"If your prime suspect is this bloke with PTSD, then I suggest you step away from the spiritual otherworld and dip into the sodding real world of science. Go and see a specialist, someone who can tell you what behaviour can be expected of an armed killer with PTSD. What would be his motivations? Do these people kill indiscriminately? Is he a bloody danger to society? If the experts say he is, then we need to act now and may be able to justify putting on more resources for surveillance, or even having him sectioned or something."

Leaning back in the leather armchair at his desk, with an intimidating bank of shelves packed with books and journals behind him, Professor Marcel d'Court considers the information put to him by his two visitors, Hardy and Stanley. Befitting the head of Investigative Psychology, the office is large, with furnishings that border on opulence compared to other offices in the police headquarters. It oozes gravitas and serenity, as opposed to the modern administrative efficiency typical of the rest of the building. Though they would never admit it, the two detectives find the surroundings — the quiet scholarly atmosphere and in particular, the professor — all a bit intimidating. They sit in awe as d'Court's dulcet tones float around the room.

"I assume you have confirmed that the person in question has been medically diagnosed with PTSD?" The detectives both nod and the professor continues. "Well, there are a range of studies, mostly, as you might guess, from the U.S.A, which have examined the characteristics of army veterans with PTSD who own firearms in civilian life. Ironically, those that do possess them are found to be the most balanced of the cohort and most able to reintegrate into society. Those soldiers who find their aggression and suicidal tendances harder to control generally have underlying historical psychological issues long before their active service. I am talking about things such as abuse in childhood. Ironically, those with pre-existing conditions are less likely to acquire firearms. Even in America."

Hardy asks d'Court what this all means in the context of what he has been told about Jenkins.

"Well, most veterans with PTSD have high levels of aggression, compared to average members of society and most have suicidal ideation to varying levels of degree. The fact that Mr Jenkins has a firearm actually means he is more likely to be in the category of those able to control their aggression and if he has a firearm and intends to use it, then he would be more likely to use it on himself than some random victim."

"If I understand you correctly, professor, you are telling me that it is highly unlikely that he would shoot a person as a result of his PTSD?"

Leaning forward and placing his elbows on the desk to emphasise his opinion, he replies, "Yes, detective, that is correct. And if he was planning to use his weapon, he would be more likely to use it on himself."

The detectives had heard enough, they thank the professor and start to rise from their chairs until d'Court takes a deep breath, signalling he is about to speak once more. They both, reluctantly, settle back into their seats.

"Unless of course, he has a motive." He paused for effect and to allow this comment to sink into the minds of his visitors, who had clearly struggled to understand everything he had previously told them. "If, I repeat *if*, he had what he considered a just complaint regarding the vicar, then his underlying PTSD aggression might come to the fore, providing he had a strong psychological motivation to cause harm. Ultimately this is true of anybody, but it is not entirely unreasonable to assume this is more likely to occur in a person suffering from PTSD, who does not have the resilience and normal societal control over the urge to be violent. There are also plenty of other categories of people who are also more likely to be violent: sociopaths, psychopaths, violent criminals and so on. That said, gentleman, studies have shown that ninety-one percent of men and eighty-four percent of women have thought about killing someone, often with very specific victims and methods in mind." The interview had turned into more like a lecture; d'Court was in his element and continued until Hardy found sufficient pause to thank the professor again and make their excuses to leave.

Hardy and Stanley leave the office both believing that the situation was now as clear as mud. If the psychic had been unclear, then the observations of the psychologist were equally as ambiguous. They agree between them that, when questioned by Parkins, they tell him that the professor confirmed that the fact that Jenkins had PTSD did not indicate he was a threat to society — more a threat to himself. The last thing they wanted was to encourage their boss to have a man sectioned with little or no tangible evidence. If that got out and it transpired Jenkins was innocent, they would be toast. Science and knowledge are a wonderful thing but despite Parkins's theory, neither had shed any light on the case nor took them any nearer to finding the killer. Doggedly, Stanley still quietly clung to his theory that Jenkins, in fact, was the man. To let it go would mean all his work to track down Jenkins was not only pointless, but worse, had been a red herring taking the investigation down the wrong track.

26

GLEEFULLY AND GREEDILY, Sebastian Henson is sucking and slurping his way through a mountain of his favourite French dish: Moules Mariniere. Errant droplets of the garlicky stock narrowly avoid his light blue Chambray shirt, courtesy of the large linen napkin wrapped around him for protection. Julia presents a more elegant picture, eating daintily, cutting small pieces of Flamiche aux Poireaux whilst picking at its side accompaniment of a small green salad dressed with a Dijon mustard vinaigrette.

Things were as good as he could have expected under the circumstances and Julia loved their new *pied-a-terre* in Biarritz. She was clearly benefitting from the break away from the village and the proximate ghost of the vicar's demise. He was not naïve and could tell that Dibley remained stubbornly close to the forefront of her thoughts, but the new surroundings and distractions had at least taken the edge off the severity of her maudlin state. As if to further assist the grieving process, he refills her glass of Sancerre to help numb the pain.

"This is absolutely beautiful, Sebastian. Thank you so much." Julia smiles at her husband and he reciprocates sensing that maybe she does have genuine affection for him.

"How are you doing today, darling, you've been quiet all morning?"

The response is preceded with a sigh. "I'm okay." Those two little words speak volumes. She clearly is not 'OK' but is working her way through her grief and trying not to bring her husband's mood down with her own. Sebastian continues smiling at his wife, who clearly has little idea that he perceives her sadness, and its true cause. The thin veil of apparent happiness is all too fragile to hide it from him.

They finish lunch and go for a walk along the Boulevard du Princes de Galles. Passing the local surf school, Sebastian feels his phone vibrating in his pocket. He apologises to her as she turns away from him to look out at the Bay of Biscay, allowing him the space to check his phone. It is a message from McCarthy. Frowning as he reads the message, his thoughts become embittered and angry. *No, Trent, she is not okay. No, Trent, Dibley's death had not re-ignited their relationship.* In fact, his death had driven the wedge of grief between them; the life seems to have been sucked out of her. *Did you bloody well kill him, Trent?* His final thought was left hanging like damp washing on the line, as his wife calls him over to re-join her and admire the bay, sparkling in the afternoon sunlight.

Dark grey clouds hang over the village, which leave Neaves sitting in semi-darkness in Mandelson's living room. His friend had shown no sign of wanting to switch on the lights, the darkness seems to compliment his mood. Though they both have a whisky in hand the atmosphere in the councillor's abode is far from convivial. There is a long list of things that Mandelson wants to get off his chest and they have spent the first two whiskies having what Neaves considers was more of an interrogation than a discussion. Accusations of complicity in the murder of Dibley have been staunchly denied by Neaves and the 'discussion' had just disappeared in a spiral down the unresolved toilet of simmering scepticism. In truth, Neaves himself is not entirely convinced and he is regretting, at his leisure, the decision to involve McCarthy. Luckily, Mandelson is ignorant of this, at least for the moment, but it would eventually come to light that McCarthy had become a silent partner in the Ayton hotel development.

Mandelson refills their glasses in readiness to address other non-Dibley matters. Leaving it hanging he has decided to move on.

"Next Thursday the auditors are commencing their review of the tendering processes. It is not inconceivable that they will ask to speak to you, as you have clearly been very successful in acquiring business from the council. So, we need to have a plan." Neaves, who is all ears, has nothing to offer, which comes as no surprise to his friend.

"So, here it is," announces Mandelson. "We need to undertake a war of misinformation, obstruction and attrition." Blank looks in response. Mandelson continues undeterred.

"Essentially, I do all the talking, I will appear to do my utmost to give them all the appropriate information. But you, my friend, will say nought. They will likely approach you and request an interview."

"So, what do I do?"

"Nothing, somewhere between *bugger* and *all*. They are just low-level bureaucrats. They have no right to question you or demand information. Just play the too-busy card and, if cornered, play your commercial in-confidence card. All your tenders were the lowest, we saw to that. Yes, they will comment on the contract variations, but I will just tell them that variations are inevitable. Until projects get underway the extent of works often is not known. It's often like opening Pandora's box."

Neaves had heard of the expression but had no idea what was in Pandora's box. All he knew was that he had to keep his distance and decline any invitations to meet, and that suited him fine, until he started to think through if there were any consequences. "But what will they do if I refuse to talk to them?"

"Pretty much nothing. They may make vague threats about recommending that you are taken off the preferred contractors list because of your refusal to cooperate, but these are empty threats and I can easily bat them away with the council. I will just point out that you charge a fair- and often the lowest – price. And so what if you have not got time to answer questions that you are not obliged to? Surely the council is interested in controlling costs to keep the rates down. Low rates mean the electorate are happy." For the first time Mandelson smiles and winks at Neaves, "If you think we are on the only gravy train in town, you are mistaken, my friend. A few people have a fair bit to lose if they make me unhappy."

Having just delivered a bag of the special mushrooms, those that they had rescued from the deluge, the boys are sitting at Jenny's kitchen table. They are enjoying a late afternoon cup of tea and one of Jenny's herbal muffins that they both love. Whatever she puts in them, it gives out a gentle, happy buzz. She calls them her *Brotherly Love* muffins. Jenny joins them at the table with a cup of her lavender tea but does not bring a muffin for herself. She tells them she is watching her weight.

"That may be the last consignment for some time Jenny. Everything else was washed away by the storm, this was all we could rescue," says Hayes pointing to the bag of mushrooms that she has placed on the sink's draining board. "But fear not, Colin here has a mate who thinks he may know of another little crop."

Hendricks nods in confirmation but gives a caveat. "Could be, Jenny, but there again this bloke wouldn't know a Death cap from a Puffball. Muffins are great though."

"Now, boys, what do you think about the poor vicar? Police asked me to help but. . . I am not sure they got much out of it."

"What did you tell them?" asks Hayes.

"Not a great deal, Purple, but I did say that the vibrations I got was that the poor vicar would have no idea why he was shot. Almost as if it was an accident. But how could anybody have shot him by accident I wonder?"

The accusatory glance from Hendricks to his friend escapes Jenny's notice but Hayes screws his eyes up to warn his friend to say nothing. Widening his own eyes slightly, Hendricks acknowledges his friend's signal and changes the subject. He looks over at a pan on the stove. It was on a low heat; occasional ribbons of steam were escaping. "So, what's that you've got cooking over there?"

In the woods the Messruther boys are in a panic and digging a hole deep enough to ensure their rifle will not be found. Billy wipes his brow and puts his hand over his head leaving small deposits of mud in his lank brown hair. His younger brother, Bobby, takes his lead from Billy and sits back, hot and flustered, making his latest attack of acne seem redder and angrier than ever. Ever since the shooting they have been monitoring the news for updates. The theory that the shooting could have been accidental had put the fear of God in them, especially as one of his representatives on earth had been at the wrong end of a bullet. And possibly a stray one.

It is mid-morning and the Old Plough is quiet, having just opened. Dolly leans on the bar, chatting with Chris Ashton who is sitting on a stool on the customer's side and nursing a lemonade. For all their small talk the conversation inevitably turns to the Dibley shooting and they mull over the events of the last few days. Practically everybody in the village had been questioned by the two detectives who were assigned to the case and over half felt that they were under suspicion. Ashton recounts how he went to the station voluntarily, but the interview had quickly descended into innuendo and accusation because he had appeared on the CCTV at the petrol station. Dolly recounts her own tale of woe, telling Ashton how they had turned a bit nasty with Ken because he did not have his rifle to hand over to them when they had asked for it. It was being cleaned and serviced for goodness sake. How was he to know that the police would need to see it?

"What about you?" Dolly calls over to Bob.

"Nothing much," Bob replies. Dolly tells him she has heard from Purple that he had been seen in the car park being marched away by the coppers. Bob acknowledges this but is noncommittal in terms of detail. He tells them that it was just a case of mistaken identity. Both Dolly and Ashton are not entirely convinced. Bob's dismissal of the event did not seem to fit in with what they had heard. That, alongside the fact that he'd been detained for a few hours. But then again, here he was, large as life, calm as you like, sipping his Guinness.

Unlike his recent conversations, Kamau is having a pleasant, good-humoured discussion with his father, who was in the most excellent of moods. Vice-President Jeffrey Kamau was no longer sinking in political quicksand; everything had firmed up in his favour. The president, who was never one to be hampered by clauses in the country's constitution, had declared a state of emergency because of a flu epidemic, and with this came a postponement of the elections until the situation was under control. When asked by a CNN reporter at the press conference, what constituted "under control" he responded that the health advice he had received from the Ministry of Health was that the country needs a much higher vaccination rate. Local reporters chose to avoid the questions that would leave them in the precarious position of challenging the president, so they were more than happy to handball it to the American journalist. The president happily revealed, in response to the American's questions, that the term 'high' amounted to ninety percent fully vaccinated. Given that the country had barely achieved fifty percent and the Health Minister who reported to the president was in charge of the vaccine rollout, then it was likely that there would be no election for months — more likely, years.

"So, Peter, it seems that your father will be vice-president for some time."

"Yes, father, which is indeed good news, I am happy for you and mother, of course."

"But there is something I wanted to discuss. Kariuki called me a few days ago and assured me your local problem was now solved. Which is also excellent news!"

Kamau wanted to say if he meant by "solved" and "excellent news," that the vicar had been killed, or rather, murdered. Well, yes, the death of a good man has indeed resolved his "local" problem. He decides that sarcasm is best avoided, seeing no value in ruining the mood by souring what had been a rare, pleasant father-son exchange.

"Yes, father, I suppose it is."

"But why I am calling you, Peter, is to ask if he is still with you? We were expecting him home yesterday, which is when his flight was booked. It seems he did not make it."

Kamau explains that he only saw his father's bodyguard for a brief time and Kariuki had told him that he would be returning to London and onward to Nairobi. He had not heard from Kariuki since. The first piece of unwelcome news threatened to darken the mood of his father, so he asks to speak to his mother to see how she was keeping.

Alone in his office, McCarthy has sought a bit of peace and refuge — or rather he did not want to be bothered dealing with the multiplicity of "problems" that were brought to him because the idiots he employed could not think for themselves. He flicks the remote and the news comes on. Not that he is at all interested in current affairs and his mind wanders as the host moans on about hospital crises, a kid in a road accident and some threat of war in between Kosnians, Bosnians, Crosnians, Serbians or whatever other 'ians' they called themselves. Eventually one news item draws his attention back from his daydream. He had barely taken in the update of the murder of the vicar; he'd crossed it off as all in the past in his mind some days ago. That is, until now as DS Hardy fills the screen. He turns up the volume.

The host was finishing off the introduction of the news item whilst the detective waited patiently.

"And so, we have DS Hardy with us in the studio to provide an update on the murder of Reverend Dibley, which we first reported over a week ago." Unsure as to whether the host was making a point about the lack of progress, Hardy pushes the dig aside and recites his rehearsed statement.

"Thank you. Yes, the investigation is ongoing, and we continue to follow several promising leads. That said I want to continue to encourage the public to come forward with any information they may have. In particular, we would like to speak with a man who was seen in the area a couple of days before the shooting, who we believe was acting suspiciously."

As the detective pauses, the host warns viewers that an image of the man that the police want to talk to would come on the screen shortly. McCarthy finds himself presented with a photofit which gave a serviceable, though not exact likeness of the stranger he is sheltering, until the hitherto undisclosed job is completed.

27

THE MORNING OF THE SHOOTING

MORNING DEW LAYS a moist silvery blanket on the fields surrounding Ashton's path as he jogs through Forge Valley. Barry is barking excitedly, circling him, running behind him, and occasionally cutting across his path as he runs. Frequently, Ashton would have to employ nifty footwork to avoid stepping on the excited Beagle.

Part of their routine involves a short rest at the stone wall bridge. Ashton takes in the sight and sounds of the green, dense woodland beyond them whilst Barry, panting at his feet, sniffs inquisitively, processing the thousand odours flowing from the rich vegetation and the wildlife that lies hidden within it. Rested, and ready for the last leg, Ashton gives Barry a pat and they both resume running. Ashton now breathes more heavily, accompanied by Barry barking as loudly and happily as ever.

Near the village, the stranger finds himself the ideal position. Just over four hundred metres opposite the High Street, he rests on the edge of a dense clump of woodland with a clear sight of all those passing through the village, whether by car or on foot. Through his rifle scope, he scans along the street from west to east. He sees the pub landlord, whom he recognises from the previous Saturday, loading what looks like his own rifle and a small suitcase into his car boot which he slams shut with gusto. Surprisingly light on his feet for a big man, he skips over to the driver's door, jumps in the car and in seconds is on the High Street, driving eastwards towards Scarborough.

Still peering through the scope of his rifle, he scans the butcher's shop, the grocers, a row of cottages and settles on the petrol station, where he watches a young woman, dressed in her nurse's uniform, filling her tank. She places the nozzle back in its cradle and disappears into the shop. The stranger continues to scan the road through his rifle scope and settles on the church. The lights were on but there was no sign of the vicar.

Peter Dibley is in the church, in his back office preparing his sermon for Sunday. He could have done this work in the vicarage, but the atmosphere of the church always seems to give him inspiration. *Perhaps divine inspiration,* he jokes to himself. It was not the easiest of times, what with a declining congregation and worse — he seems to be in the middle of several disagreements with the locals. Village politics were beginning to rankle, irritating him to the point where he was beginning to question his place in the local community.

But this was not the most serious thing that was challenging his values and mental equilibrium. Increasingly, he was thinking that maybe he was not in the right calling, and his nuanced relationship with Julia Henson had done little to settle the doubts that had begun to pierce and probe the once solid walls of his faith. Maybe the difficulty with Neaves is a sign from God? The collapsing church around him a portent, a foreboding. Maybe the ravens that had recently taken up residence above the collapsing wall was an augury. He was even at loggerheads with the Wilkes couple and certain locals seem to be vocalising their general displeasure, either at him, or the church. The *fun police*, someone had labelled the small church community.

More seriously, he had found a bullet embedded in the door frame of the church door and was now in two minds whether to report it. Already in conflict with a lot of locals, he probably did not need to add more to the list. The likely culprits were not bad people, just young blokes somewhere between stupid and careless. Nevertheless, their behaviour was dangerous, and he was going to have to talk to the idiots directly if he was not going to involve the police. Someone would eventually end up dead and he did not need to add that to his already overburdened conscience. Who knows, if they wouldn't see sense, he still may have to get the authorities involved.

A creature of habit, Ashton slows the pace of his run accompanied by Barry's bark of disappointment. Once he reaches Forge Valley Lane, which marks the end of the forest, he stops, reaches into his pocket, and fishes out his AirPods. Leaving the serenity of the forest, he likes to replace the impending jarring noise of the traffic on the High Street with his favourite playlist. Not that there was too much in the way of traffic at that time in the morning. It was a sort of musical warm down, but a warm down with a purpose.

He has a little private physical test where he must complete the distance before the song ended. Some days were more challenging than others. A four-minute song was harder than a five-minute song but, with shuffle play, it was potluck which added to his childlike fun. Yesterday the shuffle selection coughed up "Song 2" by Blur. A great tune to get the adrenalin and heart racing, but the two-minute length of the tune made it impossible to successfully complete his personal challenge. Unless you were an Olympian at the eight-hundred metre, that is — and starting fresh. He wanted redemption; he was one nil down for the week. The challenge involved a semi sprint all the way up the High Street to the church, touching the sign and turning round back up the High Street to the front door of his cottage. Self-aware, he attributes this anally retentive behaviour to his time in the army and the regime and physical discipline that this brought to his day. This final routine ensures he completes his personal daily target, a full ten-kilometre run. Anything less and the feeling of failure and cheating would eat away at him for the rest of the day. Of course, nobody else in the world was party to this and an outsider would suggest he could even run the extra nine hundred metres later in the day to make up for the shortfall. Oh no, my friend, that would be cheating, because he would have had a rest in between and therefore, in his mind, he would have to start the ten-kilometre all over again. Okay, maybe he was a bit OCD. Maybe he was massively OCD.

Dibley also had his morning routine, driven less by OCD and more by a century of custom. He would open the church every day at 7:00 a.m., check the post box and put up the daily message on the church noticeboard at the front of the grounds overlooking the main road, the one that Ashton used as his turning marker during his run. Having set up his daily message, which often conveyed something meaningful but humorous, he would then complete his final task before going back into the church. This would involve standing outside the main door at 7:15 a.m. precisely — well, not always precisely — turning to face the stained window above the front door and saying a quiet prayer of contemplation. Only the vicar knew which prayer was whispered, and the secret was passed on to each successive incumbent. This was a routine that he'd promised to honour as his predecessor had done before him. No one was sure how far back this practice went but the legend was that it had been followed religiously — no pun intended, said his predecessor — since the church was built. No incumbent had the will to break it and Dibley certainly was not going to start, no matter how ridiculously superstitious he felt it was.

A couple of days hanging around the village had enabled the stranger to find a routine. A hit was all about preparation and it helped that people were mostly creatures of habit. If you knew where a person was going to be at a given time, then the rest was easy. It was just about picking the right time and the right place, and he had both. The shot for a trained sniper was run of the mill providing weather did not get in the way; today was a bit windy, but nothing that should compromise his shot. Four hundred metres was practically point blank; he had been successful at more than twice that distance. He glances at his watch; the target is due to appear. It is nearly time, so he wriggles himself into a comfortable position, rifle loaded, only one bullet needed. A piece of cake.

Ashton jogs up the High Street passing the Old Plough, the butcher's shop and Betty's store, glancing to his left as he passes his cottage. Barry knows the routine; he recognises his home but knows the master has further to go before he is allowed to return to his favourite doggy cushion for a well-earned rest. He barks in anticipation. Passing the petrol station, Ashton scans the CCTV camera. Intelligence Corp, security junkie — force of habit. Music playing, the song, Rubber Bullets by 10cc, is reaching the halfway point. Did he catch a glimpse of Bob in the corner of his eye at the edge of the forecourt? Not sure. Keep going, the clock is ticking. Time is running out, it's touch and go if he can make it back to the cottage before the music finishes. Reaching the end of the church yard, he smiles at Dibley's daily witticism, touches the sign and turns around. Focussed on his Apple Watch, he picks up the pace, failing to notice Dibley who, having just finished his prayer, turns to face the road, spots him and waves.

Ashton sweats heavily, takes a deep breath. Focuses. Barely thirty seconds of the song left.

The stranger has tracked his target and is confident that the right moment for the shot has arrived. The cross hairs in his scope fixed on the centre of his intended victim's head. Deep breath, slow squeeze of the trigger.

Dibley waves and shouts good morning again, but Ashton neither sees nor hears him, even though the vicar is only a few yards away from him. Barry barks in excitement and surprise as his master starts to sprint still faster and the dog reflexively jumps in front of him. Human and dog legs tangle together. Barry yelps and Ashton trips slightly, stumbles sideways but recovers his balance and sprints on. The song is coming to an end. With the music's cacophonous beat blasting through his AirPods, combined with his struggle to keep upright after stumbling, Ashton is oblivious to his surroundings. He is unaware of the bullet passing within two centimetres of his head.

The Stranger removes his right eye from the scope, blinks and then returns to it, desperately staring through the magnified glass as he sweeps the scene. Ashton was in his crosshair as he squeezed — but where the hell is he? Slightly panicked, he searches for a body on the ground. He must have hit him. He swears. Through his rifle scope, his eye rests on the prone body of the vicar, who had fallen face down. It is not Hollywood, victims are not projected back several yards when shot, they simply collapse forward in a heap. Dibley is dead before he hits the ground. Ashton is nowhere to be seen. He removes the scope from his eye to get a wider perspective and find his intended target, but it is too late, Ashton has gone. The stranger is not certain, but he thinks that he catches Ashton's front door closing.

Inside the cottage, Ashton pats Barry and fills his water dish. The dog wags his tail whilst lapping greedily at the water. His master smiles at him, unaware that moments before, the Beagle had inadvertently saved his life. "Time for a shower, Bazza," he announces to the dog, who responds by pricking up his ears and looking searchingly into the eyes of his master.

The Stranger, still swearing, jogs away from his sniper's spot, through the trees to his rental car parked in solitude on the road that runs parallel to the wood's edge.

28

2:00 A.M. IN the morning and the back streets around Kings Cross station are deserted. A fine golden blanket of light drizzle sparkles in the yellow sheen of the streetlamp overlooking a small terrace of four Victorian cottages in a cul-de-sac, incongruously located in the centre of the city. The front door of the end terrace opens, and a young woman slips out into the rain clasping her purse; her last client of the evening.

As the door swings shut it is caught by a man who appears from nowhere, causing her to squeal. He puts his finger to his lips to shush her and waves her on her way. She scuttles off down the street, heels scraping on the paving stones whilst he stealthily enters the house.

After checking all the ground floor rooms, he listens at the foot of the staircase. No sound, he creeps up the stairs, pauses at the top and, once again, listens intently. The noise of snoring directs him through the open door of the main bedroom.

He walks to the bedside and uses his pistol, fitted with an Obsidian 45 silencer, to tap the man on the forehead. The sleeping man wakes almost immediately with a grunt. Struggling to make sense of the situation, he sits up with a cry of alarm when he sees the shadowy figure. The dark figure remains still, armed but not immediately threatening, pointing the gun downwards away from his body and the bed.

The intruder appears calm and still, as if he just wants to talk, reassuring the man in the bed. Confidence grows, which turns to indignation and then anger. Having regained his composure, he recognises the intruder and tries to take control of the situation.

"Oh! It's you, what the fuck are you doing here? What do you want?"

"Mr Fraser sends his regards."

Hoskins had already uttered his last words and a single bullet through his forehead snuffs out his life in an instant.

The lack of resolution to the events at Bishop's Avenue had been a cancer that had eated away at Fraser's ego. Nobody had been held accountable for the death of his girlfriend. Grief for his loss, what little he felt, was not the issue. It was the level of disrespect of some cowardly maggot thinking he could get away with it. He was Edward Fraser, not some mug from the local housing estate. The police were, as usual, no fucking use, so he would have to deal with the matter himself and it was not going to end with the scum who was responsible spending a few comfortable years in pokey. In his mind, there were only two possible candidates.

It would not have been out of character for Hoskins to get overly physical with a woman, but they were long standing partners, and few people knew him as well as Hoskins did. Hoskins was acutely aware of what he was capable of, so surely he wouldn't have had the guts to cross him. Or would he? That left Ashton. Hoskins had pointed the finger, snide innuendo, boundaries crossed, hinting that the bored girlfriend had looked for a bit of excitement alone in the house with the pretty boy bodyguard. But was this just Hoskins making an even bigger mug of him than he already had? He couldn't be sure either way. If guilty, Hoskins was never going to come clean, because his life depended upon his silence, and sticking to his story.

The stranger had been briefed to deal with both of them; it was the only way Fraser could be sure that the cancer had been cut out. Both were easy to track down. Fraser knew of the Kings Cross hideaway that Hoskins used. As for Ashton, a few questions and a financial incentive to one of Ashton's colleagues at the security firm told him what he needed to know. Convenient too, as it turned out. Well away from London and near his old mate McCarthy, who, for once, might be of some use. The matter was settled: both men had to go and one of them would just have to be collateral damage. Too bad.

McCarthy's favour to Fraser, the one that McCarthy had hinted should clear all debts, was to look after Fraser's man, who he intended to send up north to sort out a bit of business. Arrange some digs — private, not a hotel — help him keep a low profile, sort out his needs — food, drink, transport. Look after him until the business, undisclosed to McCarthy, was done. Fraser held his counsel as to how taking care of his man went towards repaying the favours McCarthy owed him. It certainly didn't get close to wiping the slate clean.

Following the Ayton debacle, the stranger had two motivations which drove his next move. His plan was to make himself scarce for a couple of weeks, allowing the dust to settle; then, he'd return to finish the job. Rectifying a botched unfinished job to maintain his reputation was his primary motivation, which in his business was everything.

If he needed a second incentive, it was the fact that his employer was Fraser who was not a man to let sleeping dogs lie after a cock-up. With a bit of luck Fraser would not have even realised he had killed the vicar accidentally, assuming, of course, that he was even aware that a vicar living in the sticks had been murdered. As it turned out, Fraser had no idea as his attention rarely crossed the M25. Too much going on in his own patch with a South American delegation to entertain for the week.

Further north, McCarthy had not made the connection either. The stranger had told him that his business for Mr Fraser was going to take him away for a few days but that he would be back to tie up loose ends. Though intrigued, McCarthy himself knew better than to poke his nose into Fraser's business. No questions were asked, no explanations offered. However, seeing an extraordinarily close likeness on the photofit that appeared on the news had more than piqued his interest. Might be something he could use to his advantage in the future. Mum's the word, for now.

29

TEN DAYS AFTER THE SHOOTING

"C'MON BAZZA, WALKY time."

Leaping off his cushion excitedly, the Beagle jumps and barks at his owner. He runs to the door and sits staring at it, patiently waiting for Ashton to grab his AirPods from the side table. Together they run out of the front door which slams behind them, closed but unlocked. There is not much in the way of crime in Ayton.

Turning up Forge Valley Lane, they are soon veering sideways onto a track which leads from the road into the woods. Sunlight beams through the trees from the clear blue sky, leaving shafts of gold connecting the treetops to the lush vegetation on the ground. Ashton begins to breathe more heavily as the run begins to take its toll, but Barry barks happily running behind him, catching him up, crossing his path and then running back a few yards before repeating the cycle again. Secreted on leafy branches, birds twitter, warble, and sing as the babble of the stream creates a serene calmness which, coupled with the warmth of the sun, brings a contented smile to Ashton's face, despite the physical effort.

Déjà vu. The Stranger parks his Toyota Corolla on a side strip, just off the road that runs past the edge of the woods. He grabs his rifle case and makes his way down the same track he had walked just two weeks ago. This time there is no searching for the prime area; he already knows where it is, and he settles himself down, waiting for Ashton to appear on the High Street. He is not leaving anything to chance this time and has taken position with plenty of time before Ashton's routine takes him to the target area, the killing spot.

Looking at his watch, he estimates he still has fifteen minutes to wait, so he sits down on a blanket he has laid out but maintains a sharp eye on the High Street and the church. Periodically he looks through his rifle scope, bringing clear vision and detail of the scene before him. Proudfoot already has his sign out, he can read the words clearly through the scope — lamb is on special. Scanning the High Street for the fifth or sixth time using his scope, he finally rests on the church sign which simply reads, "This Church is closed until further notice." The rubble from the west wall has been cleared into neat piles but there is no sign of further works taking place on the site.

At the Old Plough, Dolly is preparing the pub for the day. Although still very early, some days Bob would be hanging around so he could get a shower. She unbolts the back door and steps out, searching for him around the car park. There is no sign of him today, at least not yet. Probably still asleep with the foxes.

Betty is also up and about, cleaning and stocking shelves. Once she completes her routine, she stands at the kitchen bench with her mug of tea to one side whilst she prepares sandwiches for Bob. He is a lucky boy today - his favourite, beef and tomato.

Having put out his sign for the day, Proudfoot is at the back of his shop, cleaving limbs and slicing meat into cuts for his customers who have pre-ordered for the long bank holiday weekend ahead.

Ashton is now on his home stretch and the vista leading to the exit onto Forge Valley Lane is now less than one-hundred metres away. Even Barry is tiring and stops barking to concentrate on his breathing. They have already had their breather, stopping at the stone bridge to allow Ashton to put in his AirPods. He is ready for the final sprint up the High Street to the church and back again. He presses shuffle, a pause, then Bruce Springsteen flows into his ears, it is "Born to Run" and at around four and a half minutes long he has a fighting chance of meeting his daily challenge. Bruce belts it out. *"In the day we sweat it out, on the streets of a runaway American dream, at night. . ."* Ashton, head down, starts to speed up and Barry, refreshed, runs with renewed energy, barking excitedly. They pass the Old Plough, the butchers, Betty's store and push on towards the church.

The Stranger has already settled comfortably into his sniping body position, prone, on his belly, feet slightly spread to anchor himself. He tracks Ashton through his scope. No wind, a still sunny day; perfect conditions — he couldn't miss. Just had to wait for him to pause at the church sign to make sure. Ashton has now reached the petrol station.

The Stranger shuffles slightly to get into his final position of comfort. More habitual than necessary. Breathing controlled, body still, cutting out all sounds around him. Pure concentration. Index finger wrapped around the trigger ready to squeeze.

Ashton passes the petrol station; it is looking good. Springsteen still hasn't finished the second verse and he is almost halfway there. Can afford to pause at the church sign and take a deep breath ready for the final sprint. Barry barks happily as if he reads his master's mind. Ashton slows as he approaches the church sign.

C'mon, c'mon, almost there . . . thinks the Stranger with a triumphant smile as he prepares to squeeze the trigger. It is his last thought before he blacks out.

Bob towers above the Stranger who is unconscious and bleeding profusely from the head. Bob places the metal pipe on the ground next to him and checks for a pulse. Still breathing, and with a sigh of relief he puts the pipe back into his bag. He is more than capable of looking after himself but it does no harm, when you sleep rough, to have a bit of protection to hand. The pipe was his protection. This was the first time he had deployed it, to use the terminology of his ex-commander.

When he learnt about the shooting of Dibley, he did his own investigating that day. He was no sniper himself, but he had worked with them in Afghanistan as a spotter. It did not take a great deal of expertise to deduce, from where Dibley fell, where the shooter was likely to have been positioned. When everything calmed down, he wandered to the church and looked across the fields opposite. For anyone with a modicum of training or even common sense, there was only a couple of real options to make the shot and walking around the wooded area nearby, he quickly found the prime location. The flattened grass confirmed his suspicion. Over the last week he had used a nearby clearing as his campsite. He had relocated from his old place behind the vicarage after that night when he had heard something, or someone tramping around the woods. It had made him uneasy.

Ashton is a lucky man. Bob was packing up to make his way to the Old Plough for his shower when he heard the car pull up and the footfall of the Stranger approaching in his direction. Peering through the trees he saw that the man was carrying a rifle case and he recognised him from the Old Plough. He had not liked the look of him then and he certainly did not like the look of him now. Nor did he like the look of what he was up to. For Bob with his SAS training, covert surveillance was second nature. He easily kept himself hidden whilst able to watch the Stranger's every move. From his position a few yards directly behind the Stranger, he quickly got a clear idea of the man's intentions as he watched him pull out the rifle from its case and set it up on a tripod.

Bob had spotted the Stranger in the Old Plough that Saturday before the shooting and he could see the man was trouble. The Stranger was not relaxed, he had what Bob called 'active eyes.' He saw that the Stranger had spotted Ashton's clumsy attempt to surreptitiously take a picture of him using his mobile phone. In fact, the Stranger had smarts and left quickly afterwards. Bob surmised that he was trying to put Ashton off the scent by making a show that his focus was elsewhere. He had also made a big show of following the next person to leave the pub. Ironically, that person was Dibley. Ashton, in Bob's mind, was the most likely target, especially as Ashton himself had acted suspiciously. What sort of person spots a killer and then secretly takes a photo of him? Bob had also seen Ashton in the vicinity that day, around that time, jogging near the petrol station. That was why Bob himself had been pulled in by the coppers. He was caught on the CCTV around the same time. It was guesswork — but educated guesswork. When everything was put together Ashton had to be involved in some way or another. There was still a lot of unanswered questions, not least, thought Bob, *Why would a bloke who makes pottery be the target of a professional hitman?* Luckily for Ashton, he had a guardian angel. Not that Ashton would ever know. But as he observed the Stranger setting up and seeing where the rifle was aimed, it all came together. When he heard, in the distance, Barry's barking as he ran alongside Ashton, Bob saw the Stranger set himself ready for his target jogging towards the line of fire.

Bob's eyes follow Barry and Ashton all the way back to their home. He then looks down at the Stranger to decide his course of action. Seeing the outline of a mobile phone in the Stranger's back pocket, Bob eases it out and a swipe of the screen reveals that although it was passcode locked, the phone allows for emergency calls. After an initial discussion with the emergency operator, he is directed at Bob's request, to DS Hardy. Hardy is already on another call, so Bob is put through to Stanley. Whispering and mimicking a Scottish accent to disguise his voice, he tells Stanley everything he needs to know to locate the man who had murdered Dibley. Stanley is sceptical and tries to squeeze more information but is cut short by Bob, who warns the detective that if he delays too long the man they want might have upped and left. Time is short, he needs to come now. The killer is unconscious, but only for so long. Stanley gets the hint and tells his mystery caller that he is on his way and would be there in about twenty minutes. Would the caller be there? Without answering, Bob ends the call and returns the mobile to the Stranger's back pocket who remains motionless, unconscious, face down.

Bob sits next to the hitman, relaxed, legs drawn up, elbows on his knees and waits. As it turns out Stanley is true to his word and barely fifteen minutes have passed when Bob hears vehicles pulling up at the layby. He retreats quickly from the spot where the Stranger lays, and the woods absorb him, hiding him from prying eyes. He can see from his vantage point that Stanley and Hardy are making their way directly to the spot, flanked by two constables. Bob smiles, at least they can take directions. As soon as he is satisfied that they had found the Stranger, he secretes himself deeper into the woods and takes a circuitous route over to the Old Plough.

30

SUNLIGHT BATHES THE village as a new day brings renewed optimism and relief, with news from the previous day that Peter Dibley's killer had been arrested and charged. Betty sweeps her store, which was so clean that barely any dirt was collected in the dustpan and sets about filling the gaps in stock that she spots on the shelves.

Dolly had slept in and decides to make herself a cup of tea before tackling the daily task of cleaning the bar area. Ken is in the cellar changing a keg and taking stock of supplies before calling the brewery.

Chris Ashton and Barry have been snared by the Addinall sisters on the High Street, who are excitedly gossiping about the news that the killer has been found. Stan Proudfoot watches on, smiling as he puts his sign board outside the shop. Written in white chalk, the specials today are fresh rabbits and pheasants.

The Hensons are both asleep after a week in Biarritz. They had not got home until 1:30 a.m. due to a delayed flight but both, though exhausted, were happy to be back in their own bed.

Neaves is packing his rugby kit. The Danesmen have a match later in the day against a team from a nearby village.

Mandelson sits alone with a coffee in his living room, scowling as he reads the first draft of the report from the council auditor's new tendering processes.

*

"Clear the stages, luvvies, we're about the go live. Get ready, Warren, dear, thirty seconds." The producer waves people away and smiles as she gets the thumbs up from the floor manager.

After a final dab on the face of the host, the makeup artist runs off, following assorted studio staff already scattering off camera. Theme music rolls and as it fades away the host speaks.

"Annnnnddd, welcome viewers, to *Daytime in the Dales*. Do we have a packed show for you today."

The host's smile transforms into an expression of mock disgust.

"Now, there will be lots of you who enjoy a morning coffee, but did you know that apparently one of the best coffee beans in the world comes from the poo — yes I said *poo*, of an animal. Urrrggh, yes, I know, it sounds gross, but apparently it is true. Later on, we will be having a guest keeper from Bridlington Zoo who has brought in Carlos. Carlos is a civet cat. Apparently, undigested coffee beans are harvested from the faeces of these animals that eat the berries. It is called Luwak coffee. Not sure I have seen that on the shelves at Tescos."

The camera pans wider to reveal the host's guest, who is sitting patiently waiting for the interview to start.

"And now, I am pleased to introduce a previous guest who has some amazing news. Welcome, Detective Inspector Parkins."

"Thank you, Warren, it is good to be back on the show."

"Yes, indeed DI Parkins and you have some amazing news. We understand that you have apprehended the man who murdered the Reverend Dibley in that lovely small — normally peaceful village of Ayton. What marvellous work from your team?"

"Yes, Warren, I can confirm that the man was apprehended a day ago and has now been charged. The dedicated and unrelenting efforts of the investigating team has paid dividends and once again local people can breathe easily."

"I understand he was captured in a local woodland area, and he was armed. Were any of your officers hurt?"

"No, Warren, our officers are highly trained, and the suspect was arrested without incident. It was a testimony to their professional training and bravery."

"Tell me, inspector, do we know anything about his motive?"

"Not at this stage Warren but I can confirm that the circumstances of the arrest are damning for the suspect, and we are confident we have the right man."

"Well, thank you, DI Parkins and congratulations to your team. I understand you have a busy agenda this morning and must leave us now. But thank you once again for coming in."

As the camera focuses again on the host announcing it is time for a break for advertisements, Parkins quickly rises from his chair, handing his lapel microphone to the floor manager, who thanks him as he leaves. Three minutes later the host is back on.

"We are now going to cross over to Ayton where Sue has been talking to locals to gauge their reaction to the good news. Can you hear me, Sue?" The host disappears from the screen, replaced by the young reporter, smiling, microphone in hand.

"Thank you, Warren. I have been here all morning and the overwhelming feeling is one of relief and residents are hopeful that the village can return to its normal idyllic life. Joining me are two local women who tell me that they were instrumental in helping catch the killer. They are sisters who live on the High Street, Freda and Mary Addinall." The reporter turns away from the camera and as the shot pans out the Addinall sisters appear on screen. "Tell me ladies about how you helped track down the killer?"

The Addinalls smile with nervous excitement, repeatedly glancing between the reporter and the camera, unsure of where they are supposed to look. With relish they describe how they have helped the police on several occasions, giving information in response to requests for help from the public. The young reporter gives them encouraging nods as they speak.

"That's amazing. Tell the viewers in a little more detail what you told the police. What sort of help did you give them?" asks the reporter, who puts her microphone in front of Freda.

"Well, we told them about lots of suspicious activity and it was us who gave them the description of the man who was arrested. Didn't we Mary?"

Mary nods and the reporter moves the microphone near to her so she can speak.

"Yes, we did," confirms Mary. "We told them he was acting strange, following people about only a day or so before poor Reverend Dibley was killed." Mary's sentence comes to a strangled halt as she starts to hitch and sob. After dwelling on Mary to milk the drama and emotional impact, the cameraman scans back to the reporter. She quickly thanks the sisters and wraps up the item following instructions from the Producer through her earpiece.

"Thank you, Sue, great work," congratulates the host. "And now we have a special guest in the studio, Zookeeper Evan with his friend, Carlos."

Hardy was invited, by the local radio station, to discuss the breakthrough. He was less than pleased when he learned it was the late-night show, *Riders Brings a Storm*. An assistant eases him into the studio, settles him in front of a microphone and leaves him to wait for the DJ to finish the current item. As he closes off, Riders looks over to the detective and smiles. It feels more like a challenging smile than a welcoming one. After the previous exchange a few days earlier, Hardy wants redemption and is more than up for the fight, especially when he is reporting success, rather than failure. The verbal tennis match commences.

"Well, listeners I have a special guest tonight, who I have spoken to before when I was called in to fill in for Millsy on his morning show. Welcome, DS Hardy, I believe congratulations are in order. You have your man."

Hardy was not sure if he was getting a smile or a sneer from Riders but, whatever it was, he didn't like the vibe coming across the table. He leans into the microphone to speak.

"Yes, thank you. After a fruitful line of enquiry, we were able to locate the alleged killer in the woods near the church where the vicar was shot." Fifteen —love, he had started well.

"Oh, detective, how so? Were you lying in wait for him to return to the scene of the crime? Like in some Agatha Christie novel," mocks Riders. Fifteen all.

Hardy retorts. "At this stage his motivation for returning is unclear, and we are continuing to question the suspect but unfortunately life is not like Agatha Christie, Mr Riders, where the suspect confesses all. If it were, anybody could be a detective, perhaps even yourself." Thirty — fifteen.

This was meat and drink to the DJ, realising that he has already rattled the detective's cage.

"Oooh, listeners, we have a feisty guest tonight. So detective, the police seem to be attributing the arrest to a triumphant piece of police work. The result of persistence and well-honed investigative skills. Or was it, as rumour would have it, just pure luck?" Thirty all.

The DJ's sarcastic tone fills the airwaves loud and clear. Hardy bristles but remains calm and even in his response

"Well, I wouldn't have necessarily phrased it that way, but we have certainly worked hard and followed several lines of enquiry, which led us to the suspect. You also are aware that when we arrested the suspect he was armed with a deadly weapon. I think in these circumstances, your listeners would be particularly supportive and appreciative of our efforts." Forty — thirty, game point.

"Interesting that you say that, detective. I am given to understand that the investigation was . . . how shall I say . . . floundering. That the only reason that the suspect was arrested was that you were tipped off, by a person unknown, that the killer was in the woods and already injured. In fact, it appears he was unconscious when you found him. I am reading from the official written police statement provided to the press and I can see that it does confirm that he is now in hospital with a severe head injury. Pre-empting any accusations of police brutality, the statement does confirm he was in this condition prior to the arrest. Anyway, I digress. Let me ask you, did no one in the police think to search the woods for clues after the shooting of Reverend Dibley?" Deuce. The DJ smiles malevolently.

"Not at all, Mr Riders, in fact we were onto the suspect much earlier than the day of the arrest. It was just a matter of tracking him down." Advantage Hardy. The detective fixes his stare directly on the eyes of the DJ, who flinches uncertainly, as it was not going quite as well as he thought it might. This was new information as far as he could tell. All he could manage in response was an "oh, really?"

Hardy presses his advantage home. "You may recall, that we gave out a photofit to the press recently and as you will have seen from the real, professional news coverage on the television. That's real news based on facts, as opposed to a Mickey Mouse late night radio show, looking to lay blame with the police rather than focus on the perpetrators of this heinous crime. If you had concentrated on this, you would see that photofit is a very close likeness to the man who we have now arrested." Game, set and match as Hardy brusquely thanks the DJ, politely excuses himself and leaves the studio. Once he gets back to his car, he allows himself a private air punch in victory.

31

THOUGH NO PROMOTION resulted, DS Hardy's credibility and capital had a much needed boost, not least with his boss. As for Stanley, he basked in reflected glory, especially as it was his first murder case and the killer had been brought to justice. DI Parkins had spoken at a small event, held to celebrate cracking the case. Hardy's boss was very complimentary about him in his speech, and everybody clapped at the end, including the desk sergeant, albeit with a sceptical smile. Of course, the conviction of a killer had not done the inspector himself any harm, who had received congratulations from on high. This fuelled his own largesse when talking generously about the work and hours the detectives had put into the case.

Try as he might, Hardy never found out who'd made the call on the killer's own phone to alert them to his location. Nor could he explain what had happened to the killer, whom he'd found unconscious with a nasty head wound. The life of the killer had then been in the balance for several weeks, following the severity of the blow to his head. The resulting oedema caused further trauma as the surrounding brain tissue pressed against his skull. He was put in an induced coma for almost two months and the Stranger owed a significant debt to the medics who managed an eventual recovery, against the odds. This had delayed the timing of the court case.

When it eventually did reach the courts, much of the case rested on circumstances and, try as they might, the motivation for the killing could not be extracted from the Stranger, even with the incentive that breaking silence would shorten the judge's sentence. The Stranger decided that life in prison was better than no life at all and he knew Frasers's reach was long. He might have got a shorter sentence, but Fraser would have ensured that he would have had an even shorter life of incarceration. In fact, he would have had a shorter life, full stop. Prison was one of the hazards of the job; keep your head down and do your time.

From the perspective of the prosecution, the failure to pin down a clear motive did make the court case harder going and the defence lawyer played on this. But ultimately verdict was guilty. The accused was found in a compromising position, with a deadly weapon that was likely to be the one used to kill the vicar.

Desmond Morgan had, in Hardy's eyes, played a blinder. "No," he told the defence counsel, he could not categorically match what was left of the bullet with the weapon, but the entry and exit wounds were consistent with the nature of the weapon and the type of ammunition found with the accused. His fingerprints were on the rifle and the circumstances of where he was found were simply inexplicable, other than the prosecution's contention that he was there to cause harm. Judge and jury listened on as Morgan gave evidence with convincing gravitas, telling them that nature of the wounds was consistent with a medium range shot from the weapon found with the killer and his location. They also heard that the angle of the shot that had ended the vicar's life was consistent with the same location at which the killer was found.

Most damning of all was the fact that the killer's mobile phone contained a string of incriminating messages. Inevitably, the person on the other end could not be identified, as the number was untraceable. A burner phone. When questioned by the prosecuting lawyer regarding the identity of the other person the Stranger remained silent, and this was damning.

Ashton went about his life unaware that he had skirted death twice. Although he followed the court case closely, there was nothing really to confirm his nagging suspicion that he may have been the target the day the killer was found. Given the time the killer was discovered, and his sniping location in relation to his own as he'd completed the latter part of his morning run, this theory was not entirely fanciful. His friend in London once again tried to identify the Stranger and any connection to persons known by him but drew a blank. Neither did Ashton realise or even suspect that he had a guardian angel. Well, to be accurate, he had two. Barry who'd tripped him up at the vital moment, and a homeless man with PTSD.

Bob went about his life and hung around the village for many months after the trial. That is until one day he thanked and said goodbye to a tearful Betty, and an equally tearful Dolly. The next day he was gone, he simply disappeared. Two unlikely guardian angels, neither wanting nor expecting any thanks.

It remained a mystery to many people but not one that the two detectives dwelled on, having obtained their conviction. The killer had been found and locked away. For the villagers, a few breathed a sigh of relief for a variety of reasons — some not particularly altruistic, but a few genuinely grieving the loss of the Reverend Peter Dibley.

But life went on and once more the village became a peaceful idyll where nothing much happened – and that is the just way they liked it.

Nothing much for the time being, at least.

THE END

www.ingramcontent.com/pod-product-compliance
Lightning Source LLC
Chambersburg PA
CBHW010304100726
47904CB00011B/2734